ALBANY

Also available in Large Print
by Laura Black:

Glendraco
Wild Cat
Strathgallant

ALBANY

Laura Black

G.K.HALL&CO.
Boston, Massachusetts
1985

Published in Large Print by arrangement with
St. Martin's Press

British Commonwealth rights courtesy of
Hamish Hamilton Ltd

G.K. Hall Large Print Book Series

Set in 16 pt English Times

Library of Congress Cataloging in Publication Data

Black, Laura.
  Albany.

  1. Large type books. I. Title.
[PR6052.L32A79 1985]   823'.914   85-5803
ISBN 0-8161-3881-8(lg. print)

One

I said goodbye to my Aunt Sophia, in the doorway of the modest house where I had lived all my life. I was going away, for almost the first time; I was going, it seemed, to no modest house but an immodest castle. I was going from Mill-stounburn, near Dalkeith in East Lothian, in the Lowlands of Scotland, to a place much further away than I had ever travelled, in the high bare country of West Perthshire, more unfamiliar to me than the landscape of the moon, which I had at least seen.

Aunt Sophia would have come with me—she had been most cordially invited—but all manner of local obligations, of a tiny kind, seemed to her tender conscience to keep her at home. Old Eppie Tainsh, now quite blind, had to be read to, from the Old Testament or from the sermons of the

Covenanting Saints, twice a week; and she could tolerate no voice except Aunt Sophia's. The feckless Johnston family, said to be settled tinkers, had to be visited, and their running-nosed swarms of children inspected for signs of infectious disease. Such was a large part of Aunt Sophia's life; most of the rest, for most of my life, had been me. Consequently it was a difficult parting for us both. My gentle aunt fought to hold back her tears, and looked for a time to be succeeding. I wept also, not at our separation, which was temporary, but at her weeping. Tears were to me as infectious as yawns—as infectious as the many diseases which Aunt Sophia detected among the Johnston children.

There was a deferential cough in the middle distance, bringing to an end farewells which might otherwise have gone on until night.

The cough came from Miss Grizelda Hamilton, the stately and gorgeous elderly lady who was to be my companion on the journey. Lady Lochinver, my shortly-to-be hostess, would have come herself, Miss Hamilton said, but could not, for domestic reasons. Miss Hamilton was her ladyship's companion and confidante. Miss Hamilton sent her ladyship's most profound regrets and apologies; Miss Hamilton herself apologized, in florid language and at length, for subjecting me to so humble and inadequate a substitute. This was so ridiculous, and so astonishing, that I think my mouth inelegantly gaped open. I did not, fortunately, laugh, which would have been still more inelegant, and horridly rude to Miss Hamilton.

Miss Hamilton stood by the travelling-carriage which Lady Lochinver had sent for me. Its door was open and its steps down. The coachman was on his box; one footman stood by the horses' heads, and one by the carriage door. The varnish and brass of the carriage blazed in the moderate spring sunshine so as to hurt the eye, and so did all the buttons and buckles on the liveries of the men, and so did the pendants and lockets with which Miss Hamilton was hung about (in that year of 1865 it was not fashionable to be austere in personal decoration).

'At your convenience, Ma'am,' said Miss Hamilton, in a tone which marvellously combined humility with impatience.

Ma'am? Me?

I was not Ma'am to anybody. I was Leonora Albany, almost penniless, not quite eighteen years old. I was Leo to my friends, and Nora to Aunt Sophia. I was nobody. I did not particularly like being a nobody, but I had been one all my life, and I was used to it. I had expected to remain a nobody. I had been, for nearly eighteen years, quite, quite sure that I should die as much a nobody as I had lived. So to be addressed as 'Ma'am' by a fashionable silken lady—to be curtseyed to so reverently that the lady's forehead almost brushed the ground, like that of an Arab at his prayers . . .

By the front door of Millstounburn House,

there was a tall window, giving on to the dark little hallway. In it, on a bright day, one could see oneself vividly reflected. Whenever I left the house (whenever, that is to say, I remembered) I glanced at myself in this convenient mirror, not altogether out of vanity, but also to make sure that my hat was straight, and that I was not wearing odd gloves. Out of habit I did so now, and saw the familiar reflection which was so far from deserving to be called 'Ma'am'. I was, for a start, too small to be addressed so worshipfully —a full six inches shorter than dear beanpole Aunt Sophia (which made our parting embraces awkward) and shorter by still more inches than the stately Miss Hamilton. I had been told, recently and often, that my face and figure passed muster, to put it most mildly: probably this was bad for a very ignorant seventeen-year-old, but I cannot pretend I found it disagreeable. Also I was obliged to agree.

There was, to be sure, an oddity about my face, besides its reported capacity to pass muster: it was one which people were often in the way of supposing they had seen before. Perfect strangers fancied that they recognized me, when there was no possibility that they had ever clapped eyes on me. In the middle of Edinburgh, in Prince's Street, only a fortnight previously, a middle-aged gentleman in important clothes had raised his hat to me, in a curious uncertain way, as though he was sure he knew me, and must therefore out of politeness salute me, although he had no idea

4

who I was. I was by this time no longer surprised by this oddity; by this time I knew why my face was so familiar to so many. I had been familiar to Lady Lochinver, and Edgar Smith, and Simon Donaldson, and the Barone Lodovico di Vigliano, all the strange persons who had entered my life and were about to transform it; it had been instantly familiar to Miss Grizelda Hamilton, and caused her to perform a curtsey which would have done credit to an acrobat.

My clothes were respectable—they were the very best I had—but in terms of Miss Hamilton and of the glittering carriage they did *not* pass muster. I had been told that all that would be put right. Lady Lochinver would equip me for my new station in life; dressmakers would fight to adorn me, as an advertisement for their skill and taste. This not because of what I looked like, but because of what I was.

I was far from having grown used to it all. I was far from grasping what was happening to me.

By dint of further coughs, Miss Hamilton levered me away from Aunt Sophia's renewed embraces, and I was at length handed up into the carriage. Miss Hamilton followed me in; the steps were raised and the door closed. Miss Hamilton seemed almost reluctant to sit, as though it was taking an outrageous liberty to sit herself in my presence. Everything was topsy-turvy.

Our journey was something over eighty miles, as the roads looped, going by Edinburgh,

Stirling, Callander and Lochgrannomhead. We spent a night on the way in the tall, dismal house of persons I did not meet. It seemed they were away from home, but their servants were charged to treat us (me, at least) like royalty. I found this arrangement extraordinary, but Miss Hamilton said that it was Lady Lochinver's decision, and that it was wisest and safest.

Safest? Why should I not be safe?

Well, there came indeed a moment when I was not very safe, and not at all dignified, and by an irony it came about as a consequence of the strange precautions Lady Lochinver had taken. For if I had not been in that tall, depressing, silent house, among tall, depressing, silent servants, I would probably not have felt impelled to go in the early morning for a solitary walk in the park: and so I would not have seen a man who, with quite a small pony, was trying to drag a tree-root out of the ground. He was a wizened little man with a fringe of red beard, and one of his eyes was bloodshot. The task was very evidently beyond the pony's strength, and the man sought to give the poor beast extra power by whipping it mercilessly with a long plaited leather whip, tipped, as I saw in the early sunshine, with inches of metal. The man was in a blind rage, with the pony, and with the tree-stump, and with the task he had been set.

Dear Aunt Sophia used to lament my head-strong impetuosity, which had got me into numberless scrapes and even, when I was small, a good many fights. I did not mean to do rash and ill-judged things, but found myself carried forward by my own fury, as though by a bolting horse.

So it was this time.

I screeched at the man, not at all in the manner of a female addressed as 'Ma'am': I screeched that he was cruel and stupid, and that he was punishing his beast for his own stupidity, which was quite true, but imprudent.

What happened next would not have happened, except that he was senseless with rage. He turned, and raised the whip, to use it on me. But I was very nimble on my feet, and dodged behind the poor pony, so that the wretched beast received yet another blow. By instinct, and not thinking of the horrid possible consequences, I caught hold of the whiplash, and tugged at it, just at a moment when the man's grip had slackened with the completion of his blow. I twitched the whip out of his fingers, and in a second had the handle in my own hand. And then I did what I should not have done—I raised the whip to strike him: and he wailed and fled, which I had not expected. I had heard that all bullies were cowards; this one was only a little man, but he was a great bully and a great coward.

So I untied the pony's traces from the tree-stump, and using them as reins I rode the little beast most of the way back to the house. I found that I could not stay on, riding side-saddle without a saddle, so I rode astride, which I had never done before, and which was gravely inde-corous, because my skirt was about my waist. But I was sure that, at so early an hour, there was nobody to see me; and, having been made a present of a pony, I could not resist riding it.

When I walked, scarlet-faced and dishevelled, into the house, I found that I was still holding the villainous whip. This was not the least of my mistakes. I walked into a dreadful silence of waiting servants, and a volley of horrified coughs from Miss Grizelda Hamilton. Nothing was said about my escapade, and I said nothing. I thought that, most likely, the folk in the house would never hear of it; the man would keep quiet about his cruelty and cowardice, and his master would find him another whip, and the pony would trot home. I did not guess what frightful conse-quences my rashness would have.

By and by we resumed our journey, and the country changed from Lowland to Highland, and I looked with awe and delight at bigger hills than I had ever seen; and we came at last into a great glen, which was Glen Alban; and in its midst, high above a river, to a great castle, which was Glenalban Castle. And it was no coincidence that the obscure Miss Leonora Albany, scarce out of the schoolroom, should be come to a place al-most of her own name: for glen and castle and girl came all by their names from the same source, and that was why I was there (though, after the events of the morning, I was very nearly not there).

The glen was so grandly beautiful that it made my heart leap. The castle was so ancient and enormous that it made my heart sink into my boots. It was not a house but a medieval walled city, set on a crag for defence, towered and moated, so that one looked for regiments of archers on the battlements, and listened for the sound of drums and trumpets.

The carriage rattled over the drawbridge (which Miss Hamilton told me, to my disappointment, could no longer be raised and lowered) into a great courtyard, from which rose a flight of broad stone steps to an enormous door. At the foot of the steps I saw to my delight my friend and benefactress, the cheerful Lady Lochinver. I jumped down from the carriage the moment the steps were lowered, and hurried across the courtyard to greet and to thank her.

Her curtsey was as low as Miss Hamilton's.

By the steps stood a piper, in full Highland dress. His plaid I recognized as the Royal Stuart tartan, which I had seen in ceremonies in Edinburgh. He began to play, as I reached the foot of the steps, and his tune was that great Jacobite air *Charlie is my Darling*.

And a magnificent person in livery, bearing a staff, led me up the steps and through the door. And in a hall as large as a church a squadron of servants stood, and the men bowed so that they were bent double, and the women curtseyed so that they were all, like Miss Hamilton, Arabs at their prayers.

All this, for me.

It was as though I owned the castle: as though I were queen.

I did. I was.

My father never had any money to speak of. He never owned Millstounburn, but was tenant of some benevolent cousins in Australia, who did not need it, nor wish to sell it, nor desire to make any money out of it, and so let it to their impoverished kinsman at a peppercorn rent. The obligation on our side was to maintain the property decently: which, because it was small and solid, was seldom a heavy imposition.

My parents were wildly mismatched, but, as often happens, deeply devoted—either in spite of the differences between them, or because of them. My father was by all accounts a man strong in courage and gaiety, and weak in prudence; but my knowledge of him was all hearsay, for he fell from his horse and broke his neck when I was only two years old. I understood that the manner of his death was typical of his life: he was attempting an impossible leap, over the iron fence of a railway crossing, for a wager.

It seemed that my mother was, in total contrast, a good and frugal manager, but timorous both physically and socially. She was also an invalid, confined to sofa or bed as far back as I can remember.

It would have been good if I had inherited my mother's prudence with my father's courage; but it seemed I had not.

After my father's death, my mother's unmarried sister, Sophia Grant, came to live at Millstounburn, to keep house, to cherish the invalid, and to bring me up. Poor Aunt Sophia! As gentle and frugal as my mother, but without her competence; as enthusiastic as my father, but without any of his courage—I loved her deeply and dearly, and my gratitude to her was bottomless, but she was not the ideal custodian of a child prone to whim and wildness.

When I was seven, my mother fell seriously ill; and soon after my eighth birthday she died. Aunt Sophia and I were both heartbroken: but Mamma's death released Aunt Sophia to the charitable works in which she was thereafter indefatigable; and it released me to run wilder even than before.

We were oddly placed. We were of a class with the neighbouring lairds, and we were considered by the country folk—and considered ourselves—a class above the rich Edinburgh tradesmen who had bought places in the countryside. Yet we hardly mixed with the families of the lairds, nor yet with those of the tradesmen, because we could not afford to return their hospitality. It was a simple matter of money. Our neighbours were a purse-proud lot (it was a purse-proud age) and Aunt Sophia and I could not compete with them. She, to be sure, did not want to. I would dearly have loved to. I would dearly have loved silk gowns and jewels and parties, and I had none of these things. I did have a sound roof over my head, and a sufficiency of food. (That was highly important. I could have suffered without any qualm a bucket in my bedroom, to catch drips from a hole in the roof: but, active as I was, I could never have survived without enough to eat. My appetite amazed Aunt Sophia, and even myself, because I ate like an elephant, yet I was always as slim as a little boy; approaching my eighteenth birthday, my body had belatedly developed into a woman's, in all particulars, but I was still very slim, with small bones, and a waist about which I could almost put my spread hands.)

A consequence of our embarrassment was that I made friends where I found them. They were a raggle-taggle lot, and I was and remain grateful for the high times I had with them. Benjie Balfour the poacher's son taught me most, and got me into deepest trouble. And it was the daughter of the Wee Free Minister in Dalkeith who taught me, long before I should have known, about men, and women, and the making of babies, and the joys and perils thereof. I wondered then how she knew so much, and I wonder still . . .

Though we had only a very small income, paid quarterly by Trustees in Edinburgh, we did have some choice possessions, relics of my father and of his forbears. There were swords with gilded hilts, pictures, pieces of old furniture. There were in the attic trunks of papers, well-preserved but as far as we could see without interest or value.

At times of crisis—they occurred once a year or so—things were sold. In this connection, we had the good fortune that Aunt Sophia was acquainted with a Mr David Maitland, an antiquarian of Edinburgh, a man of scholarship and scrupulous honesty, who maintained a celebrated shop in Prince's Street. He had been out to Millstounburn to appraise some of the contents of the place. He said that, when the time came for him to retire from his shop, he should make a serious search amongst the papers in the trunks in our attic, for there might be matter there of historical value. When we were obliged to sell something, it was he who sold it for us, and I believe that he did not withhold his usual commission.

On a November day (which turned out, in ultimate consequence, so very fateful) the roof did suddenly begin to leak, so that plaster came down from a bedroom ceiling, and buckets were all over the floor. It seemed that, in a gale, a branch had broken slates and the battens on which they rested, and that the necessary repairs would be more considerable than we had at first supposed. It was not a thing which could be ignored, nor yet postponed, because of the further expensive damage that would be done. A price for the work was given to us. Aunt Sophia almost swooned, and I was solemn. From our regular income the cost could not possibly be met, and we did not receive another instalment until the New Year, and the Trustees could not or would not give us any sums in advance.

Another sale, then, to or through Mr David Maitland. So much had already gone! There were darker oblongs on the walls, where pictures had hung, and gaps in the furnishings of rooms, where tables or chests or chairs had stood. All that remained was the more beloved, and losing more household gods would have been like losing teeth or limbs.

And then I remembered the sword, which had lain for some forgotten reason always in a cowhide trunk in the attic, with the dustiest and most repellent of the hoarded papers. It had a silver scabbard—surely not valueless, we thought—and a hilt of unusual design, and the blade was engraved with indecipherable words in what seemed a foreign tongue. The sword had been handed down through the generations, and with it a scrap of its history, which my mother had had from my father, and Aunt Sophia from my mother, and I from Aunt Sophia: my great-grandmother had brought the sword back with her from France in 1770, because it had meant something of importance to her. It meant something of importance to us, too—it would pay for mending the hole in the roof, and replastering the ceiling of the ruined bedroom. Off it went accordingly to Mr David Maitland, and he acknowledged receipt by return of post, and undertook to find a purchaser at an equitable price.

Scarcely had the sword gone on display in Mr Maitland's shop, than it produced for us a visitor. Visitors of any sort were rare at Millstounburn, and threw Aunt Sophia into a flutter, so that she bleated of refreshments, and looked as though she wanted to run away. This one was not like any we had ever entertained —not at all like the doctor, or the representative of the Edinburgh Trustees, or the Episcopalian Minister, or any of the charitable ladies with whom Aunt Sophia was in league or in rivalry. He was a big, plump man, approaching the middle of his middle age (I could not be more exact than that), smooth-shaven and with a glossy look, as though polished with a leather by a servant; his manner was gentlemanly—Aunt Sophia described him afterwards as 'urbane', which I thought a good word, and one I had never before heard her use, and did not know she knew. Our visitor's face, which was somewhat moonlike, was not unhandsome, and not at all displeasing, except that it was disfigured by a purple birthmark beside his left ear: not large, but impossible not to notice, being livid in colour, and resembling in outline the silhouette of a flying bird.

It was one of those things which you do not know whether to look at, or look away from—to pretend not to see, or to show that you have seen and do not mind. At least I, not so very long past my seventeenth birthday, did not know how to react to the birthmark, and it was very evident that poor Aunt Sophia did not know either. I was in a terror lest she should say 'birthmark' instead of some quite other word; I was in some fright lest I should do so. Our visitor's affability of manner showed that he, at any rate, rose quite above his disfigurement. If he had been worried by it, he could have covered it with whiskers. That he did not deign to, I thought did him credit, and I strove to be as unembarrassed as he was.

He did not have a card about him, owing to the incompetence of his servant, but he announced himself as Doctor Colin Nicol. He was not a medical doctor, as he hastened to explain, but held some other superior academic degree; he was an historian and an antiquarian, like our friend Mr David Maitland; but instead of keeping a shop he was a teacher, scholar and writer. He was at the time engaged on research towards a new biography of Prince Charles Edward Stuart, the Young Pretender, Bonnie Prince Charlie. He explained that much new material had come to light about the Prince's life, and more was expected yet to come, which required reappraisals of this or that aspect of his career, and that this justified and even demanded a new study of a man already often studied. He was at pains, it seemed to me, to justify his project to us, and to make us agree that his labours were timely and meritorious.

We listened, puzzled, in the parlour of Millstounburn. We did not know why he thought it necessary to explain himself to us; we did not know why he had come.

He said that, whenever he was in sufficient funds, he was a client of Mr David Maitland in Prince's Street, and had there formed the basis of a collection of memorabilia of Prince Charles Edward. He had acquainted himself with the various devices, heraldic and decorative, used by the Prince at different times of his confused life; he was thus able to recognize and identify, with fair certainty, objects associated with His Royal Highness.

In Mr Maitland's shop, a day or two previously, Doctor Nicol had seen a sword. He saw at once—and Mr Maitland agreed with him—that it was not of Scottish or English craftsmanship, for the design of the hilt was of another school of swordsmiths. Doctor Nicol believed it to be French, though Mr Maitland was inclined to give an Italian ascription. Closer examination, with a glass, and after some careful polishing, revealed a badge engraved on the hilt, of a crowned leopard running; further search, of the blade, revealed part of a French inscription engraved on the steel, which suggested that the sword had been given to some great person by the citizens of a town. In sum, the evidence pointed with some certainty to the sword having been the property of Prince Charles Edward.

Doctor Nicol had been and remained greatly excited by this identification, owing to his passion for objects associated with the ill-fated

17

Prince. He had prevailed on Mr Maitland to reveal the provenance of the sword. Mr Maitland would not normally have given Aunt Sophia's name and direction to a stranger: but Doctor Nicol was not to him a stranger, and he was a scholar of repute. Mr Maitland, it seemed, after some initial reluctance, saw no harm in naming Millstounburn and Miss Sophia Grant; we saw no harm in it, either. Doctor Nicol's enthusiasm was infectious, and his manners were excellent, and he was outspokenly grateful for our kind reception of him; we could not regret that he had come.

As to the sword, we could only tell him that it had been brought back from France, as we believed, by my great-grandmother in the year 1770. We did not know how she had come by it, nor why she esteemed it so high. He wanted to know more, much more; but we were no use to him.

I had been made known to him by Aunt Sophia, at his first arrival; but at that point she was flustered and ill at ease, by the mere fact of an unexpected visitor, and mumbled my name, so that he did not catch it. Now he learned that my great-grandmother's married name had been Albany: and that her son and grandson and great-granddaughter were surnamed Albany. This unimportant fact threw him into a state of almost frightening excitement.

'Not a usual name,' he said. 'Far from a usual name, if I may be permitted to be personal. *Then*

18

felt I like some watcher of the skies . . . You say, Ma'am,' he turned to Aunt Sophia, 'that the sword has reposed, time out of mind, in a box with a collection of ancient papers? Dare I request the privilege of examining those papers? Should I discommode or offend you, if I made so bold? Nothing will be removed, nor shuffled out of sequence—but *may* I look at the contents of that box?'

Of course he might. We had both rather that he suffocated himself with century-old dust, than that we did. We had kept the papers against the eventual leisure of Mr Maitland; there was no reason in the world why Doctor Nicol should not examine them first.

I showed him to the attic, and to the cowhide trunk where the sword had lain. Politeness obliged me to offer to remain with him, but to my relief he said that he would do very well on his own, and would not inconvenience me further. I came downstairs wondering why an unusual patronym should throw an eminent scholar into such a storm; wondering also at a taste which led a healthy man to prefer dusty attics to the clean bright air of the countryside. I hardly went into our attics from year's end to year's end; they were full not only of dust, but also of spiders and scuttling things, and I suspected bats. Not all the temerity I had inherited from my father equipped me to face the notion of a bat caught in my hair. (My hair was fair—it was commonly called 'bright', which was a nice word—though, unusually in the Scottish Lowlands, my eyes were brown. To get drifts of dust in my brown eyes was almost as disagreeable an aspect of the attic, as to get a bat entangled in my bright hair.)

No sooner was I downstairs, than Aunt Sophia and I were astonished by another visitor. It was good Mr David Maitland, come galloping up in a hired carriage. With him were two sturdy men in long coats and billycock hats, whom he introduced to us as Police officers.

Police officers! Aunt Sophia put a hand to her breast, and began to make a moaning noise, like a poor cow I had once seen, on the point of death after eating a branch of yew.

'You have a stranger within your gates, Miss Grant?' said Mr Maitland.

I replied, since Aunt Sophia was plainly incapable of doing so, 'Yes. He is Doctor Nicol. He is in the attic, sneezing.'

'Sneezing?'

'He is certain to be sneezing, on account of the dust.'

'The attic. As I thought. Ha. So, gentlemen,' said Mr Maitland to the Police officers, 'our fellow is caught like a rat in a trap, and we can take our time.'

They nodded. They were like wooden men, showing nothing in their faces; but I was glad I was not a fugitive criminal.

Mr Maitland turned to Aunt Sophia. But she was still pressing a hand to her breast, and making the noise of a poisoned cow; so he turned back to me.

'Doctor Nicol, did he call himself?'

'Yes.'

'A big man, with a wee birthmark here?' He indicated the side of his face, by his left ear.

'It looks like a bird.'

'Ay, and a kind of bird he is, too. A hoodie-crow, maybe, or a thieving magpie. Your precious Doctor Nicol, Miss Leo, is a villain named Edgar Smith, who presented himself to me two weeks syne, seeking employment in the shop, and carrying letters of testimonial that made him out all kinds of a scholar and gentleman. No doubt they were forged. That's one of the matters my friends of the Police will be investigating. Well, he left my employ this morning, a mite suddenly, when I found his fingers in the cash-box. And when he left, as I discovered two minutes later, his pockets contained a gold snuff-box, said to have been the property of the great Duke of Montrose, and a set of miniature paintings of the Blair family.'

I goggled. At least, that is what I think I must have done; for my face felt as though I were goggling.

'He was in my shop when your sword arrived,' said Mr Maitland. 'He knew where it came from. He knew nothing about it, I think, because he knew nothing about anything. Fool that I was, I told him. Maybe it was vainglory, the old man showing off his knowledge; I hope it was in part

21

a kind of charity, to educate a poor body I still trusted. I showed him the badge on the hilt, and the line of French engraved on the blade, and I said it had likely been the property of Prince Charles Edward, who in his lifetime owned a muckle lot of swords. I said that there were more old papers in the place whence the sword had come, than in the library of the University of Edinburgh, and that, if the sword was in truth Prince Charlie's, then some of the papers were maybe his also. I said I was proposing to devote a part of my retirement to a thorough examination of them. All that I said to the villain, for which I should throw dust on my head.'

Though almost speechless with astonishment, I somehow said, 'How did you know he was coming here today?'

'We did not know, for certain, but it seemed a likely guess. He was bent on coming here, because I had told him what treasures I thought might lie in your attic (*I* told him! Idiot that I was, *I* told him!) and he knew that if he did not come here quick, he would not come at all, because I would have warned you against him. I thought he would come at once, today, and my friends of the Police agreed. Ha, my mannie! We'll have the Duke's snuffbox back, and the Blair miniatures, and your wrists in a pair of handcuffs.'

Mr Maitland was fairly dancing with satisfaction. The constables remained wooden. One of them said that he would go round to the back of the house, to prevent Edgar Smith's escape by the back door.

Aunt Sophia had stopped moaning, but still she clutched her breast.

There was a man's shout. There was a scream, which I recognized as that of Morag the little housemaid. I sped round the house, followed by Mr Maitland at almost equal speed, the second constable more slowly, and Aunt Sophia more slowly still. I was in time to see 'Doctor Nicol', no longer so glossy in appearance, hitting the first constable a tremendous blow in the face, which knocked the man flat. 'Doctor Nicol' had a bundle of papers under his left arm. He had stolen them, from the attic. He jumped over the fence which divided the kitchen garden from the little paddock; he jumped without dropping any of the papers. He ran to our old horse Virgil. Pulling him by the mane, he led Virgil to the gate out of the paddock. Mr Maitland and I and the second Police officer ran to catch him, but he was far ahead of us; and none of us jumped the fence as nimbly as he had done, for all he was a big fat man. He opened the gate, and jumped on Virgil's back; holding the mane with both hands, he kicked the old horse into a canter. This he could not do, while still holding the bundle of papers under his arm—the papers flew away in a cloud, drifting behind him like the leaves of a plane-tree in a gale.

The constable and I ran after Virgil, quite fruitlessly. Mr Maitland ran after the swirling papers, with more success. Aunt Sophia subsided against the fence, which she did not try to climb.

Mr Maitland was more than ever anxious to examine the papers, but had less than ever time to do so. We returned them to the trunk from which the sword had come. We locked the trunk; but we were sure that we would not see Edgar Smith again, the urbane 'Doctor Nicol' of the unmistakable birthmark.

Virgil was found by the Dalkeith railway station. Edgar Smith was not found.

These melodramatic events put our little household most strenuously on its guard. Never again would we be hoodwinked by a plausible rogue, especially one pretending to be a student of history, and most especially one pretending to be preparing a life of Prince Charles Edward.

Consequently, our reception of poor Simon Donaldson was suspicious and hostile in the last degree.

The first we knew of him was a rattle of hooves and a rumble of wheels, as a dog-cart turned the corner of the road. John Anderson, the gardener, straightened from his digging, to watch the dog-cart go by on the road—like all the rest of the household, old John was alert to identify and repel marauders. The dog-cart drew up at our gate, which was nowadays kept closed, though it had always before stood open. John

Anderson picked up his fork, and advanced to guard the gate. He carried his fork before him, as though it had been a partisan; he was a big man; watching from an upstairs window, I did not think any stranger would care to dismount from his vehicle and enter.

It chanced that David Laurie, the nearest farmer, went by at this moment in a trap, on his way home from market. He was a good friend of ours (though he had been no friend of mine, in my lawless childhood) and of course he knew all about Edgar Smith. Seeing the stranger, seeing John Anderson with his warlike garden fork, he pulled up, jumped out, and approached the dog-cart from the other side. He was a big man, too, and he carried a stick as gnarled and heavy as a cudgel.

Through the upstairs window, and divided from the scene by the front garden, I did not hear what was said. But the progress of the scene was plain enough, in dumb-show. The two big old men with their weapons were telling the stranger to get himself away and to stay away. And he was expostulating, and showing them pieces of paper; and they were unimpressed by his expostulations and his papers; and John Anderson brandished his fork, and David Laurie brandished his cudgel; and I was glad that we were protected from robbers.

This robber, still perched unhappily on the box of his dogcart, was much unlike Edgar Smith. He was a young man—in his middle twenties, I thought—and at a distance he looked like a gentleman. (So, to be sure, had Edgar Smith; but this one looked like a gentle man, as well as a person of breeding.) He wore an ulster over tweed knickerbockers, and looked like a laird on his way to a superior shooting party, instead of a robber on his way to our attic.

I continued to watch this scene being played, in silence and at a distance; perhaps I should have run at once out to intervene, but the weather was raw, and the house was warmer than the garden, and I did not want chapped lips or a purple nose.

It seemed, after a time, that John Anderson and David Laurie were impressed by what the stranger said—when at last they allowed him to say anything—or by the way he said it, at least so far as to allow him the benefit of the doubt; for John Anderson opened the gate for the dog-cart. But still he held his garden fork at a threatening angle, and David Laurie came into the garden, with his cudgel on his shoulder like a musket.

When the stranger jumped out of his dog-cart, I saw that he was much taller than I had supposed; and, when he removed his hat before ringing our doorbell, I saw that he was much fairer than I had supposed. His hair was thick, of the sort that can never be made to look perfectly tidy, and buttercup-yellow. Since I was standing in a window directly over the front door, all I could see of the newcomer was this hair. I liked it. A doubt entered my mind, provoked entirely by unruly buttercup hair, about whether he was in truth a criminal.

Little Morag answered the front door (for we kept no manservant within doors), and there was at once a very Babel of voices: John Anderson, whose voice was a deep bass, was thundering out warnings and suspicions; and David Laurie, who for all his bulk had a high tenor voice, was calling out his own fears and doubts, in a kind of musical counterpoint; and the stranger, whose voice was a light baritone, was trying to announce himself, and to ask for Miss Sophia Grant; and Morag, whose voice when excited was a peahen shriek, was saying that her mistress would admit no stranger at all, and at the same time telling John Anderson and David Laurie the story of Edgar Smith's assault on the constable, every detail of which they already knew. And then a moaning noise joined the chorus, by which I knew that Aunt Sophia had entered the hall: and I concluded that it was time I descended.

Well, he was called Simon Donaldson, and he had documents to prove it. And he had a letter, addressed to Aunt Sophia, from no less a person than Mr David Maitland, that established him as a *bona fide* scholar, and introduced him to Millstounburn as a person to be welcomed and trusted; and another letter, addressed 'to whom it may concern', from a Professor of the University of Aberdeen, that established Mr Donaldson not only as a scholar but as a gentleman of irreproachable character.

I was the first to be convinced, by his face and

hair and manner and voice and clothes, and by these letters, that he was an honest man on an honest errand. David Laurie was next to be convinced, perhaps because he wanted to get away home to his dinner. Aunt Sophia was slower to be convinced, because she could not at once find her spectacles to read the letters, and there was too much disputation for my reading of them to be audible. John Anderson was reluctant to be convinced, and cross when he was obliged to admit himself convinced, because he admired himself in the role of soldier, and wanted to save helpless ladies from a footpad. Morag was never convinced, then or later.

It was almost unbelievable. Simon Donaldson's story was word for word identical to that of 'Doctor Nicol'. He was a scholar and an antiquarian. He was a customer, when he could afford it, of Mr Maitland's shop. He was engaged on a study of Prince Charles Edward Stuart, which he believed justified by the new facts which were continually coming to light. He was keenly interested in any objects or papers associated with the Prince. He had seen our sword in Mr Maitland's shop.

It seemed a coincidence too gigantic to swallow. But, of course, it was no coincidence at all. In Mr Maitland's shop, Simon Donaldson had met Edgar Smith, who was still at the time employed there as an assistant. Simon Donaldson had talked to Mr Maitland, in Edgar Smith's hearing. They talked about the sword, and about

Simon Donaldson's researches into the life of Bonnie Prince Charlie. Edgar Smith then invented a name and a doctorate for himself, and otherwise came to us and performed an imitation of Simon Donaldson. So it was that Simon Donaldson's account of himself so closely echoed its own pre-echo; and so it was that Simon Donaldson was nearly impaled on John Anderson's fork, and cudgelled with David Laurie's walking-stick.

It was some time before we could fully grasp that Simon Donaldson was in reality exactly what Edgar Smith had pretended to be. I spent that time inspecting him, as well as listening to him. He was tall and slim, not with the scholar's scrawniness, but with the athlete's wiriness. His face was open and pleasing; he had wide-set grey eyes, an aquiline nose, and a cleft chin. His voice was educated; he was indeed a gentleman. His manner was a little hesitant and shy, far from the confident ebullience of 'Doctor Nicol'. I liked what I saw, and what I heard.

More covertly, he was inspecting me, which is something of which it is impossible not to be aware. He looked at me with a kind of astonishment. I understood, in part. It was this face of mine, which people fancied they had seen before. Perhaps it was more than that (I hoped it was more than that) but it was certainly that.

Once again, Aunt Sophia's social embarrassment caused her to mumble when she told him my name. It came into the conversation, as it was bound to do, in connection with my great-grandmother, who had brought back from France the sword which was the reason for his visit.

He seemed staggered.

'A family called Albany,' he said, 'have lived in this house since 1770, and the first who came here of that name, came here from France? Is that right? Do I understand you perfectly correctly?'

We assured him that he did.

He seemed to forget Prince Charles Edward, and to embark on a new line of research, of lesser importance. He wanted to know about my family.

I said that, on my mother's side, I had numerous Grant relatives; that on my great-grandmother's father's side, I had numerous, but remoter, Bruce relatives; that it was a descendant of the Bruce connection who owned Millstounburn, and allowed us to live in it.

'But Albany!' he said. 'Albany! What of Albany cousins?'

'There are none,' I said. 'It is odd, but my grandfather was an only child, and my father was an only child, and I am an only child.'

'You are therefore the single living descendant of your great-grandfather, who was named Albany?'

'Yes,' I said, greatly surprised by his excitement. 'But we do not know anything about him. We suppose he died abroad, and so my great-grandmother came back to Scotland with her baby son. She lived here with her brother. He was John Bruce. Whyever is that interesting, Mr Donaldson?'

He took a great shuddering breath. His eyes burned and his hands trembled. 'This,' he said softly, 'is going to rock the stones of castles. To humble the mighty and elevate the humble. I have believed for a long time, and my patron too, that there was an earlier marriage, perhaps with issue, but it has been impossible to prove . . . Great heaven, Miss Albany, do you not know who you are? Do you not know why your face is recognized? Do you not know who your great-grandfather was? Of course you do not. And we are running ahead of ourselves. That trunk of papers in the attic, which we suppose came back from France with the sword—that should, that surely must, include documents which will prove that you are . . .'

'What am I?' I asked nervously, not knowing in the least what he was talking about.

'I think,' he said, 'that you are Queen of Scotland.'

Two

THE ONLY SOUND in the parlour was the fluttering of a baby flame in the grate. The ticking of the grandfather clock would have been deafening, but the clock had not worked in my lifetime. We were struck dumb.

My brain began to recover from the shock it had been dealt, and began to work normally. And, as soon as it did so, I was immediately convinced that our visitor was either a lunatic or a prankster.

Simon Donaldson was looking at me intently: and I suppose that my feelings showed on my face, as they always unfortunately did.

He said, 'You are thinking, Miss Albany, that these are either the ravings of a maniac, or a cruel practical joke. With God's help, I shall prove to you that they are not. I shall prove to you and to the world that this is sober truth.'

Still his words held no meaning for me.

I was an obscure little creature, who dwelt in a modest house in an unimportant corner of Scotland. I was used to being so. I contrived, on the whole, to be resigned to being so.

Queen?

Simon Donaldson and I rushed at once to the attic. But the men who were mending the hole in the roof occupied all the attic with their tools and materials, and had buried the cowhide trunk under all manner of rubble. It did not do to interrupt their work, because even queens need mended roofs over their heads. They said that, by noon the next day, the rubble would be removed, and we could get at the trunk.

I was close to screaming with impatience, and Simon Donaldson looked close to screaming too. Aunt Sophia moaned at the unholy disorder the builder's men were making.

Of course, we asked Simon Donaldson to stay in the house, for the night and for as many nights as his researches would take. He thanked us warmly, but said that he would not stay. He had established himself at an inn in Dalkeith, and his razors and changes of clothes were in a chamber there, and he was expected back. He did, however, accept our invitation to dine: and over dinner, and afterwards, he told us an extraordinary story.

'You must know,' he said, 'that Albany is the ancient name for the major part of Scotland, that

33

occupied by the Pictish folk, the Scots from Ireland, and by numbers of invading Angles. Albany, Albania, Alban—the name comes in many forms. In the fourth century, Albany was taken to be all of Scotland east of Drumalban, which was the name they gave to the mountain barrier which reaches from Loch Lomond in the south to Cape Wrath in the north. West of Drumalban the Norsemen came, as they came to Orkney and the Hebrides.

'Now the Norsemen were always rebellious and turbulent, so that the boundary was held by castles in which the Kings of Scotland put their most loyal feudatories. I speak of King David I, and Alexander II and III, and I speak of the thirteenth century. Those castles, at that period, were built for the first time of stone. They were very massive. They were entirely military in design and function; we believe they must have been odious to live in, most squalid and uncomfortable.

'Am I tiring you? Is this history lecture as odious as a thirteenth-century castle?'

We said that he was not; that it was not.

'The first great leader who aspired to a truly united Scotland was Robert the Bruce,' Simon Donaldson went on, almost dreamily, reliving history that was to him evidently as vivid as the events of yesterday. 'He fought the Comyns and the Balliols, the autonomous and turbulent lords of the North and West. His son-in-law, who married Bruce's daughter Margery, was Walter

34

Fitzalan, hereditary steward of Scotland. Steward became Stuart, and Stuart became king.

'And then a younger branch of the royal house became Dukes of Albany, in the late fourteenth century. They rebelled, and were captured and executed, and their lands and titles reverted to the crown. Albany became as royal a name as Stuart.

'Another remarkable man came to the throne, which was King James IV of Scotland, who married the daughter of Henry VII of England. In the earliest years of the sixteenth century he travelled everywhere, making and keeping the peace. He built far finer and more comfortable castles than any Scotland had seen before, on a French plan. One of these was in Glen Alban, renamed so, by the king, as a symbol of the extension of his power. In the Castle of Glenalban he installed a grieve, as you would say a factor or agent. Then he was killed on Flodden Field, in 1513, and the nobles waxed fat and rebellious, and chaos descended again on Scotland. And the grieve of Glenalban had a son, who succeeded him in the appointment, and they became the family of Grieve of Glenalban, and nobody remembered that they were only royal servants. But the Grieves were not the rightful owners of Glenalban then, or at any time, and they are not its rightful owners now. They are Earls of Glenalban by one royal patent; and they are the tenants of Glenalban by another.'

'How can you know this?' I asked.

'Because I lived and worked there for months.

Three years ago I graduated from the university, somewhat qualified to handle and assess ancient documents, and, through the good offices of one of my professors, I was engaged by the present Earl of Glenalban, descendant of the original grieve who became Grieve. I was engaged to explore and catalogue centuries' worth of documents, deeds, charters, account-books and the like, which had piled up in the muniment-room in the castle. It seemed likely to my professors that there might be much valuable historical material in those oaken chests.

'They were right.

'King James VI of Scotland, who became King James I of England, was a canny and cantankerous kind of man, not at all inclined to let anything go that was his. He confirmed the Grieves in their stewardship of Glenalban, but he also confirmed his own ownership of it. The documents are in the castle, of course, where they belong; I have copies of them. James I's son had his head chopped off by the Roundheads; his son in turn was the Merry Monarch, who did not have time for remote Scottish castles; and his younger brother was James II, who tried to turn England Catholic, and was packed away abroad for his pains. Now I am not pleading a Tory or Jacobite case, but I am saying that on a strict reading of the law the 'Glorious Revolution' of William and Mary was a piece of the most barefaced usurpation. It saved the Church of England and the Kirk in Scotland from the Romans, but it was not lawful. It was arguably good and necessary, as we have all been taught all our lives, but there was no shred of legality about it. James II was rightful King of England and Scotland, to the day of his death, though he lived out his days an exile in France.

'In that exile, he was visited by many well-wishers and some ill-wishers, especially from Scotland. One of his visitors was Duncan Grieve of Glenalban, whose motives were probably mixed. We may guess that Duncan Grieve swore fealty to his rightful sovereign, and touched the hilt of his sword in homage, and so forth, and that he was as two-faced and treacherous as his family have been before and since. Anyhow, James II, from his exile, once again confirmed the Grieves in Glenalban, but with the qualification that if any descendant of his own body had need of the castle, then castle and estate were his, and the Grieves no more than caretakers—never more than caretakers—for the royal house of Scotland. This document, too, is in the muniment-room of the castle, and I have a copy of it.

'James II's son was James Edward, known as James III to his friends and as the Old Pretender to his enemies. The Earl of Mar raised his standard in Scotland in the winter of 1715, and James Edward arrived himself for a couple of months. Nothing came of it. By all the rules of chivalry and loyalty, the Grieves should have been among the first to rally to that standard. They did not. They sat tight in Glenalban, as greedy and cowardly as ever.

'So we come to James Edward's son, Charles Edward, whose mother was Maria Clementina Sobieska. He was born in Rome in 1720, to a diligent, dullish, bookish father, and a pious termagant of a mother. He was a skilful sportsman, a linguist, a musician. He had light brown hair that was called 'bright', and he inherited brown eyes from his mother. He was slender. His nose was high-bridged and his chin pointed. Yes, Miss Albany. There are many paintings of him, and from those paintings very many engravings, and the people of Scotland know these features well, as part of their national inheritance. Of course you are recognized!'

'But I . . .' I began: but I choked, and ceased.

'Charles Edward was not much educated and not much disciplined. He was spoiled and wilful. He was highly attractive to women, but not apparently, in his youth, much interested in them. He travelled extensively. As early as his seventeenth year, he travelled with a guardian. He adopted, when he travelled, the style of Count of Albany. He continued to do so, off and on, all his life.'

'Oh,' I said.

'Conte d'Albani, Comte d'Alban, and other variations.'

'Oh.'

'He came to Scotland in 1745, and declared his father king; and the little people rallied, and some of the great; and most of the great played as safe as they knew how, being concerned with saving themselves, and enriching themselves, and paying off a few scores; and, if the Grieves were no worse than most others, they were certainly no better. Charles Edward went to Glenalban about the middle of August of 1745, on his way to Blair Atholl, knowing full well from his father that the place was his, and the people his tenants and servants. No doubt every kind of protestation of loyalty was made to him, and every kind of treachery afterwards committed.

'Well, you know the end of that story—the Prince escaped to the Isle of Skye in a little boat with Flora Macdonald, and spent the rest of his life doing nothing in particular. He was involved with various ladies, quite aside from which he tried to marry various princesses. He began to drink heavily about 1750. He had an English lady-friend thenabouts, a passionate High Tory Catholic called Clementina Walkenshaw. She bore his daughter Charlotte, in 1752 or '53.'

'Who rightly owned Glenalban?'

'No, because she was illegitimate. Clementina ran away a few years later, taking the child. They were protected against Charles Edward by King Louis of France himself, which suggests that he was given to violence . . . He was all over the place in those years, drifting round France and Italy, sometimes in much better health, but often drinking heavily. In 1766 his father died. Thereafter he was rightfully King Charles III of England and Scotland. Yes, he was. Make no mistake about that. But nobody took him seriously, except some romantical Scots. He was an embarrassment to every government. He was a hopeless case. But he was King Charles III.

'People came across him from time to time, travelling obscurely, begging and borrowing money, calling himself usually Count of Albany. And those people wrote letters, and some of those letters are preserved, and there is in them a persistent rumour, round about 1768, that he had married at last. There is mention of a countess of Albany, and elsewhere of a Contessa d'Albani. This is not conclusive, you understand, because a lady with whom his union was not regularised might have adopted that style. But it has led my patron and myself to believe that there was a secret marriage. We have assumed that his wife died, and without issue, because he did un-doubtedly marry in 1772. Either he was a widower, or this second marriage was bigamous. In any case, it ended in divorce ten years later. After which his natural daughter Charlotte was legitimized and made his heir.'

'Oh,' I said.

'She never married.'

'Oh.'

'So the search continues.'

'For . . . ?'

'For evidence of that previous marriage, about which there were so many rumours. For evidence of living and legitimate descendants of that marriage. For evidence which will return Glenalban to its owner, and take it away from the proud and cruel and treacherous usurper who sits there now.'

We had the trunk brought down out of the attic by the builder's men. Morag swept a bucketful of dust off the outside, and another off the papers inside. They were all in a muddle after Edgar Smith's piracy, and it was three full days before Simon Donaldson had put all in order.

Much of it was valueless. Some was of only specialized interest, old household accounts, and the like. And mounds of it were the intimate journal of a young girl who left Millstounburn in 1766 as Leonora Bruce, and returned four years later with another name and with an infant son.

The hand was spidery and strange. Simon Donaldson was trained to decipher it, and did so with ease.

'3rd of March 1766. Calamity! I was never so distracted! Brother J. saw me in the Larch Plantation with my Beloved, embracing as wee cannot forbear to doe whenever wee meet in Secret, and told Papa, who has forbid me to see or meet my Ralph, on pain of my being sent Away to Cousin Henrietta in that Detestable City, and of Dearest Ralph being deprived of his Position on the Estate. Papa and J. were to be gone on a Great Journey about the Nations of Europe, J. to complete his Education and Papa to commence his, not having had the Opportunity of Voyaging when he was young, and now the plann is that I am to go with them, so that I may be Saved from the Contagioun (as they call it) of my Ralph. So to one distraction is added this Other, because I shall need a Host of Gowns and Cloakes and Shifts and I do not know what, and where are they to be hadd in this desert at a few Weekes Notice?'

The next many pages were devoted to preparations for the journey, and visits to dressmakers, and the packing of cloak-bags; and to lamentations about Leonora's separation from her unsuitable lover (Ralph was apparently a clerk employed by her father on the farm). These passages were full of underlinings and marks of exclamation; certainly the writer convinced herself she was passionately in love with her Ralph. The breaking of her heart, I thought, was losing nothing in the telling.

'I think she was a conventionally romantical girl,' said Simon Donaldson, after we had subjected ourselves to some pages of miserable outpourings, 'with a clear idea of how she ought to feel in such cruel circumstances, derived from works of fiction.'

'You mean, you think she was not truly in love with Ralph?' I said.

'She was very young.'

'She was older than I am now.'

He smiled. His smile was most warm and friendly. He had overcome the shyness with which he had first made our acquaintance: but still his manner was gentle and unassertive. His smile said that I too, like my namesake, was too young to know my heart, but that he was not going to risk my wrath by saying so.

Leonora Bruce showed the passionate enthusiasm of her nature, in a new and surprising way, amongst her outpourings about gowns and about Ralph. She recorded in her journal the news, which was come from Rome, of the Death of James Edward Stuart, called James III, called also the Old Pretender.

'Ah Black Day!' she wrote with frenzied strokes of her pen. 'My Rightful Soverain is extinguished, in Lamentable Exile, far from the Purple Heather of his beloved Land!'

There was much more in the same strain. It appeared that Leonora was a romantic Jacobite; the effect of these effusions was to make her seem younger—a silly schoolgirl, in fact, with a head full of maggots.

From the dead father, her romantical ramblings went to the living son. To her, he was a kind of god, a paragon of beauty and courage, a living legend. I knew from Simon Donaldson that Prince Charles Edward was in fact, by his time, a drunken ruin, a beggar and a sponger: but to Leonora Bruce he wore shining armour, and was her Champion and her King.

I think there were a lot of young ladies in Scotland then who felt the same girlish loyalty to the 'Young Chevalier'. But most of them, fortunately, did not go to Southern Europe with their brothers and Papas.

Leonora in due course did so, and the next piles of her journal were a record of coaches, postillions, inns, sinister travellers, beautiful and mysterious travellers, flies and cockroaches, unfamiliar dishes which affected her digestion, and descriptions of scenic and artistic beauty which had an air of being written from a sense of obligation. She was more interested in clothes than in cathedrals, in mantillas than in mountains; she *was* a silly schoolgirl, though, when she wrote what we read, she was older than I.

It was difficult to keep remembering that all this girlish stuff had been written down almost exactly one hundred years before.

We skipped rapidly through pounds of material, some of which made us laugh but much of which made us yawn: and so followed the family and their servants down through France to Avignon, where Leonora dutifully described the famous bridge, the Palace of the Popes, and the fine eyes of an ostler at the inn.

'August the Third. It is vexatious beyond anything, but our coach is broke down on the road between Avignon and Nîmes, and we are to be Obliged to shelter in an Humble house by the side of the road, where I am writing this in a Bed Chamber no bigger than a Privvy, and no Cleaner. The House is indeed a kind of Inn, but has an Insufficiency of Chambers, and those too small, so that my poor Wench Sarah is Obliged to lie in a kind of Attick, with the serving girls of the House, and I must make shift to Dress and Disrobe myself . . .'

These complaints continued for a page or two, the worst aspect being that no blacksmith was immediately available to mend whatever part of the coach had broken (on mechanical details Leonora was silent).

'August the Fourth. Exploring this place, for want of any other Employment, I saw that the Building is larger than we had supposed, having a sort of Wing extending out at the back, in which there is a much Larger and Finer Bed Chamber. Papa tried to engage this Chamber for himself, but it is Bespoke by a Traveller who is expected, Whos Servant is all ready here, making preparations against his Master's coming. The Inn Keeper speaks of "Milor", but I cannot determine from him, what Lord is expected, of even of what country, from the fact that in this Region of France, they speak all through their noses, so that it is nigh impossible to understand a Word. The Servant is a Strange and Gaunt old man, with a grey Beard. I heard him speaking in a kind of French to the People of the House, but I think he is not French, and he and the Women did not at all understand One Another.

'Evening. We have just eat Dinner, which was Ill, as the Host and his Wife and all the Folk of the Inn are devoted entirely to the new Arrival, who came quietly in, so that Wee did not see him, and they say that he will keep to his Chamber, which makes me suppose that he is a person of

High Importance, on an Embassy, or Secret Mission.

'August the 5th. The most mad and Freakish night just past, which has left me Dropping for want of Sleep. Long after Dinner, when we were all abed, but I do not know what o'clock, there rose up from the Yard behind the house, a Dreadful Droning, and Groaning, and Shreaking, which Presently Resolved itself into a kind of Rough Musicke, and to my Compleat Amazement, I understood that I was listening to a Scotch Bagpipes! Nothing could be, that could Astound me more, than to hear this of all Noises here! I threw on a Dressing Robe, and ran downstairs, to see a thing that could not be Believed. The secret Milor's Servant was Marching up and down, as Pipers do, beneath the window of the Milor's Chamber. On his Head was a Scotch Bonnet. And the Yard Filled up with people, Papa and Brother J and the Host and Hostess and Servants, all in dressing Robes and Night Caps, calling on the old man to stop his Noise, but he would not, and Marched on, Playing on his Pipes. Papa called out to him in English, Forgetting in his Rage where we were, to let Decent People sleep, and the servant stopped his Piping long enough to reply, in a thick and broad Scotch Voice, Syne ma Maister canna sleep, he'll hae the soond o' the Pipes. And indeed there was a candle in the window of the great Bed Chamber, and a face beside it, but we could not well see the face.

'Later. Papa has spoke to the Servant, who is in Truth a Scotchman, but he has followed his Master for twenty years, travelling the cities and Villages of Europe, and Papa says the old Man was Moved almost to tears, to heare a Scotch voice, and see a Scotch Face.

'The Servant called his Master "His Highness", but he would not say more who he was.

'Later. There has been a Battle about the Inn, going from the Kitchen to the Hall, and so to the Yard, and backe again, between the Scotch Servant and the Host and Hostess. Papa, thinking to go to the Aid of a Distressed Fellow Countryman, discovered Milor cannot pay his Reckoning. It is not a great sum. At last, upon his knees, the old man begged Papa to assist his Master, and all would one day be repaid, when his Master came into his own, which he would Surely Do. Papa said that he would Assist any Creature in Need (which is not entirely True) but that he must know who he was Helping. In sum, he would not part with any Gold, until he knew who "His Highness" was. The Servant whispered to him, looking round as though for fear of Eavesdroppers. Papa said "That is just as I thought," and gave the Servant more than he asked him for.

'Later. Papa has told Brother J and me, in the Greatest Confidence, what we will remember all our Lives. I can scarce hold the penn, for Agitation, for "Milor" is no other than the King Over the Water, to whom I have in my Secret

Heart, and in the Hidden pages of this Journal, vowed *Lifelong devotion,* and in whose Cause, I would *sacrifice all!*

'August 9th. Three Days have past, when I have not known if I was on my head or my heels, my Mind and Heart being in such a Whirl, that I could not find Time or Strength to take up my Penn. but now my Beloved Lord sleeps, and in Tranquilitie I sett down the Strangest Events that ever Overtook a Young Female.

'I was making myself ready for my bed, though was still for the most part dressed, when came a knock on the door, which I thought must be my wench Sarah, or one of the Maids of the House. I went to the door, and to my great amazement there stood the old Scotch Servant, whom I now knew to be named Wedderburn. He bowed to me, holding his bonnet in his hands. He said that his Master had seen me from the window of his Chamber, as I crossed the Yard, or was about some business behind the House, and desired that I should Present myself to him, for that he wished to make my Acquaintance, and to hear news of Scotland, and how it went with those that had Followed him twenty years before.

'I trembled at the Thought of making my Reverence to a Prince, that should have been a King, and was almost too alarmed to have followed Wedderburn, but A request from this Prince, was to me the most Absolute and Binding Command, so I summoned my Feeble Courage, and followed the old man through back passages, to the Door of the Princely Apartment.

'Of my Graceful Reception by His Royal Highness I can not write without a flood of grateful Emotion. He rose as I entered the Chamber, and by the Light of his Candles I saw him to be moderate tall, no longer perhaps as Slender as I had seen him Pictured in his hot Youth, but still elegant, and Well Formed in all Particulars, with Features sufficiently pleasing, though shewing Signs of the Manifold Hardships and Deprivations which it had been his Lott to bear. I curtseyed deep, but he took my hand, and raised me, and with the Greatest Affability, conducted me to a chair, desiring me to sit, and take my Ease, and then with his own hands (for Wedderburn had left the Chamber) poured out for me a glass of Wine, which I knew I should not take, but which from the Royal hand I must accept. His condescension then, as he sate near to me, is what I despair of being able to Express. He pressed me for Details of the Situation in Scotland and in England, of which alas! I shewed a wofull ignorance; and was so obliging as to express a lively interest in Myself, and in my family and life, and whether I were in Love, and whether Betrothed. He pressed more Wine upon me, which I knew I should not take, for fear of Inflammation of the Nerves, and of becoming too Free with my Speech. And after some Glasses of Wine, I told him about Ralph. Answering his Questions, I admitted that Ralph had kissed me with Ardour, and that I had felt his hands on my

Bosom, but not quite inside my Clothes. Then, to my Stupefaction, I found that he was upon his Knees before my chair, Speaking very rapidly and Hoarsely, praising what he called my Beauty of face and figure. And then he said, Did your Ralph touch you so? And so? And placed his Royal Hands upon my bosom, and kissed me! And then he asked me in a low Tone, about my Sympathies, and whether I were Loyal to the Hanover Rats of England, and I cried out that I was His Loyal subject and servant, at which he gave me more wine, which I knew I should not have taken. I made so bold as to kiss his hands, as Token of the Reverent Loyalty I felt for Him, but he raised my head, and kissed my lips, and Embraced me with a mounting Passion, to which my Loyal Fervour inspired me to respond, as also did the Wine, so that he carried me, overcome by my emotions, to the bed, and there undressed me, and had his Will of me, and I could not resist, and would not if I could, for I was Honoured above all Females.

'So he fell at last asleep beside me, and I watched over him with Adoration, and slept at length also. In the dawn I woke, my head thick with sleep and with Wine, but he slept on, breathing with a great Noise.

'Then suddenly below there was a Hubb-Bubb, and in dismay I heard Papa's voice, and old Wedderburn's, and I thought blows struck, and Brother J's voice raised up very high and Furious. In a moment there was a great pounding on the door, which burst open, and Papa was within,

50

shouting of Disgrace, Treachery, Fornication, and such stuff, which was an Ill way to speak to a Prince, and Brother J had drawn his sword, and was shouting also. The Chamber was quite full of People, all shouting, and all saw my Lord in his Bed, and me with him unclothed. Papa said something behind his hand to my Brother J, who nodded, and rann off, still carrying his Sword.

'I thought nothing would have woken my Beloved Lord, so profound was his sleep, but at last he Stirred, and groaned, and looked with the greatest astonishment at the Croud which had gathered in his Chamber. He sate up in the bedd, and commanded silence, and that all those present should at once depart, but Papa would not, and with his sword prevented Wedderburn and the Host from removing him, at which I screamed.

'So matters rested for a time, during which I began to feel increasingly Ridiculous, and then at last Brother J returned, from the next village, with a Priest. And Papa said that the Priest should immediately Marry us, and if he did not, there would be Breasts spit on his Sword.

'So there was at once a Ceremony, of which I understood Nothing, for it was conducted part in Latin, and part in French. And at the end of the Ceremony, I was the Lawfull Wedded wife of His Royal Highness Prince Charles Edward Stuart, rightfully King Charles III of England and Scotland. But he was not married under that name, but under another style he used, which was Count of Albany.

'There was a Paper give me by the Priest, which sets forth that we were Wedd, and shews if ever I am challenged in the matter that I am indissolubly the Wife of the Prince.'

'This is the paper, I fancy,' said Simon Donaldson, drawing a yellowed document from between the pages of the journal. 'Oh yes. I have seen just such certificates before. That marriage was entirely legal and valid.'

'Let us get on,' I said, choking.

'This must have been a shock to you, Miss Albany. I am sorry you should learn so—so brutally about your great-grandmother's . . .'

'Immorality? You have not been brutal. Did the, hum, improper events of that night take place because she was drunk, or because she was a Jacobite and he her king, or because she fell in love with him?'

'I would say equal parts of all three,' said Simon Donaldson slowly. 'He was an experienced man of nearly fifty, who had had a number of mistresses, and who had been, if he no longer was, highly attractive to women; and she was a very green girl. He was a royal prince, and her greatest hero. He filled her with wine, to which she was unused. It was all very easy for him. It does him no credit. I wonder if it does her father credit, that he forced them into instant marriage at the point of his sword?'

'Let us see how they fared, and then we can tell.'

Well, the new Countess of Albany's Papa and

brother John stayed on a few days at the same inn, and then resumed their travels. Leonora, of course, stayed with her husband, and began to share with him the obscure and purposeless travellings which had been his life since the defeat of his rebellion.

The journal became scrappy and allusive. It seemed to us that, after a sober period, the Prince began to drink heavily again. Money was a constant and degrading worry; mostly, this extraordinary royal couple lived on what the old servant Wedderburn begged on their behalf.

It seemed, to Simon Donaldson and me, that Leonora sometimes begged on her husband's behalf; but this was reading between the lines. She remained steadfastly loyal to him, even in the secrecy of these pages.

A son was born to them, in an Italian city; and this, as the diarist wrote, at once changed everything.

'The Course of Life, which my Royal Husband has adopted, is one which I have been able to Stomach, tho often it has been hard, and often laid me open to Humiliation and Despaire. But an Infant cannot travel Europe like a Parcel, nor be exposed to the Dirt and Fatigues of everlasting coaches and inns. I have writ to Brother J, Papa being dead, for a Draft to pay for my journey home.'

Home was Millstounburn, where her brother John now reigned.

Of her parting with Prince Charles Edward,

Leonora wrote pages of script that seemed to us to be shaking with emotion. But we read that she was writing them in the coach that carried her north from Genoa, and the rattling of the coach was what caused the waywardness of her pen. She was not so very grieved; all too clearly, this was because the Prince had become a hopeless case. Her feelings, as she revealed them, were very much the mixture that might have been expected —part of her still revered the Prince, part could no longer tolerate the man. And it was no life for a baby.

Of course she wanted something to remember him by. He had almost nothing: everything, even to his pistols, had been sold to pay for wine. He gave her a sword, presented to him by the citizens of Carcassonne, on the occasion of his birthday.

We read of her homecoming with the infant James Edward. She resolved to say nothing to anybody, then or ever, about her husband, but to let it be assumed that he was a foreigner, now dead. This was out of loyalty. Out of loyalty also, she retained the name Albany, but abandoned the title of Countess, although she was perfectly entitled to have used it.

James Edward Albany was baptised only after his return, in the Episcopalian church in Dalkeith. His mother had not become a Roman Catholic on her marriage, and did not wish her son to be so.

'That baptism will be recorded in the church register,' said Simon Donaldson. 'Put beside these pages, it will absolutely confirm that your

54

grandfather was the son of Prince Charles Edward.'

Well, we read the rest of Leonora's journal, Simon Donaldson and Aunt Sophia and I, during those thin midwinter days, in the search for anything else that would throw more light on our discovery. There was nothing. James Edward grew up, married, and had a son. John Bruce died; his son went out to Australia, like many Scotsmen at that time, and James Edward became his tenant at Millstounburn. Leonora lived on obscurely until her death in 1818, keeping up her journal until her final illness. She became increasingly devoted to religion, and the later parts of the journal contained many long extracts from sermons and from the Scriptures.

There was a final note, in what Aunt Sophia said was my father's hand, recording Leonora's death. It was evident that neither he nor my grandfather had ever read any of the journal, or knew anything of its contents. This may have been because they thought they would have been guilty of prying; or because they were not much given to reading.

Simon Donaldson made copies of the relevant pages of the journal, and of the marriage certificate; he also went to the church in Dalkeith, and copied the entry in its Register recording my grandfather's baptism. With these copies, he went away to Edinburgh, promising to return.

And, when he had gone, I found that I missed him dreadfully. He had almost lived at Millstounburn, all during the time of our reading, often arriving early and leaving late, often sharing our dinner, more and more becoming a member of the household. To Aunt Sophia he was always gentle and considerate, so that she was at ease with him as with almost no one else, and she talked freely with him, and even laughed. To me he was also gentle and considerate, but bit by bit he was more—much more. He became my intimate companion and confidant. He became my closest friend. He became more—much more. By looks as much as by words, he declared the warmth of his feelings for me. And by my looks I, no doubt, declared that I returned those feelings.

It had never happened to me before. I felt as drunk, on those warm looks of Simon's, as Leonora Bruce on Prince Charles Edward's wine.

In those dragging days either side of Christmas, my mind was in a rare muddle. I could not begin to guess what the implications were, of what we had discovered. That was muddle enough: and there was the memory of Simon himself, to muddle me further.

And, to muddle me further still, Simon reappeared in the middle of January, far sooner than he had given us to expect.

'This is a fleeting visit,' he said. 'There are some more pages the lawyers want to see, so I must copy them.'

I thought he was glad to have an excuse to

come to Millstounburn. In my vanity, I thought he was joyful to see me again. He looked joyful, as he took my hand. I am very sure I looked joyful.

His copying was done quick—so quick, that I wondered if there was truly any to do. Aunt Sophia had asked him to stay for dinner, and it came about that Simon and I had some time together in front of the parlour fire.

He said, very quietly, looking into the fire, that he was in a daze of happiness to see me again, and to be with me.

'I am happy too,' I said.

'But for two reasons I cannot speak my heart to you, Leo. The first is, that I gave my word to your aunt that I would not speak until after your eighteenth birthday. I suppose she was right, to extract that promise from me. Think of what befell your great-grandmother! As you yourself said, she was older when she went off to France than you are now. But soon you will be older than she was then . . .'

'It is bad enough that there is one reason why you cannot—speak your mind,' I said. 'I do not want another reason.'

'But you must have it. At the moment, I am hardly able to support myself. I am living on charity. My patron would not put it like that, but honesty obliges me to. You must see that, even if I had not given my word to Miss Grant, I must altogether change my circumstances before I say—anything to you.'

'You could perhaps,' I said anxiously, 'give me an idea of what you are going to say, when you come to say it, so that it will not come as a shock to me. Shocks are bad for people, you know, and lead to disordered nerves . . .'

He smiled. In the firelight, his smile seemed to me enchanting. There was something of a renewed shyness in his smile, because he was talking about his feelings for me.

He said, looking away, with a choke in his voice, 'You know very well what I shall say, dearest Leo.'

'And you know very well what I shall reply,' I said.

'I am in imminent danger of breaking my word to your aunt,' said Simon. 'And of acting dishonourably in that other sense, too. I can earn a living, you know. I have done so, and will do so again, when this project of ours is complete.'

'Yes, of course. I do not doubt that.'

'Things have gone strangely for me.'

'Tell me.'

'There are more interesting things to discuss than my poor affairs.'

'Not to me,' I said.

'Well, if you must subject yourself to my story, at least it is quite brief. As you know, I went from the university almost directly into that position as archivist at Glenalban. I believed then, and I believe still, that I was doing competent and valuable work in that muniment room, and I had and have reason to think that my labours were appreciated by my employer's aunt, the Dowager Lady Lochinver, who has lived at Glenalban since her husband's death. She was unfortunately away, visiting her married daughter, when the Earl of Glenalban suddenly and summarily dismissed me.'

'Why did he?'

'For no reason. A man like that needs no reason for what he does. In that place he is an autocrat, a whimsical tyrant, a Tiberius, a Borgia, a Napoleon. Perhaps he resented my being younger than he, and—dare I say it?—cleverer and better read than he. It is repugnant to his philosophy that anyone should be better at anything than he. All his life, I think, his family and friends have allowed him to win games, because he has made life so disagreeable if he was defeated. I was—I am—demonstrably better at matters historical and archival than he. I was a daily reminder of his own ignorance and stupidity. Thus I became first an irritant, and then a reason for fury.'

'But that is ridiculous,' I said.

'Many of the things the Earl of Glenalban does are ridiculous. His reasons are childish, laughable. But the results are often tragic. I do not mean in my case—I am alive and well and happily occupied: I am not swimming in a soup of self pity. But in the case of the tenant farmers suddenly evicted, without justice or humanity—men barely able at the best of times to feed their children . . .'

'He does that?' I said, appalled: for, like everybody else who ever saw a newspaper, I knew of the frightful sufferings of crofters evicted by cynical landlords, who wanted the land for deer-forest, or grouse-moor, or sheep-walk, from which more money could be made.

'He has come near to doing it countless times,' said Simon. 'He has, mercifully, often been restrained by his own family from acts of arbitrary barbarity.'

'Is he mad?'

'No. Not in a medical sense. But the effect of almost unlimited domestic and local power, on an indifferent intellect, produces results which look like the work of a wicked madman.'

'Can nothing be done to curb him?'

'All that is possible is continuously done, by many decent people. But they are not Earls of Glenalban.'

'Did he give any reason for dismissing you?'

'He said that I was incompetent, which I believe was not true. It was a point, moreover, on which he was himself incompetent to judge. He said that I was dishonest.'

'But that is absurd!'

'I am glad you think so, Leo. You have the benefit, if it is one, of knowing me moderately well. The people to whom the Earl wrote, when I was seeking other employment, did not know me. Consequently, they believed the Earl.'

'But that is vicious!'

'The mildest of the words I have used about it myself,' said Simon. 'I felt physically sick, when I was shown one letter he wrote about me, in response to an enquiry. The gentleman who showed me the letter did not quite believe it himself. But he could not take the risk of engaging me as tutor to his sons—a man branded by his only previous employer as a scoundrel. Of course, he was right. He could *not* take that risk. I do not blame him at all. The whole fault lies elsewhere.'

'I did not think such things happened.'

'Nor did I. I have always been optimistic. I have—I had—always believed in the essential goodness of humankind, which is the working of the Holy Spirit. An episode like that shakes one's faith in God and man.'

'Perhaps I can help to restore it.'

'Yes. You, your aunt, my patron, Mr David Maitland, the eminent people I have been seeing in Edinburgh—I have been more fortunate recently.'

'I do not understand about this patron.'

'Ah. He is a fascinating man. An Italian aristocrat, the Baron Vigliano—il Barone Lodovico di Vigliano. Highly educated, highly civilized, himself a scholar, much travelled. The point is that he is descended on his mother's side from Princess Louise de Stolberg.'

I looked blank.

'The wife, whom we now know to have been bigamously married, of Prince Charles Edward Stuart.'

'My great-grandfather.'

'Just so. This relationship inspired the Baron to

focus his abundant energies and his formidable scholarship on the Europe of the late eighteenth century, and in particular on its various royal families, and most particularly on the sad outcast among them whom his ancestress had married.'

'Good gracious. Is he producing a book to be a rival to yours?'

'On the contrary, he is assisting in and financing mine. By a staggeringly lucky chance, he wrote to a professor at Aberdeen, with whom he had been corresponding for years, asking to be recommended a person who could conduct research in Scotland, while he conducted it in France and Italy—and the professor received this letter not long after my dismissal from Glenalban. Very kindly, the professor submitted my name, not being in the way of believing slanders about his former students. The Barone wrote that he must meet me, before any firm arrangement was made. He could not at that time come to Britain, owing to pressure of business, so I must go to Turin. My fare and all expenses were paid— fortunately, for I could not have paid for them myself. I was enchanted by him. You will be, too.'

'How will I be?'

'Did I not tell you? He is coming here, for the first time in his life. He speaks good English, but he has never used it in England or Scotland. He is coming because he is fascinated by what I have already been able to tell him, about our discoveries.'

'Yours.'

'Without you, none of this would have come to light.'

'Without your having seen that sword . . . Which was only in Mr Maitland's shop, because we needed money, because of a hole in the roof . . . How oddly things turn out. When is your Baron coming?'

'He writes that it will be as soon as possible. He himself does not know when he can get away. I warned him of the Scottish winter, but I do not think ice or fog will deter him, especially in view of another reason that he has for coming. He is avid to meet the single living legitimate descendant of Charles Edward.'

'Oh.'

'Of course he knows exactly what the Prince looked like, from engravings. So that, although he has never seen you, he will recognize you at once, and would do so from a thousand girls. In fact, he would not need to be aware of your uncanny resemblance to your great-grandsire, to recognize you straight away. I told him you were the most beautiful girl in Scotland, so he would pick you out from any crowd, with no difficulty, from that description.'

'Um,' I said deeply pleased but not having had any experience of making a proper reply to such a remark.

'I am forgetting myself again,' said Simon. 'I wonder if, after all, you have an immoral influence on me?'

'We are not allowed immoral influences on one another yet,' I said. 'But when I am eighteen . . .'

The conversation was taking a lovely but disquieting turn; perhaps it was as well that Aunt Sophia returned from a charitable errand, to interrupt it.

'I do not think,' said Simon at dinner, 'that there would be any profit in your pursuing claims to the crowns of England or Scotland.'

'Mercy,' said Aunt Sophia, rattling her knife against her plate in agitation at the thought.

'We are all loyal subjects of Her Majesty Queen Victoria,' said Simon. 'We had better remain so, I think.'

'Yes,' I said: for I was not going to admit to some of the wild dreams I had had.

'What, then, does all this mean to you, Leo?'

'Well, what does it mean to me?'

'The Lord Lyon King of Arms, in Edinburgh, accepts the probability, which can shortly be turned into certainty, that you are Countess of Albany in your own right. It was a legitimate title, legitimately used by Charles Edward, and it can descend in the female line if there are no male heirs.'

I pondered this. I thought I would like to be a Countess, but there were difficulties.

'To make any sense of being a Countess,' I said, 'you need all kinds of things. Things I have not got, and cannot get. How can I be a sensible Countess, living here, and wearing what I wear, and eating boiled mutton twice a week? To make any sense of being a Countess, you need a castle and a lot of money.'

'You have those things.'

'What?'

'You are the owner of Glenalban, castle and estate. You are one of the richest individuals in Scotland. The lawyers have examined the evidence, and your claim is as solid as the Palace of Holyroodhouse.'

'Mercy,' said Aunt Sophia.

Three

SIMON CAME AGAIN, two weeks later, with a little shrivelled man who was some important kind of lawyer. What the lawyer had to do, was to confirm that Simon had accurately transcribed my great-grandmother's journal and marriage certificate; the courts would then accept the documents as genuine, without having to inspect the originals.

We were moving gradually closer to my claiming the abeyant Earldom of Albany. I could not yet picture claiming the castle and estate of Glenalban.

The lawyer was always with Simon, during that visit. There was no chance of another lovely and disquieting conversation. My feelings towards the lawyer were consequently mixed, resentment of his presence striving against gratitude for his labours. My feelings towards Simon were not mixed at all. I know now that I was not yet truly in love with him, but I thought then that I was.

Aunt Sophia was right. I was far too young for all this. The hole should have been made in the roof a year later, so that the sword would have gone to Edinburgh to pay for the repairs a year later, so that Simon Donaldson and his discoveries would have come into my life when I was well into my nineteenth year. Then I would have brought at least a smattering of experience to bear on these new problems—at least a wisp of maturity, to keep cool and calm. But I had no experience and no maturity, and I did not keep very cool or calm.

Of all the seventeen-year-old girls in Scotland, I was the least qualified for greatness of position, or for emotional storms. But, of all the young girls in Scotland, I was the one who would shortly be Countess of Albany.

The lawyer confirmed this, when he left with Simon. He was the first one who called me 'Ma'am'. I was completely startled, because seventeen-year-old-girls are not called 'Ma'am'. But ladies of royal blood are.

They left; and life at Millstounburn returned, to all appearance, to normal. But it was not normal. Nothing would ever again be as it was.

Presently word came from Simon that dates had been fixed for my formal petitions to the courts. They were not in the very near future. This was fortunate, for the legal processes of pursuing gigantic claims like mine would be hideously expensive, especially the fees for the leading

67

advocates we would require.

Hearing of these, from our own solicitor in Dalkeith, made Aunt Sophia moan and myself goggle. We concluded that we must at once abandon the entire project, and forever.

But Simon wrote that, long before my petitions were presented, the Barone Lodovico di Vigliano would be in Scotland, and that he could and would pay every penny involved. He would be delighted to do so—proud to do so—said Simon. And we should not worry about accepting money from him, because he had a very great deal of it; and, by and by, I would have a very great deal of it too, and could pay him back.

Simon wrote again, in excited and delighted terms, that he was expecting the Barone before the end of February, and that, the minute he arrived, Simon would bring him to see us.

He came to Millstounburn, with Simon, in a fine hired carriage—a big, ebullient man between forty and fifty, with long glossy black hair touched at the temples with grey, and with a beard of such magnificence that it could only have belonged to an Italian aristocrat or a French poet. He was dressed in a frock coat, with pale coloured trousers, and button boots, and a prodigious cravat of silvery material with a large jewelled pin in its midst. He wore the tallest top hat I had ever seen, and he carried an ebony cane with an ivory knob bigger than a cricket ball.

He was in the most total contrast to Simon, who

was quietly dressed in his usual tweeds, and looked like a laird of serious tastes. Yet, although the Barone was exotic, his appearance was no more incongruous (after the first moment of shock) than Simon's was, because his clothes suited him, and he them. Like Simon, he was dressed as himself; he was not pretending to be in any particle different from what he was.

He jumped down from the carriage, very active for such a big, plump man: and I thought he would bounce as he met the ground, as high as the carriage roof. Indeed he had the appearance of bouncing, as he walked with Simon towards the house.

He bowed over Aunt Sophia's hand, and kissed it. She was too amazed to speak. Hands were not commonly kissed in East Lothian. Probably Aunt Sophia's hand had never been kissed before.

Nor had mine; but it was kissed now.

'It is not correct, Contessa,' said the Barone, 'to kiss the hand of a young lady not *sposata*. But it is most correct to kiss the hand of a royal princess.'

He spoke English very rapidly, and somewhat loudly, in a strong accent that was not at all displeasing; this was because, like his clothes, it suited him; beard, button boots, tiepin and accent all fitted together; for such a gorgeous exotic to have spoken normal English would have been the incongruous thing.

He straightened from a bow lower than I would have supposed such a portly man could make. He stared down at me, from an impressive height. (He

69

was a little taller than Simon, and Simon was tall.) He stared at my face, with a frown that held no hint of anger or disapproval.

'My friend Simon is right,' he said at last, more softly. '*A ragione, come sempre.* Your face, *piccola Contessa,* is the face of that great man who was a king and not ever a king. Simon is right, that I should know your face among a thousand. I do not know if he is right that you are the most beautiful of all the *signorine* of Scotland, because I have not seen every one of the young girls of Scotland, but I guess that he is right, yes. *Indovino cosi.* Of the Prince you have the *capelli chiari,* the bright hairs described by people of his time, the brown eyes from his mother, the chin with a kind of point. Now—haha!—we have another *revoluzione,* my little Simon. We shall gather up all the clans! We shall march ourselves upon Edimburgo, with our *piccola Contessa* riding in the frontal on a white horse, and you and I, little Simon, shall ride close behind on other horses, and all the clans will march behind, full of *valore* and love of their true Queen . . . There will be horrible noises, which you call music, from those goatskin bags which you call *pipi,* which I have heard once in Mentone, but all revolutionaries must suffer hardships with courage, and I shall suffer the music of your bagpipes . . .'

Simon began to laugh—the infectious, husky laughter which, when he had overcome his shyness, we had heard so often at Millstounburn. I began to laugh. The Barone, after a moment of

70

pretended anger, laughed loud and long at his own fooleries, a rich baritone trumpet-call of laughter, which threatened to shiver the windows of the house.

Even Aunt Sophia, overwhelmed by the Barone, managed a little strangled giggle.

We conducted the Barone to the unoccupied bedchamber where my great-grandmother's trunk had been put. We showed him the journal. He did not attempt to read it, because Simon had, weeks previously, sent him copies of the pages that concerned us. But he was most anxious to see and handle the original strange document, and did so with a kind of reverence.

Even while he turned the pages of Leonora's spidery handwriting, he continued his fanciful and ludicrous account of the new Jacobite rebellion we were to lead. He had us fortified in Edinburgh Castle, then throwing an army down into the Borders. He had flying columns of cavalry striking deep into Northumberland, and at last myself being crowned in Westminster Abbey, with poor Queen Victoria going off into exile in Holland.

Turning suddenly serious, he said, 'Signorina Principessa, I think you will not wear a crown in London. But I think you will wear a coronet in the Castello di Glenalbani. I think we shall make it so.'

'Why?' I said. 'I mean, why are you helping me?'

'Because I am poet. I am lover of art and of justice. I am lover of Carlo Eduardo and his

71

Highlanders. Poetry and art and justice and politics and history, all these things say to me that a wrong must be made right, and a fairy story must have the happy endings.'

I thought that really was what he meant. He wanted to be the one to turn, if not a frog into a prince, then a mouse into a Countess. It seemed to me a good reason, a nice reason for helping me; and I thought that a man who spent a lot of money for such a reason, was a nice man.

Besides, as Simon had said, I would one day be able to pay him back.

Of course, they both stayed for dinner. The Barone was extravagant in his praise of the beef, of which he ate many slices. He said that Scotland was to be admired above all nations for the beauty of its women and the succulence of its cattle. He insisted on meeting Mrs Murray the cook, and gave her a gold coin; she tucked it away so rapidly, that I did not see of what country it was. Morag shrank away from him, in horrified astonishment, but Mrs Murray was a-flutter with delight.

It was just at this moment that I had the silly idea that I had seen the Barone before. I knew I could not have done, because he had never been across the English Channel. But the notion persisted. I said to Simon that, as the Barone recognized me from pictures of Charles Edward, so I thought I recognized him from something.

'Many people do,' said Simon. 'There is a sort of similarity to your own case. The Barone bears a certain likeness to Garibaldi, of whom you are

72

bound to have seen pictures. To tell you the truth, I think his beard is deliberately modelled on Garibaldi's, to increase the resemblance.'

This seemed eminently probable. The Barone was nothing if not theatrical. That great swash-buckling patriot would have appealed immensely to his romantic notions, as my own royal great-grandfather did. And this fitted, too, with his ambition to manage a happy ending for our fairy tale, and turn the country mouse into a castellated Countess.

It was all very endearing, as well as being very convenient.

And, because I was thinking on these lines, I said, as they were gathering up their things to leave, 'Is that a swordstick?'

With his face comically solemn, the Barone twisted the great ivory knob of his cane, and pulled it out, revealing a few inches of narrow, highly polished steel.

'There are many *banditti* in my country, small Contessa. A wise man goes armed.'

'Have you ever used it?'

'Yes! Surely! There was one time when I had deep need of my sword, and I was thankful that I had it.'

'You were attacked by bandits?'

'I was by the *Lago di Como,* far from help, far from any houses or any person. I was in despair.'

'How many bandits?'

'There were no bandits there. I had a melon, which I wished to slice. It was a very good melon.'

73

He burst out into his trumpet-call of laughter. I thought he carried a swordstick simply as part of his play-acting. I thought it was not exactly childish, but child-like. It was odd to find this trait, in a man so clever and learned; it was all of a piece with the other things I had learned about him. It was, as Simon said, rather enchanting.

Simon's letters were written on such odd scraps of paper as he had by him, I suppose, when he was working. They were addressed jointly to Aunt Sophia and myself. I would have liked a private letter, directed only to myself; but I accepted that this would have been a breach of Simon's vexatious promise to Aunt Sophia.

Now a letter came which was addressed to me only; and it was not written on an odd scrap of paper. In the envelope, it was so heavy, that I was surprised it could be carried by the penny post.

I could not think who in the world would write to me, that would use such paper. My surprise at receiving it was nothing to my astonishment at reading it.

Glenalban Castle
February 8th, 1865
My Dear Miss Albany,
    Next week I shall be making one of my rare visits to Edinburgh, after which I am to go for two nights to Dalhousie. I understand that you live only a few miles from that place. I am anxious to meet you, and believe that we

have much to discuss. May I propose to call on Miss Grant and yourself on Wednesday next, in the early afternoon?

If this is *not* convenient, perhaps you would be so kind as to convey a message to Dalhousie Castle, in time to stop me making a fruitless journey. If I do not hear from you, I will take it that my arrival with you is expected.

I am greatly curious to meet you and, from what I have heard, shall greatly enjoy doing so.

Until Wednesday next I remain, dear Miss Albany,

Yours very truly,
Rosanna Lochinver.

It was another moment for goggling.

Aunt Sophia was watching me, with what was clearly unbearable curiosity. I handed her the letter, and presently she found her spectacles.

She moaned as she read.

'Rosanna Lochinver,' she said. 'Who can she be?'

'Let me think,' I said. 'Simon has mentioned her. She is the aunt of the Earl. She is a widow. She lives at Glenalban. When Simon was there, she knew he was giving good service. I think he liked her. Yes, he spoke as though he liked her, as though she was kind to him.'

'Lady Lochinver!' wailed Aunt Sophia. 'Straight from Glenalban! I cannot entertain such a person here! What will she think of us?'

I wondered, too. I wondered what on earth she wanted with me. The tone of her letter was formal, but affable enough.

She had befriended Simon. That suggested that she was a civilized person. It also raised the possibility that they had kept in touch—that she knew something of what had been engaging Simon these past weeks.

From this possibility, a thousand possibilities sprouted. She might know what we were about, the Barone and Simon and I. She might most bitterly oppose it, on her nephew's behalf. In spite of the friendliness of her letter—which might have been deliberately adopted so that we would be disarmed, and receive her—she might be bent on threatening or terrifying me out of the course to which I was now committed. She might be intending to buy me off, to bribe me into silence. She might be simply curious. She might be favourable to my claims, though this seemed the remotest possibility. She might know nothing of Leonora's journal, nothing of the true ownership of Glenalban, but merely be curious to see the person of whom Simon had written—whatever he had written. If, indeed, he had written.

It was barely possible, I supposed, that she was curious to inspect me for some quite other, unguessable reason, having heard something about me from some quite other, unguessable source.

The following Wednesday afternoon was perfectly convenient. I was prepared to abandon, for as long as Lady Lochinver honoured us, the course of reading which Aunt Sophia had set me. Aunt Sophia could postpone (she would never abandon) the charitable errands for which those hours had been earmarked. No message therefore went to Dalhousie. We steeled ourselves to receive a lady as august and frightening as Boadicea.

Anyone less august, anyone less frightening than Lady Lochinver could not be imagined. She was the kind of person whom one likes from a distance, and who makes one smile before a word is said.

I put her age at fifty. In person she was plump, in height moderate, in dress untidy. Her clothes were doubtless expensive and certainly fashionable, but she had the air of wearing them as a joke. Her face was round, with a high fresh colour like a Ribston pippin. Her hair, which was a thick bundle of pepper-and-salt, looked on the verge of tumbling down from under a hat which looked on the verge of falling off.

Where the Barone had seemed to bounce on his way from his carriage to the house, Lady Lochinver seemed to hop. I do not mean that she literally proceeded across the gravel on one leg, but she advanced with the perky eagerness of a bird, of a plump redbreast certain of a welcome.

I curtseyed to her. She stretched out both her hands, and took mine. She smiled, very broad and warm.

She said, 'They were right. You are the image of

77

the Young Chevalier. And you are the most beautiful girl in Scotland.'

I challenge anyone to make a reply, unrehearsed and on the instant, to such an opening from a total stranger.

She drank tea, and ate an astonishing quantity of Dundee cake; she chatted to Aunt Sophia about household expenses, and whether vegetables grown in the garden were in truth an economy, considering the wages of gardeners.

Aunt Sophia was put at her ease by Lady Lochinver even more quickly than by Simon Donaldson. One would have said that they were friends of thirty years' standing, as they discussed the respective merits of wood and coke in a kitchen range, the scandalous cost of feeding servants, and the dangerously advanced views of a certain Episcopalian bishop. Lady Lochinver was garrulous, kind, and I thought essentially simple in the nicest way. She was like a country neighbour of our own station of life, if we had been lucky enough to have any such neighbour.

She finished the last crumbs of cake on her plate; she finished her third cup of tea. She turned to me and said, 'You must have guessed that I have had word from Simon Donaldson.'

'I thought it might be that,' I said.

'I have remained in his confidence, and he in mine, since that horrid business with my nephew.'

'What did happen?'

'I scarcely know. I was away at the time, which was so unlucky. Simon wrote to me that he did not really know why Glenalban turned against him. Glenalban said Simon was incompetent and dishonest. I know quite well that he was neither. You do too, I think. So, to answer your question, what happened is simply that Glenalban behaved as he is apt to behave, when I am not there to stop him. Reason doesn't come into it. Justice certainly doesn't come into it.'

'Why do you live there, Ma'am?'

'I do so reluctantly. I do so out of duty. I was brought up, as I can tell that dear Miss Grant was brought up, to very strict religious and moral principles, which I pray God I have not lost. Glenalban Castle has hundreds of tenants and servants, every single one at the mercy of a . . . common bully. You will think it more than odd that an aunt should talk so of her nephew, of my own sister's son. He does not inherit his qualities from that unfortunate creature, who I think died of misery. It is the damnable Grieve inheritance of cruelty and stupidity. Like father, like son. That is why I do not like living there, but why I am bound to live there. It is why I have come to see you.'

I looked at her, puzzled, not understanding this new turn.

'What Glenalban needs,' said Lady Lochinver, 'is a new owner.'

'That is what it has,' said Aunt Sophia, most unexpectedly.

'That,' said Lady Lochinver, 'is what it will have, God willing, thanks to a secret wedding near Avignon in 1766, and to Simon Donaldson and his

Italian colleague—who is delightful, I am told, and whom I am most anxious to meet. It will be a very pretty turn-up, my dears, and I shall be standing by applauding.'

Lady Lochinver sat back beaming, after this amazing speech. It came to me that the word for her was 'motherly'.

She went on to say that there was no conflict or confusion in her mind, in the way she reacted to the explosive news Simon Donaldson had confided to her. She scarcely felt any kinship with the Earl, although he was her nephew, and so was unmoved at the thought of his expulsion from Glenalban. She violently deplored his character and actions, and so, from this point of view, actively welcomed the prospect of his expulsion. She knew me to be the rightful owner of Glenalban, so the strict moral principles of which she had spoken drove her to champion my claim to my inheritance. And although she was perfectly realistic, and perfectly loyal to the Queen, she was a romantic Jacobite almost in the mode of my earnest, silly great-grandmother.

'You are the legitimate heiress of the Bonnie Stuarts, Leonora,' said Lady Lochinver. 'You cannot have the crown that is yours, more's the pity, but you can and shall have the castle that is yours. That will serve the Grieves right, for their treachery to our Prince in the Forty-Five.'

I understood that she was well read in the Waverley novels of Sir Walter Scott, and they had heavily influenced her view of history. Rob Roy came into her conversation more than once. This was, for me, yet another prodigious stroke of luck, and made Lady Lochinver my ally from every possible point of view.

Because she was garrulous, her own history came tumbling out, as I thought it probably did to everybody she met. She was one of three sisters, daughters of General Sir George Frith. They were widely spaced in age, because of her father's prolonged absences on military duty. She had married moderately well in a worldly sense, and brilliantly well in the way of personal happiness. Her much older sister had married brilliantly well in a worldly sense, becoming Countess of Glenalban and mistress of its Castle, but miserably in every other way. In contemplation of that marriage, Lady Lochinver thought, her youngest sister Louisa had never married.

'Although,' she said, 'Louisa was a beautiful girl, and is still a very handsome woman, as I was not and am not. And she is one of the people who achieve perfection in their dress, which is a trick I have never mastered, how ever much money I spend . . . She has lived at Glenalban since our older sister's calamitous marriage, I only since my dear Lord died.'

Lady Lochinver's son had inherited their property, in Sutherland in the far north-west of Scotland; her daughter was married, and lived near Perth. We heard a good deal about their childish ailments, their beauty, their astonishing precocity. Lady Lochinver was clearly one of those mothers, round the shoulders of whose children the sun rises and sets. She was a creature of the greatest goodness of heart. I thought I was supremely lucky in all my allies.

As though divining my thoughts (or perhaps they showed once again plainly on my face) Lady Lochinver turned from Aunt Sophia to me. She said, 'In the courts of law, my dear, I shall stand your friend. But in my heart I am something quite different. I am your subject.'

This was graciously said. But I thought it was carrying romantic Jacobitism a shade far. It verged on the ridiculous. The Barone had talked in such terms—and then roared with laughter, because he was exaggerating my importance in order to construct a comic fantasy. Lady Lochinver looked completely serious, her broad smile for once quite wiped away by solemnity.

Glenalban would have a new owner, who would be just and humane. That was one thing. It was an awe-inspiring prospect, but it was more and more evidently within the realm of the possible. We were talking of stones and mortar, of tenants and servants, practical matters, susceptible of a practical resolution. But that the widow of a Peer of the Realm should describe herself as my 'subject'—that was bordering on the bizarre.

I did not even like it very much. I wanted Lady Lochinver to be my friend, not my subject. In my life, I wanted friends rather than subjects. I did not feel myself of an age, of a size, of a character, to have people thinking themselves my subjects.

Of course there was something intoxicating about it. How could there not be? But I was wary of intoxication, remembering the awful example of my great-grandmother.

When presently Lady Lochinver took her leave, I curtseyed to her—and she curtseyed to me. Her curtsey was deeper than mine, which was an ordinary little curtsey, in which I descended a few inches. She descended most of her height. She was more graceful than one would have supposed such a dumpy person could have been. On her face was a kind of radiance. She made me feel like a queen. She made me feel a part of the Barone's wildest comic fantasies.

Yes, it was intoxicating, and I fought with uncertain success against the intoxication.

'Do you mind very much, dear,' said Aunt Sophia, with an unusual touch of dryness in her voice, 'if I do *not* curtsey to you?'

I burst out laughing; and she smiled.

And so she gently and wisely reminded me that I was still an obscure nobody, whatever I might become; and she stopped me getting a swelled head, and a silly notion of my own importance.

Two crawling weeks later, another letter came to me from Lady Lochinver, which made me wonder if she were entirely sane.

Glenalban Castle
March 1st 1865
May it please your Royal Highness,

(For so I regard you privately, and so in a private letter I address you.)

My nephew Glenalban will be in London next month, for Parliament is sitting and he will be attending the House of Lords. His sister will be with him. It is an opportune time for your Highness to claim her own!

In all humility, I deplore that I should find myself in the false and invidious position of inviting your Royal Highness to your own castle; but that will be put right on your arrival.

I venture to suggest that your wardrobe can also be put right, if I may venture the audacity of the observation. I beg you will allow me the honour of introducing to you some dressmakers and milliners that I believe to be not without merit; and I beg that you will do me the honour to allow the reckoning to my affair.

The lawyers are busy, and matters march.

My grief is that I dare not invite our friend Simon Donaldson to share your triumph, which would be only just; Glenalban's servants, on Glenalban's orders, would do him harm, even to serious injury. No doubt the time will come, when your Royal Highness will honour him with a summons; but it is not yet.

My sister and I pray that you will honour your own house with your gracious presence about the beginning of April. Of course we trust that the estimable Miss Grant will also give us the keen pleasure of her company.

Presenting my humble duty to your Royal Highness,

I remain, yours most obediently to command,

Rosanna Lochinver.

'She is two different people,' I said to Aunt Sophia. 'And only one of the two is sane.'

'You should not mock such kindness, dear.'

'No, I do not mock it, exactly, but you yourself have told me not to take all of it seriously.'

'Take the kindness *very* seriously, Nora. Take the reverence with a pinch of salt.'

Well, I did, and I did not. I was still a distance short of my eighteenth birthday.

Aunt Sophia would not, as it happened, give Lady Lochinver and her sister the pleasure of her company. Once we got to Glenalban, there was no knowing how long we would stay. I, perhaps, forever. Aunt Sophia felt that she could not be spared about Millstounburn. Her conscience was indeed as lively as Lady Lochinver's.

I thought that she did not altogether want to go to Glenalban. She did not want to see me treated as royalty, because she thought it would be thoroughly bad for me. (As it is apt to be, no doubt, for other royalty: as it certainly was for my hapless great-grandfather.)

She was frightened of the size of Glenalban, and its rules and protocol; she was frightened of making herself ridiculous, by losing her way between one room and another; she was frightened of using the wrong fork, and of curtseying to an upper servant in the belief that she was a visiting duchess.

So was I. But I was going.

So, on the 31st of March, came Miss Grizelda Hamilton, humbly representing Lady Lochinver; and Aunt Sophia and I made our ill-matched farewells.

And, on the journey, I brooded about what had happened, and what was to happen.

I rejoiced in the friendship of the Barone Lodovico di Vigliano; and in the much-more-than-friendship of Simon Donaldson. I rejoiced in the goodwill of Lady Lochinver, although I thought she had a streak which was silly to the point of embarrassment.

Remembering, I thought for the first time in weeks of Edgar Smith, 'Doctor Nicol' of the birdlike birthmark, that greedy and violent man. I wondered what had become of him, and whom he had been robbing. I thought we would not hear of him again—that he would attempt his crimes in another place, under yet another name.

We came to the gaunt house with the gaunt servants, and my indiscretion with the whip.

86

We came to Glenalban—to Lady Lochinver's reverential curtsey, and the Jacobite screaming of the piper, and the obeisances of the army of servants.

All Aunt Sophia's fears were realized. It was very bad for me. How could I not feel somewhat glorious, when the whole visible world was treating me like an empress?

The liveried grandee with the wand of office, who had led me up the steps into the hall, now presented to me, in a graveyard voice, the housekeeper. It seemed she was Mrs McKim. She kept her face averted from me, first by the depth of her curtsey, and then by what I took to be awe. An awestruck housekeeper was something new to me—all those I had encountered inspired terror, rather than felt it. To strike awe was also new to me, and not altogether agreeable.

Mrs McKim said, in a strangled voice, 'Will her Highness be pleased to follow me upstairs?'

It seemed they were all romantic Jacobites in this place. I thought life would be simpler, if they accepted me as their mistress, without raising me up on to a throne.

I looked round for Lady Lochinver, with whom I had hardly yet exchanged a word. She was not to be seen. Evidently I was, now, a royal parcel, given into the charge of Major Domo and House-keeper.

'Your Highness wull occupy the King's Room,' said Mrs McKim, still in a strangled voice. 'It will no' hae been slept in, syne the last veesit o' King

James the Sixth o' Scotland.'

'Prince Charles Edward came here,' I said, suddenly remembering Simon's history lesson.

'He didna bide the nicht, your Highness.'

I was startled at the notion of a bedchamber, doubtless the finest in the castle, unused for more than two and a half centuries, because it was reserved for the exclusive use of royalty. To be sure, there was a sufficiency of other rooms.

The very fact of there being a 'King's Room' bore out what Simon had discovered. It was kept for the use of the owner, as might be a room in a laird's outlying farm.

It was a great climb to the King's Room, and after the great climb a long walk, down a corridor as wide as a church, carpeted in tartan, and hung with old pictures. I made an effort to remember the turns we took, and the landmarks we passed, so that I should be able to find my way back without a guide.

We went very slowly, as though it had been a royal progress. To those old upper servants, I supposed that that was what it was.

As we reached another flight of stairs, which rose from a great archway, a pale young man in black came hurrying along the corridor after us. He was not dressed as a servant; I took him for a kind of secretary.

'Ma'am,' he panted, bowing, 'Lady Lochinver sends infinite regrets, but she has just been summoned post-haste to the bedside of her daughter.'

'Is her daughter ill?'

'She is, er, in an interesting condition, Ma'am, and we understand that there are complications affecting the imminent confinement. It is to be her Ladyship's first grandchild, and she humbly begs—'

'Of course she must go!' I cried. 'Of course her place is with her daughter at such a time!'

'So she feels, Ma'am. In fact she has already gone. Her Ladyship's sister, Miss Louisa Frith, will venture to entertain your Highness, when you are pleased to descend to the drawing room.'

'That is kind of Miss Frith. But I hope mother and child will be safe.'

'They will be better for Lady Lochinver's presence, Ma'am.'

'That is certainly true.'

He bowed. He murmured something to Mrs McKim, who glanced at me and nodded. He bowed to me again, and hurried away. From his way of addressing me, he was yet another Jacobite. I had not supposed there were so many, in all Scotland. In fact, I had not supposed there were any.

I wondered if the air of the glen, or perhaps the drinking water, caused a mild form of hereditary insanity. Well, it did not do any harm; least of all, did it do me any harm.

We reached the King's Room at last, and it was superb.

It must have been new, when James VI used it, for the windows were great expanses of leaded glass, in the Tudor style, not medieval slits in the stone; and it must have been newly furnished and fitted then, for even to my ignorant eye the great bed and the hangings and chairs were of the Elizabethan period.

A thin, dark-haired woman with a sallow face curtseyed as I came in. I understood that she was Mary MacAndrew, and that, if I pleased, she was to be my personal maid.

I had never had such a thing. It was an aspect of my new situation which I had not considered. Aunt Sophia and I had always done all our own sewing, and much of our own ironing. And dressing and undressing myself, and arranging my own hair, had never seemed to offer any problems. I thought Mary MacAndrew would have an idle time of it.

I walked over to the windows, and looked out. The prospect took my breath away—it was magnificent. I had been seeing great hills for much of the latter part of the journey to this place, but from ground level. To look at them from an eminence was splendid, and to look far down to the descending sequence of terraces—some paved, some grassed and close-mown, some with intricate geometrical parterres—which merged into parkland, still descending, and so to the silver rapids of the river far below.

I looked across the glen at the high tops opposite, still covered in snow, though it had melted on the lower ground. The air was clear; the distances I could see were huge. I caught myself wondering how much of what I could see was mine.

A door opened in the side of the enormous room, which gave to another and much smaller room. Through it came, bowing, a burly young man in livery. I understood that he was Kenneth Doig, and that, if I pleased, he was to be my personal footman.

This was becoming too much for me. To what possible use could I put a personal footman? Was he to run with messages? To whom? Was he to fetch books, or embroidery? Move my footstool? Shade me from the sun?

It occurred to me that the very rich made their lives needlessly complicated; and that when I became very rich I would simplify things. I would not dismiss such as Mary MacAndrew and Kenneth Doig, because that would be just the kind of cruelty which Lady Lochinver trusted me not to commit; but I would find them more useful things to do than dogging my footsteps and picking up things I dropped.

I smiled at the maid and at the footman. The maid did not return my smile. Her face remained completely solemn. She bowed her head. I thought that, if I must have a personal maid, I should prefer one with a more cheerful air. Perhaps in Glenalban no one wore a cheerful air, on account of the Earl; perhaps even Lady Lochinver, when she was here, lost her blithe garrulity.

That too I would change.

The man Kenneth Doig did begin to smile to

answer mine: but he wiped it off his face almost before it had started. He composed his features, so that he looked as wooden as the police officers who had come to catch Edgar Smith.

Mrs McKim said that, if it pleased me, I should look at the wardrobe. I was surprised. I was not much interested in inspecting any wardrobe, until it contained the fine new clothes I had been promised. But, in order not to offend her, I looked about for a wardrobe. There was none. The small room from which the footman had come was the wardrobe. The clothes of kings would not fit, I supposed, into a piece of furniture; nor would my new clothes.

I went obediently into the little room, out of consideration for Mrs McKim's feelings. In fact, I saw that it was furnished as a bedchamber, though barely. There was a small cot, low to the floor, with a thin mattress and a single blanket. There was a wooden chair and a small wooden table. There was an enamel washbowl on a wooden stand in the corner, and under it a bucket. That was all. There was one small high window.

I looked round this dreary little cell, pretending interest, out of politeness. I did not understand why such a point had been made that I should see it. Surely Mary MacAndrew was not going to sleep in it, so that she could look after me twenty-four hours of the day? I did not think any servant would be subjected to such discomfort.

I turned to leave the 'wardrobe', having, I thought, done all that politeness required.

At that moment, the door slammed shut. I heard a key turn in the lock.

I twisted the doorknob, and rattled it. I knew it was useless. I shouted out. I knew that was useless too.

It was not Mary MacAndrew who was going to sleep in the cell.

Four

It was a long time before I could quieten the turbulence in my head, and make any sense of what was happening to me.

When I was a child, the punishment I most detested was being shut in. I had a horror of confined spaces—of being accidentally imprisoned by the latch of a cupboard or the bolt of a shed. It was not so much that I was frightened of the dark, or of suffocation—I had no morbid fears, of the kind to which the Faculty gives long names—as that I needed to be forever free to move, to dart about, to go in and out and about and up and down. Of course I could sit still to my sewing or my book, when I was obliged to, but I needed to feel that I *could* get up and dash out of the house.

This was one reason for my extreme dismay at being locked in the wardrobe.

The other was that I had, simply and stupidly, walked into a trap.

I tried to understand, and by and by I thought I did. All those servants I had seen—at least those I had met—were the creatures of the Earl of Glenalban, and loyal to him. From what I had heard of him, they were either bribed into being so, or frightened into being so. Thus, as soon as Lady Lochinver was called away to her daughter's bedside, and her benevolent influence removed, I was tricked into my prison. That was what the young black-suited secretary was about. That was what the Major Domo, and the Housekeeper, and the lady's maid, and the footman were about.

I thought it highly probable that Miss Louisa Frith had been kept in complete ignorance of the doings of her nephew's servants. I thought she would be told some story that I had run away, too awed by the size of the castle and the numbers of its servants to stay. Something like that. And so she would raise the alarm, and there would be a search for me up and down the glen, and perhaps the river would be dragged; and it would all be pretence, because there would be those who knew that I was fast in the wardrobe of the King's Room.

Of course I might not be here long. I might be kept to await the punishment of the Earl for my temerity; or I might not be kept at all, but knocked on the head and sunk in a peat-hag.

I was very angry, and I was very frightened.

Obviously, Lady Lochinver would not have

breathed a word to the Earl her nephew about me—about my claims, or about my coming. But, as soon as the Earl was away, she had told those servants, who had pretended to agree with her, so that they should greet and treat me as she thought proper. And most gloriously they play-acted, for her and for myself!

As soon as they knew about me—it might have been only that very day—word would have been sent to the Earl. No doubt the secretary had seen to that. I imagined a courier had galloped to the nearest railway station, wherever that might be, and a special packet had been handed to the guard of the London train, for urgent delivery into the Earl's hands.

The Earl's sister was with him in London. I had no mental picture of her—Lady Lochinver had hardly spoken of her. That suggested that she was cut from the Earl's cloth. Presumably she was entertaining for her brother, at his London house. That meant that he had no wife. Either he was not married, or he had driven his wife in misery to the grave, as his father had driven Lady Lochinver's sister.

What would the Earl's sister make of these events? What would she make of me? Quite likely, I thought, she would never see me. Nobody would see me, except my guards and executioner.

For, trying hard to bring logic to my predicament, I did not see that the Grieves would have much choice. If I remained alive, my friends would still press my claims on my behalf, amply financed by the Barone. What mattered was the proof of my ancestry, and the title to Glenalban; my face was not needed in the courts. But if I were dead there was no case, because there was no claimant; there was no legitimate descendant of King James II's body. The Grieves were safe in Glenalban for ever.

And they would be spared the cost of defending their title in the courts.

The one other thing they could do was to keep me prisoner for ever, in this little cell, or some other little cell. In a place as big as Glenalban, that would be perfectly possible. But it would be cheaper and safer to kill me. It was their prudent course. There was nothing whatever I could do about it. Being forewarned was not being fore-armed.

I examined my cell minutely. It did not take long. I did not know what I was looking for. I did not find it.

I thought the wooden chair might have a loose leg, that I could pull away and use for a club. It did not. All the furniture was simple, even rough, but extremely solid.

I stood on the table, to look out of the window. I leaned far out. I thought I could have wriggled through, with a squeeze, though I think not many persons could have done so. But below the window the wall fell sheer to the stones of the highest of the terraces, a very long way down; and it rose sheer above to the battlements; and it stretched smooth and unbroken by any projection to a corner on my right, and to the great windows of the King's Room on my left.

I had never felt unnerved by heights. As a child, I spent much time in the tops of trees, frightening Aunt Sophia half to death, and I wished I was a poor working boy, so that I could have become a steeplejack. But the thought of climbing out of the window of the wardrobe made my head spin. It was certain death. There was no escape that way. There was no escape any way.

I stayed hanging out over the window-ledge, my toes just touching the table-top; because, although it was alarming to look straight downwards, it was better to look at hills and glens than at the white-painted walls of my cell. I could see nobody. It was as though the world were suddenly deserted; although I knew that the castle below and about me teemed with people.

Then, as darkness gradually fell, pinpricks of light appeared here and there in the distance, as folk lit their lamps; and below me some light washed out from the castle windows on to the stones of the terrace.

My little room grew very dark, even while the sky outside was still pale, because the window was so high and small. It grew cold. Reluctantly, I shut the window. I nearly tumbled, climbing down from the table in the dark.

I was frightened and angry, and I was cold and hungry.

Two people who wished me well knew where I was. Aunt Sophia would not expect to hear from me for some days; she would be happy to think that I was under the protection of Lady Lochinver. Lady Lochinver herself would be preoccupied with her daughter; she would be happy to think that I was under the protection of her sister.

It was conceivable that Simon Donaldson knew where I was, from Lady Lochinver, or would know, from Aunt Sophia. But he would not show his face within miles of Glenalban; and he would think me perfectly safe, with the Earl away.

It was conceivable that the Barone Lodovico di Vigliano knew where I was, from Simon. He would expect one day to come to Glenalban, but not for many weeks yet.

There was no help to be hoped for, from any of those well-wishers. The only help was to be prayed for. I prayed for it, there in the dark by the cot. I hoped my prayers were strong enough to pierce the massive granite above me.

After a long time—I could not guess how long—I heard the key in the lock of my door. Light flooded into my cell. Mary MacAndrew the sallow maid came in quickly, carrying a tray which she put on the table. Behind her, blocking the door, stood Kenneth Doig the sturdy footman.

Well, they had been described as my personal attendants. In their fashion, they were attending to me.

I said, with what must have been some violence, 'Why am I being treated like this? Will you please give me a reason?'

The maid made no reply, nor showed any

emotion. The footman, who had started to smile when I first saw him, maintained his face of wood.

They had been told to say nothing. They were frightened to disobey. They were not frightened of me.

On the tray was a bowl of meat stew, a piece of dry bread, and a burning candle in a short brass candlestick. There was only an inch of candle. It would do for me to see to eat my supper, but it would not last long after that.

I thought there was deliberate cruelty in these arrangements.

I was locked in again. I did not hear their retreating footsteps, because of the depth of the carpet in the King's Room. There was no carpet in the wardrobe.

I sat to the table, and ate my stew greedily. It was good, but there was not enough. To be sure, that might not be deliberate cruelty. Nobody in this place had had a chance to study my appetite.

The maid came back, with the footman always behind and blocking the door. She put a jug of water by the washstand, with a towel. She put another blanket on the cot. She put a white cotton nightdress on the cot. She put a comb and a toothbrush on the table. I recognized them as mine. My scanty luggage had been opened and examined, then. The nightdress was not mine.

'Do you know that what you are doing is a crime?' I said. 'I suppose you have been ordered to do it, but still you are committing a crime. Do you understand? You will go to prison, when I tell the police what you have done to me.'

They were silent. Their faces were as impassive as before. They did not think they would go to prison.

They left me alone, in the dark.

I thought I had not been sensible, telling them they would go to prison when I had reported them. They would make sure I never did report them.

I think I had never prayed so hard as I did that night. Aunt Sophia was used to say that one's prayers should be for other people, not for oneself. Mine, that night, were for myself.

My great concern was not to weep. It would not have mattered—God knew, nobody was there to see me. But as a point of pride, I was determined not to weep, and I did not.

I did not sleep, either, although I found I was deeply exhausted. For one thing, I was cold, although I spread my clothes as well as the blankets over myself on the cot. For another, unanswerable questions screamed at me from the black corners of the room; and I wondered where I would be the next night, and whether sleeplessness would ever again be a problem for me.

I thought not. In my more rational moments in that dreadful and endless night, I thought that whoever had been left in charge by the Earl— bailiff, factor, housekeeper, steward, secretary —would think it best to solve the problem posed by my existence, and permanently, while the Earl was far away. Then he need never even know the squalid details, and never be implicated at all. If all bullies were in truth cowards, then he would not wish his hands dirtied. His creatures would earn his gratitude, if he came home and found the nuisance removed.

Drably, in the small hours, I wondered who they would pick. I thought either a forester, with an axe, or a gamekeeper, with a sporting rifle. I prayed that I would face either with courage and without tears. But I was frightened that I would break down, and shriek, and weep, and beg for mercy. I think I was as frightened of that humiliation, as of axe or rifle.

I wondered what they would have done, if Lady Lochinver had not been called away. I wondered what they would do, when at last she came back. They could explain my absence by all sorts of stories, if I was not there. How could they explain my presence, and in a cell, if I was there? This seemed, in the small hours, a remote possibility.

The little high oblong of the window paled, at long, long last. Presently, a-tiptoe on the table, I saw the big hills take shape in the pearly air, and then the rim of a chilly sun behind them.

As well as I could with cold water and without a looking-glass, I washed and dressed and made myself tidy. Whatever was coming to me next, I wanted to meet it with dignity.

What came next, to my relief, was breakfast. The same servants, in the same silence. The maid emptied the washbowl, and gave me a ewer of fresh water. She gave me a bowl of porridge, and a cup of tea. She looked as though she did not enjoy giving me even so much. The footman looked as though playing prison warder came naturally to him.

I tried to talk to them, with the same success as before. They might have been deaf mutes.

An hour passed. The sun climbed higher, but there was no other change at all. I spent most of the time tiptoe on the table, looking at the profiles of hills which were becoming terribly familiar. My thoughts spun round in my head, like peas in a tambourine, and of no more use.

Sometimes I was enraged almost to screaming, sometimes frightened to prayer. I did not weep.

Almost worst, was the contrast between the enormous and glorious landscape spread before my window, and my world of twelve feet by ten feet—between terraces, park, river and snow-capped hills, and a table and chair and cot and washstand.

It was too early in the year for flowers to be bedded out in the parterres, but I thought they had already been dug and made ready, and the shrubs pruned. So there was nothing for the gardeners to do on the terraces below me, and I still saw no one.

Then I saw a man far away in the park, crossing in front of the castle, with a dog at his heels. He was surely part of the Glenalban establishment, but, as an outside man, he might not be part of the conspiracy which had imprisoned me. At least it was a chance worth taking, and I had nothing to lose.

I waved and shrieked. If he saw and heard, he would at least know that there was someone in distress in the great tower of Glenalban. Very likely he knew already; there was a possibility that he did not.

The wind was blowing gustily from the river towards the castle. If the man I saw had shouted loud, I would have heard his voice carried downwind to my window. But my shrieks were puffed back into my own face.

He saw me, though. He waved back. He was too far away for me to see his face, but it seemed a cheery wave, a friendly gesture of 'good morning'.

He thought I was a saucy maidservant. He went about his business with his dog, and I was alone in the world again.

How the time dragged! How my thoughts whirled!

I heard the key in the lock, and scrambled down from the table.

In the doorway, with the footman on guard behind her, stood a lady I had not before seen. But I knew at once who she was. My heart leaped —and then sank again, because immediately one of my tiny sparks of hope was snuffed out.

Miss Louisa Frith had that certain, small resemblance to her sister which is usual among sisters; but she was a creature of a different kind.

She was much younger than Lady Lochinver— hardly turned forty, I thought. She was still beautiful, with the kind of strong and well-boned face which the years are most kind to, and which even increases in handsomeness with age. She was slim and elegant. As Lady Lochinver had described her, she was superbly dressed, and carried her clothes superbly. I had seen enough grand ladies in Edinburgh to realize that Miss Frith was very grand indeed.

But the greatest difference between the sisters lay in the manner in which they regarded me. Miss Frith looked at me with unmistakable disgust. To her, I was a cockroach, or a rat, unclean vermin to be despatched by someone wearing gloves.

She stared at me long and intently, frowning.

I stared back. I attempted dignity.

I said, rashly, 'I have been subjected to an outrage.'

'No, not you,' said Miss Louisa Frith. 'An outrage has been attempted, by you and your confederate. He chose ingeniously, when he picked you as his candidate. He has throughout been ingenious. He forged old documents purporting to relate to the ownership of this property. He forged pages of a spurious journal, and planted them where they would be found. He searched Scotland for a young woman who combined brazen audacity with a need for money, and a fleeting resemblance to Prince Charles Edward. One might say another forgery, a false Stuart, an impersonation. No, Miss Albany—your real name, whatever it is, is of interest to the police rather than to us—you have been subjected to no outrage.'

'You have got everything completely wrong!' I cried. 'Simon Donaldson—'

'Was dismissed from this place for most dastardly and cruel behaviour, by which he had hoped to enrich himself. Unfortunately, the folly of a person here very nearly allowed him to succeed, and in order to protect the reputation of that person, we have not broadcast the whole truth about your friend. The folly of another person here has given you grounds to hope that Donaldson's new piracy would succeed. It will not.'

'Simon Donaldson is a learned man!'

'Yes. He could not have attempted this fraud if he were not.'

'He has testimonials from his professors!'

'Whose noses are so deep in their books that they do not observe the devices of confidence tricksters.'

'Lady Lochinver says of him that—'

'My sister is good-hearted and infinitely gullible. Because Simon Donaldson is a pretty young man with cajoling manners, and a most adroit pretence of bashfulness, she will not be shaken in her faith in him as a pure knight. The evidence of his treachery here, where he had been shown nothing but kindness, would convince a blind lunatic. It will not convince my sister. She is a goose. She took one look at your face, I imagine, and was instantly convinced that you were of royal blood. She stuffs her head with romantical claptrap from cheap novels, and thinks life imitates them. It does

106

not, Miss, er, Albany—'

'My name is Leonora Albany,' I said.

'We will indulge that fiction, if you wish. It is the only wish of yours which is likely to be indulged. Even from your point of view, perhaps, it was providential that my sister was suddenly called away. The sentence of the judge will be less, I imagine, because your scheme was stifled almost at birth. I shall make myself responsible for you, until my nephew's return from London. It will be up to him, then, to decide what to do with you. You will find him just, but I do not think, in a case like this, you will find him indulgent. The fact that you are the confederate of Simon Donaldson is of itself enough to brand you.'

'This is all lies! The Earl—'

'Acted, in the matter of Donaldson, with what seemed to me excessive tolerance. Donaldson did not go to prison. Subsequent events have confirmed that he belonged there.'

'The letters the Earl wrote, poisoning people's minds against Simon—'

'Were written with distaste, and from a sense of duty. Great Heavens, girl, would even you have permitted such a man to enter other households, to take charge of young children, to cheat the unsuspecting and rob the preoccupied?'

'The Barone di Vigliano—'

'Is either another impostor or another dupe. I suspect the latter, but we shall know better when enquiries have been completed. If he has been duped, it is by you as well as by the man

107

Donaldson. Knowing the explosive Italian temperament, I imagine the Barone will be angrier than the Earl of Glenalban.'

'If you are making enquiries,' I said angrily, 'you will come to learn the truth. You will not wish to admit it, but the courts will make you do so. Then you will apologize to me, and when you have done that you will pack your bags and go.'

'A creditable performance, Miss. Righteous indignation almost convincingly played. Bah. Your bluff has been called, and your histrionics are wasted. And so has a sufficiency of my time. I shall leave you to your thoughts. I should, if I were you, direct them to methods by which you may reduce the term of your prison sentence.'

I opened my mouth to make a defiant reply, with no clear idea of what I was going to say; but before any words came she was gone, and the key turning again in the lock.

Then nothing happened, nothing at all, until they brought me luncheon. Again it was quite good, and again not enough. But I would not humiliate myself by asking for more.

Miss Louisa Frith was wholly in the Earl's camp, then. I wondered at Lady Lochinver's sister being so. Then I thought that, as a dependent spinster, she knew on which side her bread was buttered. By following the Earl, and working for the Earl, she assured herself a life of elegance and luxury. To have flouted the Earl—to have taken an honest and independent line—might have threatened her with life in an Edinburgh lodging house, without any of those silks and jewels she wore. Perhaps she had contrived to convince herself that the Earl was in the right, in all things. If not, she must have woken up in the middle of many nights, and lain in the dark sickened by self-disgust.

I thought it was a kind of prostitution, to live as she lived.

I thought it was a kind of purgatory, to live as I was living and to look out on the great hills.

In the afternoon, some people came out of the castle, to stroll upon the terraces. They too had had their luncheons—more than I had had, I supposed—and they were enjoying the clear April sunshine. They were free. They were Miss Louisa Frith's guests; they were not in the pay of the Earl.

So I screamed and waved from my window. I screamed that I was a prisoner, that I was blameless, that I must at once be released.

The people looked up, far up to where I hung out of my window. The dark of hats turned, below me, to the white of questioning faces. I seemed to see an air of sympathy. I screamed again, begging to be helped. They looked down and away, and strolled on. I seemed to see that they shrugged, with pity, or with indifference.

'Your demonstration to my guests,' said Miss Louisa Frith the following morning, 'was purposeless. They had been told that a young maidservant is crazed with grief, after the death by drowning of her lover in the river, that we consider it more merciful to keep her here, locked up but well cared for, than to throw her into the public lunatic asylum. She is an orphan, you understand, with no family to go to.'

'And so you earn a reputation for charity,' I said bitterly.

She looked at me coldly, gave a quick cold smile, and left me.

I asked for pen and ink. They were brought, though not until the following day. The writing paper I was given, was of the sort on which Lady Lochinver had written to me.

At least they did not stint me, as to the quality of the paper they gave me.

I wrote to Aunt Sophia, saying that there had been a horrible misunderstanding, and that I was being held prisoner on suspicion of my claims being fraudulent. I begged her to get in touch with Simon Donaldson and the Barone di Vigliano, so that something could be done to free me, and to establish as soon as possible that I was no imposter, and that my claims were at least sincere.

I had no real hope that this letter would reach Millstounburn. But there was a tiny chance that it might find itself in a pile of others, and be stamped and sent off with them by a servant to whom 'Miss Sophia Grant' meant nothing.

There was also a chance that Miss Louisa Frith, reading my letter as I was sure she would, might be given a jolt by the truth, and reconsider her course of action. I thought this a much smaller chance, than that of the letter being sent off.

Days passed. I did not know how many days. I became muddled, and lost track, because every day was exactly like every other. The weather outside continued glorious. Into my cell crept a little morning sun, but only a little, and that not for long.

I began to feel like a plant that sprouts in a cellar, and grows white and weak.

'The servants have reported to me that you seem in indifferent health,' said Miss Louisa Frith. 'I suppose you are accustomed to vigorous exercise, running about the streets of a city and picking pockets. Or perhaps you are already a member of a still older and more dishonourable profession.'

I did not realize, until I thought about it later, what she meant by this observation. This was probably lucky. I would have lost my temper completely, with grievous results.

'You will be given thirty minutes' exercise on the battlements, guarded, at dawn and dusk,' said Miss Louisa Frith. 'If you attempt to abuse this privilege in any way, it will be withdrawn. I have made myself responsible for your health and safety, as well as for the restriction of your movements. I am not in the way of shirking my responsibilities, and I shall not do so now. I am not acting out of kindness. I feel no kindness towards such as you.'

So, that evening and thereafter, I promenaded

up and down a kind of avenue of stone, behind the battlements, and dividing them from a steep-pitched roof made of mossy stone slabs. A few paces behind me came sallow Mary MacAndrew. At each end of my promenade, which was some forty paces long, stood a footman, Kenneth Doig and another. None of the three ever said a word to me. So, after a time, I never said a word to them.

As far as possible, I made sure that I took the exercise which I so desperately needed. I fairly sprinted along my promenade, with Mary Mac-Andrew panting behind. Or I strode; or I strolled, breathing in deeply, thankful to have the heavens above me.

The dawn was the better time. Sometimes it was very cold, but the air was as sweet as a nut.

What was miserable was that the battlements were too high for me to see over. A man of normal height could have done so, which I suppose is why they were built as they were built. I could have jumped, and caught a split-second glimpse of hills; but that would have brought my guards on to my head.

My footsteps were dogged, and each end of my walk was guarded. But they did not post a guard on the ridge of the roof. They did not think I could climb the roof. I thought I could. But I did not know what I would find, when I looked down from the top on the other side. I risked fresh air and exercise, if I uselessly went like a spider up to the ridge, and then sat there helplessly waiting to be caught.

The roof remained a faint possibility of escape; the only possibility.

I did speak to one person, who listened to me, and replied at length, and preached to me, and prayed at me. He was the castle Chaplain. He was the Reverend Joseph Cardew, a skinny little man of about thirty, with amazing white hands, which he flapped as he spoke, as though trying to fly.

He would have come on a pastoral visit to see me before, he said, but he had been away on leave of absence, visiting his widowed mother in Glasgow, by gracious permission of his Lordship, who was always so liberal to those who worked for him.

It was easy to see to which camp the Chaplain belonged.

'I beg and implore you, my child, to consider your conscience.'

'There is nothing on my conscience,' I said.

'Ah, contumaciousness! To persist in this scandalous and audacious folly will bring the vials of wrath upon your head! You are too young and too comely, my child, to consort with notorious evil-doers—'

'Comely' was a word I had never been called. Indeed, I think I had never before heard it used. I was interested to be termed 'comely', but I did not want compliments from this sanctimonious little man. And I did not care to listen to yet more slanders on Simon Donaldson.

'The first evil-doers I have met in my life,' I

said, 'have been here.'

Even as I spoke, I remembered Edgar Smith, who smote the policeman and tried to steal the journal. But I thought it would be better not to bother with qualifying my statement.

'Deny, before me and before God,' cried Mr Cardew, 'your insolent and mendacious claims! Confess, to me and to God, that you are not what you have audaciously claimed yourself to be, and that you do not have a title of right to the property that you claim to own! Make humble confession, meekly kneeling upon your knees! Then I will attempt to intercede with his Lordship, as we are assured that Jesus Christ will intercede with God the Father. Admit, my child! All will go better for you, in body and in spirit, if you make a full confession now!'

'I will tell you the truth,' I said.

'Blessed be the name of the Lord, that the lost sheep is returned to the fold!'

'I am the great-granddaughter of Prince Charles Edward Stuart. I am Countess of Albany. I am the rightful owner of Glenalban Castle, being the single legitimate descendant of King James II.'

'Alas!'

'I am,' I said incautiously, having worked myself into a passion of rage, 'rightful Queen of England and Scotland, and would be so in fact as well as in law but for the usurpation of William and Mary.'

'Alas, alas!' Mr Cardew flapped his hands, like a nestling trying to fly. That was when he began to

114

pray at me. He prayed that my obduracy might be softened by the Holy Spirit, my proud head humbled, my wild folly disciplined by reason, my maniacal ravings forgiven.

His prayers were not answered.

I thought the Chaplain's position in the castle was even worse than Miss Louisa Frith's; because a dependent spinster could more readily be forgiven for hypocrisy than a man of God. But after some time of thinking about this (it may not have been truly worth thinking about, but I had nothing else to do) I concluded that Miss Frith was worse. The Reverend Joseph Cardew was stupid. Miss Frith was many unutterable things, but she was not stupid.

I had no means of discovering what lay beyond the ridge of roof behind the battlements where I walked. There was no one I could ask who would answer. And there was no one I could ask who would not at once realize, from my question, what was in my mind.

I did not know how the tower in which I was lodged joined on to the rest of the castle. I tried to remember the complicated route by which we had reached the King's Room, but my confused memory of the interior gave me no picture of the exterior. There might be a slope of roof, then a sheer drop to a courtyard. There might be battlements; if so, a way out, for the ancient defenders of the castle must have been able to come and go. Those ways might be locked or

guarded. If they were not, I would find myself in a
warren of upstairs passages, and would most likely
run into a squadron of servants. In all these
eventualities, my last state would be worse than my
first. Any attempt I made to escape must be less
hit and miss.

I needed guile. I thought I was not gifted with
guile. I was better at running than at thinking.

Then I had an idea of the purest genius, and it
made me gulp with terror. I did not know how the
idea had come to me; at the same time, I could not
understand why it had not come to me days
before.

I considered the materials I had at hand. The
towel I had been given was only a yard long—too
short by far. The curtains over the window were
no larger; and I needed those curtains. I would
have cut a blanket into strips, but I had no knife
or scissors, and there was no sharp projection in
my cell by means of which I could cut anything.
The mattress had no loose cover over it. All that
remained of fabric were my clothes. I wondered if
they were strong enough. There was only one way
to find out. I undressed myself. I tried my
stockings for strength, for they would have been
ideal. They would not take my weight. My shift I
did not at all trust, for I had sewn it myself. The
only thing that would bear my weight, and that
was long enough, was my dress. It was not such
very heavy material; but I was not so very heavy
either.

I climbed on to the table, and hooked the back

of the dress over the catch of the window. Then I took hold of the dress, and hung by it over the floor. I found that if I tucked up my shift, I could grip with my legs as well as with my hands, and it was no great effort to hang so. The good Scottish wool held me. It might stretch a little, and so be baggy when I put it on again. That was not one of my major worries.

This must be done in the dark. I might not be so frightened, if I could not see the ground. And they were far less likely to see me, where I should be. And nobody outside the castle would see me. And I was more likely to get through the castle, and clear of the castle, when there were more shadows in the corridors, and fewer folk in them.

The two servants had to react exactly as I planned for them to react. This was the weakest part of a plan none of which, on examination, was so very strong. People behave in unexpected ways, and when you think they will run away shouting, they stand and stare, and when you think they will leave doors open, they lock them . . .

I had the impression that the servants came with my meals like clockwork. But I could not be sure, as I had no clock. I thought my supper would arrive about an hour after it was full dark. I was lucky it was only April, with the evenings still falling early, and not June, when it would be light until very late, and in the north not so very dark even when it was full night.

I waited with a tearing impatience for the sun to go down. At the same time, a part of me, which grew an increasingly large part, wanted the sun to remain as long as possible in the sky, because I was frightened of what I faced.

The nearer the moment for action came, the less I relished it.

But I could not stomach any more of this dim half-life in the wardrobe; and I think the Reverend Joseph Cardew's prayers had been the last straw.

I had my evening promenade on the battlements. No word was said. I was locked up again.

I watched the last of the sun on the snow on the hilltops. They turned from gold to blue to purple. Sparks of light showed from crofts up and down the glen; and the nightly wash of light spilled out from the castle windows on to the terraces.

I would have moved at once; but my shift was white, and would show against the stones of the tower like a moth on a gravestone. I made myself wait. And, when the time came, I had to make a very great effort to make myself stop waiting.

I thought the servants would come with my supper in a quarter of an hour.

I did not want to hang from my dress a moment longer than I needed to, for the sake of the dress as well as for my own muscles and safety. But I must be ready before the servants actually came into the room. With a great effort, I heaved the heavy metal cot across the room, and against the door. It would not delay Kenneth Doig long, but I thought it would take him long enough to push it out of the way with the opening door.

I fixed the collar of my dress again to the catch

in the window-frame. I lowered the dress out of the window, so that it hung behind the curtain, and then out of sight down the wall.

I wanted to go out of the window feet first; but I could not. I put the chair on the table, and climbed on the chair. I pushed my head and my shoulders through the window, and held fast on to my dress, hanging beside the window. I kicked away the chair, so that it fell off the table on to the floor. Nearly all my weight was on the windowsill; I could safely stay where I was for ever, or until I died of cold. The thought of my next movement made my heart jump in my throat; and the thought of the flagstones far below me.

I waited for the sound of the key in the lock.

It seemed to me that the servants were much, much later that evening, and that I hung on the windowsill for hours. Probably they were no later, and I was just there for five minutes. I gulped at the prospect of the immediate future. I prayed. I found myself bitterly blaming the Reverend Joseph Cardew, for driving me to risking my neck. Even at the time, it occurred to me that this was scarcely fair, as neither he nor anyone else could have predicted that a few prayers would have such a desperate effect.

I heard the key.

I wriggled through the window like a rabbit, clutching my dress, so that I hung in a void. I heard an exclamation outside the door, and a man's gruff reply. I heard a violent screeching, as the cot was pushed inch by inch across the floor.

By this time I was completely out of the window. I lowered myself so that I was below it. I gripped with legs as well as with hands. Holding with one hand, I reached up and closed the window. I could not close it completely, because of the fold of my dress on the catch. But nobody would think, it seemed to me, that anybody would have thrown themselves out of a closed window. I was thankful to grasp the dress with both hands again. I prayed that the curtain hid the part of my dress which was still inside the room; and that the dress was strong enough; and that I was strong enough.

There was a final shriek of the iron feet of the cot on the floor, and the servants, furious, were in the room. I saw the flare of the candle through the window above me, and heard the jabber of voices.

'She didna lep,' said Kenneth Doig. 'Yon windie's closit.'

'She had nae rope.'

'A cateran wi' a key hae let her oot.'

'Ay.'

They poked about, searching. To search that room took two seconds. They ran away, to report to their mistress. I did not hear them lock the door. They had reacted as I had planned. Neither stayed to guard the room, since the horse had evidently bolted.

They took the candle with them, but left my supper on the table, as I discovered when I hauled myself in again, and put my foot in a bowl of soup.

I unhitched my dress from the window-catch,

and struggled into it. I would have liked to take my comb; but I could not spend time groping for it in the dark.

I slipped into the King's Room, and wondered where to go next. The castle would be searched from top to bottom. Probably every one of the indoor servants had seen me, when they were drawn up in the hall at my first arrival, and acting that cruel play. I could not pass myself off as a visitor, or a new maidservant, or a milliner come with a hamper of hats.

I peeped out into the corridor. There was no one, yet. To the right were the stairs by which we had come up, which led by stages into the public part of the castle, the great corridors and rooms and grand staircases. To the left, what? Back stairs? With servants already pounding up them?

Either way might be safe, or perilous.

They must think I had left the room by the door. I wondered how many keys there were to that door. Suppose Mary MacAndrew had the only one, or the housekeeper the one other? They must think an accomplice had somehow crept into the castle, and secured the right key; or that I had bribed or persuaded a servant.

They could not know when I had left the room. It might have been at any moment after my evening promenade. Therefore I might by now be miles from the castle, from the glen, going in a fast carriage in any direction. But equally, in their minds, I might be exactly where I was, dithering in the door of the King's Room, and wondering which way to go.

I turned right, because I had at least been that way, when I still thought I was a Queen.

I turned the first corner, and ran straight into the arms of Miss Louisa Frith.

She said nothing. I said nothing. Nobody said anything. She inspected the collar of my dress, which was pulled out of shape where I had hung from it. A servant took my arm, and I was led back to my cell. Mary MacAndrew came in with me, and Kenneth Doig stood in the doorway. Mary MacAndrew took my untasted supper away.

Almost at once, two men in leather aprons came. One had two heavy iron bars, of a little over a yard long; the other tools and a trowel and a bucket of mortar. They put the bars in my window.

Next morning, and next evening, I did not have my exercise on the battlements.

I heard the boom of a cannon.

I wondered dizzily if civil war had begun, and the Barone Lodovico di Vigliano were leading the clansmen to Glenalban to free me and proclaim me, as in his fantastical jokes.

On tiptoe on the table, peering through the bars, I saw far to my left, where the carriage-drive curved into the outer courtyard beyond the terraces, a carriage arriving, surrounded by outriders.

The Earl?

A little later, craning my neck, I saw below me people coming out of the castle on to the terrace; and one was a tall man, hatless, with black hair and broad shoulders. That was all I could see of him, for I was directly above.

The Earl?

He did not come to me. I was taken to him. I was expecting an arrogant bully, and that is just what I saw and heard.

He was undeniably handsome, if you liked that style of masculine beauty, which I did not. I supposed he was something over six feet tall, slim but with broad shoulders. He looked hard and much exercised; how would he not, since he was usurping so many of my acres? His hair was thick and black and sleek; many people perhaps admired it, but I did not, for I preferred unruly fair hair. His mouth was quite broad, which might have been considered an attractive feature, bespeaking humour and generosity; but his lips were thin, bespeaking cruelty and coldness. His eyes were grey and set wide apart, which was conventionally a good way for eyes to be; but they contained an expression of chilly disdain, which made them repulsive. He was about thirty years old; he bore himself with the ponderous gravity of a man three times his age, which I thought ridiculous.

He was in a kind of study, behind an enormous desk. The room was lined with books, and the desk covered in papers. He gave himself an air of busy importance. As I was thrust into his presence by the footmen who had brought me, the black-suited young secretary disappeared through another door.

I stood in front of the desk, my chin at what I intended to be a defiant angle.

He said, in a voice which would have been a pleasant baritone, if it had not been marred by a sneering harshness, 'Do you not curtsey, Miss Albany, when you are presented to the Earl of Glenalban?'

As an opening speech to a new acquaintance, I thought these words intolerable. I therefore incautiously replied, 'Do you not rise and bow, Lord Glenalban, when you come face to face with the Countess of Albany?'

He gave a sigh, and shrugged.

He said, 'Let us recommence. Under circumstances which I am beginning to understand, my remark was ill chosen.'

I nodded. It seemed to me the most dignified thing to do; and I did not trust myself not to say something unfortunate, if I opened my mouth just then.

He said, 'I must say first that I regret the necessity of the treatment you have been accorded. It is not our habit here to incarcerate strangers, and the thought of a young girl being shut up is as repugnant to us as it has been, no doubt, to you. I must however add that my aunt Miss Frith acted according to her conscience, and I cannot think that she could have acted differently. She has been, as always, correct in all things. I should welcome the opportunity to set you free, or to lodge you differently, but that opportunity can only be provided by yourself.'

I looked at him with raised eyebrows. I wondered how I was to provide the opportunity for my being let out.

He said, 'You know, as I know, that your pretensions are fraudulent. You have only to say so, and you will be taken home. You know, as I know, that your confederate Donaldson is a criminal. He was dismissed from his position here for evil, immoral and greedy behaviour which was not, in strict point of law, illegal; what he is now attempting, with you as cat's-paw, is illegal and is punishable by condign sentence of imprisonment. You also are in danger of such a sentence. You will escape all danger of it, if you sign a statement setting out the truth. I cannot be fairer than that, Miss Albany, so to continue to call you. I cannot be more merciful. Write and sign, in the presence of my Chaplain, a full and frank account of the inception and development of this ingenious attempt at gigantic fraud, and you are free as air. You will not subsequently be pursued or troubled. You have my word of honour on that score.'

My face probably revealed how I regarded his word of honour.

I said very slowly and in almost total control of myself, 'You are asking me to perjure myself, in order to save my own skin, and send an innocent man to prison. You are asking me to abandon a claim which I think you know is just. I am not

125

used to lying, my Lord, nor to lying down. Do your worst.'

'I shall not do my worst, Miss Albany, to a girl I judge barely eighteen years old. You shall be exactly as you have been, until we persuade you to abandon this criminal folly. You will be adequately fed. You will resume your periods of exercise. If you fall ill, you will receive the best attention from my own doctor. I can think of nothing else at this moment. You will return to your chamber.'

And so I returned. And that was it. And there seemed no end to any of it.

Five

THE EARL HAD been fully informed about my claims, the moment they were known to his creatures in the castle. He had no doubt consulted lawyers, probably in London and Edinburgh. He must know that my claim was good. He was simply trying—as he would have been expected to try—to bludgeon me into surrender. And into betraying Simon Donaldson, with perjured evidence.

It was lucky that I had met Lady Lochinver, to have been given confirmation of what Simon had said about the Earl. But that was the only lucky thing in the whole situation.

I was not long back in my cell, when I had another visitor, another lady—another whom I had not seen before, but whose identity

I knew at once.

The Earl's sister was very like her brother, in a gentler way, with the same dark hair and the same wide-set grey eyes. She was much taller than I, though almost as slender. I thought she was two years older than I was. She was very, very much better dressed.

'I have been talking to my brother,' she said. 'He did say you were beautiful, but I had not expected you to be quite so lovely.'

'He said that?' I said, startled.

'Yes, of course. That is why he has not sent for the police, to hand you over.'

'I am only out of prison,' I said slowly, trying to digest this extraordinary new morsel, 'because your brother thinks I am beautiful?'

'He hopes he can persuade you to admit that what you are doing is wrong and deceitful. And, oh, I hope so too! It is dreadful that a girl like you should be shut up!'

'I think so too,' I said.

'But it is better than prison.'

'Is it so different?'

'Oh, Leonora, have you ever seen the inside of a women's prison? And the kind of women there? You are a lady, and I doubt if you are quite eighteen.'

'Not quite eighteen.'

'Oh dear, the younger you are, the worse it makes everything. Won't you please, please, do as my brother asks?'

I thought Lady Flora Grieve was genuine. She

was ten or more years younger than her brother, and she was a gentle creature; of course she immediately and blindly accepted everything that he said. But I thought she was the one person —with Lady Lochinver far off—whom I might convince.

'What is so odd about this situation,' I said, 'is that my story is true and my claim is genuine. The lawyers have said so.'

'Tell what lies you like to everybody else, but could you not, please, tell me the truth?'

'How can I convince you that I am telling the truth?'

She pleaded with me, begged me, to free myself by saying that it was all a fraud.

'Yes, and send an innocent man to prison?' I said.

'You mean Simon Donaldson? Innocent? that man?'

She believed her brother about that, then, too.

We stared at one another, she on the wooden chair, and I on the edge of the cot. We were scarce a yard apart, but we seemed to be divided by the breadth of the glen I could see from my window.

'You will not be helped,' she said at last, with a sort of desperate pity in her voice.

'Not in your way,' I said.

That night, Mary MacAndrew took my supper away as usual, but left behind a candle of decent length. I saw the hand of Lady Flora Grieve. She wanted me to have light by which to contemplate my sinful folly.

Some time after the door was once again locked on me, and I was thinking of preparing for bed, I heard the key again. And after it had turned I heard, with astonishment, a knock. You do not knock on the doors of prisoners' cells; at least, no one had knocked on mine.

I said, 'Come in.'

I blinked at the new arrival, and he at me.

He was a man of the Earl's age, not as tall but broader, with a pleasant, weather-beaten face. His hair was sandy and his eyes green. He was in full evening dress, but he looked as though his favourite clothes were those for shooting and fishing.

'Miss Albany?'

'There is nobody else in prison here.'

'My name is Avington. Jack Avington. Lord Avington, to put you fully in command of the facts. I am staying here for the salmon fishing. I mention that to reassure you that there is nothing strange or sinister about my being here.'

'How did you get the key?' I asked.

'From the place where keys are hung. I shall have it back there, before anybody notices it has gone. I have been talking to Lady Flora about you, and she filled me with the most burning curiosity to see this beautiful, miniature visitant that they are all convinced is a cunning criminal. Are you?'

'As Lord Glenalban's guest, you had better

follow his line,' I said.

'I don't take anybody's line. I think as I find. And I find it hard to believe all that they say of you. People say the eyes are the window of the soul. What do yours reveal, I wonder?'

He stepped closer to me, and stared down into my eyes in the candlelight.

'No serpents there, that I can see,' he said. 'I begin to be prepared to believe that a dreadful mistake has been made. Tell me your side of the story.'

His manner was commanding, but not in a way I could resent. What he said was beautiful music.

I told him all my story, by the end of which the candle was guttering. He lit another from it. I probably allowed a good deal of passion and outrage into my voice.

'Hm,' said Lord Avington, when I had brought matters up to date, including my visit from Lady Flora. 'We have here what the lawyers call a diametrical conflict of evidence, on every single point. Simon Donaldson. That is a new name to me. He was not here any of the times when I have been here, and nobody has mentioned him. I am unable to judge between your opinion and Lady Lochinver's and your Italian friend's, on the one hand, and the accepted Glenalban view, on the other. As to Duncan Glenalban himself, I have known him since we were lower boys at Eton together. But never very well. I always admired him as a sportsman, and still do. I find it difficult to think ill of a man who rides a wild horse as he does, and throws a salmon fly as he does, though I know my attitude is short of logic . . . Your Barone sounds a delightful soul. What a tangled story! Edgar Smith's birthmark, your great-grandmother's indiscretion, all the ingredients of something from Mrs Radcliffe. I am English, you know. I only come to Scotland on occasional visits. They are good long visits, to make the journey worth while, but I cannot pretend to know the country very well. I realize now that I do not know it at all—I had no idea that such desperate events took place.'

'Nor had I.'

'Oh God, what am I to believe?'

It was as though these words released a champagne cork, after the bottle had been violently shaken. An impassioned appeal spouted out of me, unstoppable. It contained no logic, I think, and not much coherence. But it must have carried conviction.

'By heaven, I believe you,' said Lord Avington, after a long pause, during which I wondered with anguish what his verdict would be.

'Then help me to get out of here.'

'Yes. Not now, because I must make a number of preparations. Tomorrow night.'

'Oh God,' I said. 'That will give you twenty-four hours in which to change your mind. You will talk to Lady Flora and the Earl and Miss Frith and the Chaplain—'

'I don't see why I should be obliged to talk to

132

Glenalban's domestic parson.'

'Get me out tonight!'

But he would not. Of course he was right. A carriage had to be engaged, and a hiding place found for it, and a way out of the castle made passable.

'I swear I will come,' he said. 'No one will change my mind. No one ever does, once it is made up. You have made it up for me, and it will not be unmade. Not so much your words, my dear, but the fury in your face and voice. It was genuine. It could not have been assumed. Whether everything you have said to me is quite exact I do not know, but I am very sure you think it is. I am at your service. I am in your service. I am your new Jacobite. I claim kinship with Flora Macdonald, who saved your great-grandfather.'

He kissed my hand when he left. There was a look in his eyes which reminded me of something. Of the look in Simon Donaldson's eyes, when he did not kiss my hand because of his promise to Aunt Sophia.

I do not know how I lived through the next twenty-four hours, without betraying the suffocating excitement that I felt. As far as I could, I kept my face averted from Mary MacAndrew and Kenneth Doig, for fear that they would read in it suspense and hope and joy. That is the worst of a face that reveals feelings.

Lord Avington's was such a face. *His* eyes

were the windows to his soul. I was deeply flattered, and touched, and proud. I did not know how I felt in return. Ignorant as I was, I knew that gratitude was not to be confused with love. And I still thought often, often about Simon Donaldson.

I wondered where I would go, when Avington had got me out. It was a problem for later. The thing was to get out. He might have ideas. I thought they would be sensible and kind ideas, because he was sensible and kind.

I had another generous candle with my supper. But it burned completely out while I waited for deliverance. I sat on in the dark. Presently, exhausted by excitement, and by the effort of pretending that I felt no excitement, I lay on my cot.

And my shoulder was being gently shaken. I started up, puzzled, confused, frightened, with a stifled scream.

'Hush,' said Lord Avington. 'What a cool customer you are, to be able to sleep at such a moment.'

'It is the last thing I expected to do,' I said, rubbing the sleep out of my eyes, and yawning enormously.

He had a dark-lantern, and a traveling cloak for me.

We locked my cell behind us when we left it, to puzzle my goalers; and we put the key back on its hook in the basement passage outside the housekeeper's room.

There were night-watchmen patrolling the castle in the hours of darkness; but they were not coy or secretive; they clashed about with keys and lanterns, and were easily avoided. I was immediately lost, but Lord Avington knew his way. He took me by the hand, and led me at last to a little door through which, he told me, vegetables were brought in from the kitchen gardens. He uncovered the beam of his lantern briefly, and seldom.

It was glorious to be outside those walls. I drew huge breaths. I danced where I stood. I wanted to shout in triumph. But I followed Lord Avington, like a mouse, through walled gardens and so across the park. There was a brisk breeze, to hide any small sound we made; clouds hurried across the moon. The carriage-drive showed white when the moon came out from a cloud. It went black, when it curved into a small wood. There, hidden under the trees, a carriage was waiting for us.

'Hired from Lochgrannomhead,' said Lord Avington. 'The owner wanted a reason, but he didn't get one. Have you considered where to go?'

'Home,' I said. 'Millstounburn.'

'If you insist. But I wouldn't advise it. It's the first place Glenalban will look for you.'

'Oh. But it is the only place I have to go to. I can go nowhere else. I know no one else.'

'I suggest Lady Lochinver.'

'Yes! . . . But her daughter is in some trouble, and she will not want to be bothered with me.'

'She cannot leave her daughter, I daresay. But, from what you told me, she will indeed want to be bothered with you. She believes in you as warmly as I do. And she will want to make amends, surely, for what her family have been doing to you.'

I thought that was true. Still I was dubious, to trouble Lady Lochinver at such a time.

'I don't think I can take you to my house in Berkshire,' said Lord Avington. 'A pretty scandal that would make, doing your cause no good, and not doing me much good. Besides, the house is being painted inside, and everything is under dust-sheets. In any case, you must be here, to fight your battles. I could take you to my sister, but she lives in Somerset, and her two youngest children have measles.'

'I think I have no choice,' I said slowly.

'I think not much. And I think you need not be a great trouble to Lady Lochinver. All she has to do is keep you hidden, until we have worked out the next step.'

'We?'

'Your friends and yourself. A council of war is the first need, I think—you and I, Lady Lochinver, this fellow Donaldson, and the Italian gentleman. They will know how things are going with the lawyers. With that knowledge, we can plan what to do and when to do it.'

'Are you coming with me now?'

'Of course. Young Countesses cannot cross Scotland alone in the middle of the night.'

'Then Glenalban and the rest will know you let me out.'

'Glenalban and the rest can do nothing about it whatever, except deny me hospitality in the future. That is a pity, because the fishing in the Alban Water is excellent—'

'Oh, you are sacrificing your sport for me!'

'I would sacrifice much more than that, my dear.'

And, in the carriage, he embroidered this theme. There was nothing he would not do for me, because he believed in me and admired me.

'But on that subject,' he said, 'I believe that honour obliges me to remain silent until your eighteenth birthday.'

It was as though he had been talking to Aunt Sophia. I did not know whether to be relieved or disappointed. My eighteenth birthday was going to be a busy time.

It was only my second meeting with him, yet already we were on most friendly and unembarrassed terms. It might have been embarrassing for him to say, and for me to hear, how much he admired me; but he was so frank and simple—without being in any way stupid—that there was no constraint or difficulty.

It was far too early for me to judge my feelings about him. I felt overwhelming gratitude, of course; and I thought it would be most easy to feel much more. But Simon's face was in a corner of my mind, and it would not go away.

We broke our journey for breakfast at an inn. The folk there thought we were eloping, and they treated us frostily. I called Lord Avington 'Uncle', for the sake of respectability, which made him angry, and made him laugh, so that he choked over his kipper.

We reached the house of Lady Lochinver's son-in-law in the later morning. He was Sir George Stevens, known a little to Lord Avington, at the time away in London on urgent affairs. His absence was one of the reasons, it seemed, why Lady Lochinver had to be there. The house was a few miles west of Perth. It was long and low and white, and had a most welcoming and friendly look.

It was nothing like as welcoming and friendly as Lady Lochinver. We were ushered into a sunny morning-room, where she was writing letters with Miss Grizelda Hamilton; and she treated Lord Avington as an old friend, and she treated me as a queen.

She was speechless when she heard what they had done to me. It was what she might have expected from her nephew; it was astonishing in her sister; Lady Flora had no mind of her own, and followed her brother blindly; the Chaplain was a time-serving nothing; the upper servants and those guarding me were all terrified into doing exactly as they were ordered.

Avington was a hero and a saviour, a rescuer of damsels from dragons. I was boundlessly grateful for what he had done for me, but I thought Lady Lochinver overstated the dangers he had run and the sacrifices he had made. As he himself said, he had run no danger except falling downstairs in the dark; and there were other salmon rivers in Scotland.

Lady Lochinver's daughter, Lady Stevens, was confined to her room, and could not receive strangers. Through her mother, she asked to be forgiven, and sent her duty.

Her duty! This exaggeration—gratifying if a little silly—had been caught by daughter from mother.

I was to stay in the house as long as necessary. The time I was there would, of course, depend on the lawyers. I would be hidden, but I would be free. The servants were completely to be trusted. Lord Glenalban would not know I was there. My lodging would not be as grand as the King's Room, but it would be much more comfortable than its wardrobe.

Lady Lochinver was as garrulous and motherly as I remembered, and—when she remembered— as solemnly reverent to me. I preferred the moments when she forgot, and treated me as a young girl whom she liked.

Lord Avington could not stay in the house, owing to the demands of the sickroom. Lady Lochinver was distressed at having to send him away, when he had acted so magnificently; but he understood, and had not expected to be asked. He said he would stay somewhere nearby, and would keep in close touch with us.

When he left, I tried to express my gratitude. He brushed it aside. He tried to express his admiration, without putting it into words. He entirely succeeded. I did not brush it aside, but lapped it up. The picture of Simon Donaldson I carried in the side of my mind wore a reproachful look. Simon had not saved me from a dungeon.

I stayed hidden in the house for a week—hidden, but free as air. In the dawn and at dusk I made up for my imprisonment, by taking gigantic walks, revelling in the mere fact of putting one foot in front of another on the open road.

I wrote a long letter to Aunt Sophia. This one would reach her. I asked her to make urgent contact with Simon and the Barone, and to tell them what had happened and where I was.

I did not see much of Lady Lochinver, and nothing of her daughter. Once again, Miss Grizelda Hamilton was an apologetic substitute.

It was as though my time at Glenalban had never been.

I found that I missed Lord Avington as much as I had missed Simon Donaldson—as much as I still missed him. Utterly ignorant of all these things, I wondered if it were possible to be in love with two people at once; and, for the first time, I had the sense to wonder if I were really in love with either.

'I have had a letter from your friend the Barone,'

said Lady Lochinver.

'Oh, good! What news is there? May I see it?'

'I think I cannot show it to you, dear. It contains highly confidential material—in plain terms, some grossly slanderous material which he probably should not have written, and which I certainly should not share, even with you.'

I understood that the Barone, his exuberant Italian spirit having been roused, had written intemperately about the Earl of Glenalban. I would have liked to see his outpourings on the subject; but I had to respect Lady Lochinver's discretion.

The important thing was, that we were to go to Crieff to meet two lawyers who were deeply involved in my affairs, and who wanted to hear my own story from myself. The Barone and Simon hoped to attend this meeting also, but might not be able to get away from Edinburgh.

I was excited. Matters were marching.

The office was dark, and a little musty. There was a shelf of dark books, behind glass. Behind a desk sat two clean-shaven men in black coats. I was surprised that they were so young—neither as much as thirty, I thought—having expected grey-beards. They were serious. Their voices were low and their faces grave. They asked me all manner of questions, and watched me closely as I answered. One took extensive notes of all I said. Lady Lochinver listened in silence. It appeared that Simon and the Barone had not, after all, been able to get away from Edinburgh.

They asked me how I knew that I was Countess of Albany. They suggested that I was, or should have been, Queen of England and Scotland. I agreed. They asked me probing questions, as though to test my sincerity and certainty. They covered ground I had covered so often, with Simon and the Barone and Lady Lochinver and Lord Avington.

At last one turned to Lady Lochinver, and said, 'What we have heard today amply confirms the deposition you have made to us. You did right to bring this unfortunate young woman to this place. Goodwill is no substitute for correct treatment. A simple delusion is sometimes susceptible to drugs and other techniques, but there are worrying aspects to the case. This Italian Barone, who is evidently the purest figment of a disordered imagination. His resemblance to Garibaldi confirms that he is a wish imaginatively fulfilled, a hero and deliverer to a kind that is the product of day-dreams. Then there is the equally fictitious aunt, a kindly relative longed for and so supplied by the brain to the brain. We understand that you heard an apparently lucid account of such a person, at a place called Millstounburn, and with relief sought to transfer the waif you had found, wandering and raving, back into the care of her own family; but that Millstounburn is in fact the property of a Mr Bruce, and there is no such person as the supposed aunt.

'Still more worrying is the violence, and the attendant unseemly display. We have a sworn statement from a woodman, brought here by your friend Miss Hamilton, that the patient threatened him with a whip, utterly without reason or provocation—a phenomenon of sudden, mindless violence which is all too likely to be repeated. Miss Hamilton herself was approached by the patient who was still carrying the whip; she was obliged to take to her heels. We have a statement from a servant who saw the patient riding a pony in a grossly unseemly and exhibitionist way—a form of revolt, of a patient drawing attention to herself, which is, again, in nearly all recorded cases repeated.'

'Are you saying that I'm mad?' I asked, hardly able to speak.

'It is a kind of illness, child,' said Lady Lochinver.

They were not lawyers. They were doctors. They were the two doctors who, by law, had to sign the paper certifying a person a lunatic, and committing her to an asylum.

'Give me any test!' I shouted.

The doctors glanced at one another. It seemed to me that they edged further round the desk, for safety.

'You say, your Ladyship, that the unfortunate girl is virtually a pauper. She appears to have no family. Her real name is unknown, since her delusion leads her to claim the name she uses. You yourself cannot undertake the charges of private institution, and you do not feel able to ask your nephew to do so. We regret this decision, but of course we are obliged to accept it. As you may know, by law admission to a public asylum can only be made from a workhouse, at which a patient must have spent at least one token night. It is usually more, depending on the availability of beds in the local institutions. The patient must accordingly be taken to the workhouse today, and kept there under restraint until we have arranged for her admission. She had better have a name. It had better not be the one she has been using, as that will only foster the delusions of which it is to be hoped that she will eventually be cured. Can you make a suggestion, your Ladyship?'

'Smith,' said Lady Lochinver, shrugging. 'Mary Smith.'

Mary, the name of my gaoler at Glenalban. Smith, the man with the birthmark, who tried to steal my great-grandmother's journal.

'I will not be Mary Smith,' I said.

'You will be what you are told to be,' said one of the doctors, with a new sternness. His face softened. He looked at me with pity. 'If you do exactly as you are bid, we may be able to make you quite better. But you must want to be better. You do want that, do not you? You will try, will not you?'

I could not answer.

Lady Lochinver rose and left, without a backward glance at me.

I was taken to a small, bare room, and left there in the charge of a nurse. She was a powerful woman. Her job was to subdue dangerous female lunatics. She could have subdued me with one hand.

Lady Lochinver had duped me from the very beginning. She had duped Simon Donaldson. She was as completely the creature of the Earl of Glenalban as her sister, and his sister.

Because he trusted her, Simon had committed the appalling blunder of confiding in her. She came to Edinburgh to see lawyers, as she wrote to me in her first letter. Indeed she was seeing laywers, on her nephew's behalf; she was finding out whether I had a case. She found out that I had a complete case, and that she and hers were likely to be expelled from Glenalban. Armed with this knowledge, she came to inspect me. She disarmed me in all ways—by her manner, by her motherliness, by her pretended regard for Simon, by her pretended determination to help me, by her pretended disapproval of the Earl—and, now that I thought about it, by the silly exaggeration of her pretended romantic Jacobitism. She overdid that part of her performance. And I rose to the fly like the stupidest trout in the river.

The affair of the whip; my bare-legged ride. She had done some sleuth-hound work there. That, no doubt, was why I had spent a week in her daughter's house, to give her time to collect all the evidence for the doctors.

My second letter to Aunt Sophia had not been

sent, any more than my first.

There had been no letter from the Barone. Neither he nor anyone else would ever know what had become of me, or even under what name I went.

No doubt those servants had been told that I was a lunatic suffering from delusions of grandeur, and that I must be locked up for my own safety.

I made another discovery. Lady Lochinver, I thought, had not been called away at all. She had simply kept out of my sight. That was so that I would continue to trust her, which might be useful to their side.

It had been. I had continued to trust her, and I had led Lord Avington to trust her.

A new and dreadful thought struck me. Was Avington in the conspiracy too? But why should he bother to rescue me, simply in order to betray me? Why not leave me where I was? So that I would trust him, too, in case they needed that ploy?

But I remembered the look in his eyes, and I did not think it was counterfeit.

And now Lady Lochinver, the falsest friend anyone ever had, was subjecting me to the workhouse, and to the public asylum for pauper lunatics.

Lady Flora had said to me that women's prisons were terrible, and the women in them terrible. I thought the places I was going to would be worse.

In the workhouse I was stripped and scrubbed, and my hair inspected for lice. I protested that I was clean, but so the rules were, and those grim women were not in the way of listening to lunatics. My clothes were taken away, and I was given a coarse shift, and a woollen dress that had the look of a uniform. Both garments were faded and thin with a hundred launderings. For my feet I was given wooden clogs, the soles worn thin by generations of pauper feet.

I was Mary Smith. I had to answer to this name. If I had not, I would not have been fed.

I was taken to the 'Infirmary Ward' of the workhouse, where the inmates were watched over. There were fifteen beds, all but one occupied. They were close together. There were no cupboards between them. Apart from the beds, there was no furniture at all. There were no carpets on the floor, or curtains in the little high barred window.

On thirteen of the beds, old women crouched or sat or lay. One clutched her knees and moaned incessantly. Another, in a high sing-song whine, uttered a stream of gibberish, in which the only clear words were obscenities. Most stared in front of them, not moving or speaking, as good as dead. I wondered if they were all going to the public asylum, and if so, whether they were going to the same one where I would be. (But I later learned that, as these pathetic creatures were incurable, it was judged pointless for them to occupy beds in a place where cures were attempted. It was cheaper to keep them in the workhouse.)

The one other inmate of the Infirmary Ward was an emaciated young girl, who twitched and dribbled. She looked very mad. She was even more pitiable and horrifying, because her life was before her, and that was the life it was.

How could doctors, trained professional men, have confused me with such as these? Even if I told a story which was nearly incredible? I thought one answer was that they were very young, and so largely inexperienced, and had been chosen by Lady Lochinver on this account. I thought another reason was the power and influence of the Earl of Glenalban, who was doubtless Chairman of Hospital Boards and suchlike, and could help the career of any doctor who pleased him.

The ward was cleaned by inmates of the workhouse who were not sick or insane. They were sluts, foul-mouthed and dirty. They made no attempt to clean the room properly, so that, because of the helplessness of the crazy old women, it stank abominably. The sluts were casually cruel to the old women. They jeered at them for their incontinence and helplessness, which made my blood boil. But I controlled my anger, because I was frightened for myself.

I am not proud of that. But, given everything, I am not so very ashamed.

Food was brought to us, nearly all turnips and

potatoes. I never saw meat, or any green stuff, or even bread. Many of the old women could not eat. They could not hold their spoons. They dropped their bowls in their laps, and stared apathetically at the mess. Some I tried to feed, spoonful by spoonful, but it was slow work, and all the food was quickly taken away. So, while I was there, I went round the ward, hoping that I could get some nourishment into each one of them. The only one I entirely failed to feed was the young girl, who pushed away the spoon, making the only sign of activity I ever saw from her.

My own mental state was odd. It seemed to me that this could not be happening. It was too terrible, too grotesque, to be true. It was a bad dream. I was numb. I came to let everything bounce off me, the jeers of the sluts and the brisk indifference of the attendants.

I could not escape. Knowing that, I knew I was wise not to try.

I was not precisely ill treated. I was not treated at all, as anything. I was a vegetable, to be moved to another place at some future moment, and for the time being ignored.

Leonora Albany no longer existed. Mary Smith was a friendless waif swallowed up into a foreign world, where she would never be seen by anybody, or heard of again.

Time lost all meaning. A day was not 'Tuesday', but the day on which I tried to shovel some turnips down the mouth of the old woman whose turn it was. An hour was not 'five', but that at which we were fed.

Place lost all meaning. I might have been in Timbuctoo, for all it mattered where I was.

I began to wonder if being treated as mad would send me mad.

Years later, because of my experiences, I was shown two fat volumes called *Care and Cure of the Insane,* written by Doctor J. Mortimer Granville, and published by Messrs Hardwicke and Bogue for the Royal College of Surgeons. The author had visited a large number of lunatic asylums, and described them in the minutest detail, in a series of articles in *The Lancet;* and then put them all together, and made them into this extraordinary book.

I could scarcely believe what I read.

Wise and kindly men had succeeded incompetent and cruel ones, in the management of public asylums for the insane paupers. They had fine new buildings, in healthy places, with extensive gardens and farms. The wards and dormitories were healthy and airy, with much space for each patient, and with bright and cheerful furnishings. The day-rooms were also airy and cheerful, sunny in summer and warmed by open fires in winter, with charming wallpapers, curtains, pictures, aviaries, and pianos and other musical instruments. The attendants were superior people, and under the strictest discipline. The diet was carefully arranged to be both nutritious and attractive, and it was often varied. The 're-straints' of the bad old days had been, almost everywhere, almost completely abandoned—padded cells, strait-waistcoats, leg-irons and the like—in favour of kindly persuasion. Certainly these things were never used as punishment, and never simply to save the attendants trouble. Opiate drugs were hardly ever used, and when they were it was for good medical reasons, and not, again, to save trouble for the staff. The patients were not dressed in clothes like prison uniform, nor the attendants dressed like prison warders.

They believed in giving the patients fresh air and exercise, and the 'airing courts' were planted with flowers, and the people could play bowls and croquet, and those that could worked in the gardens and farms, and it was very good for them.

And the centre of it all, was the idea that lunatics were ill, and many of them could be cured. And many of them were cured.

This was because the Medical Superintendent examined each lunatic as he arrived, and studied his behaviour and what he said, and gave special treatment to each case. And this was possible because there were not too many patients for one man; and because curable cases were kept separate from poor old incurables, and from criminal lunatics.

It all sounds so very obvious. It made me think that what the very wisest and best people have is common-sense.

There were still things wrong, said Dr Mortimer Granville. And the two worst things were these: the way people were certified as mad; and the fact that there were still some asylums as bad as the worst of the past.

'Not one in twenty of the average practitioners one meets is either qualified to form an opinion on a case of insanity, or justified in filling up a certificate . . . On this malady, whereof he knows nothing—can know nothing, and in regard to which he may so readily make a mistake, perhaps worse than fatal—he is positively required to form and pronounce an irrevocable judgement off hand, without either time for thought or opportunity for reference.

'Certificates of insanity are legal instruments of civil disability. They deprive the person named in them of the power to control himself and his property. They have proved worse than a death-warrant to many a poor wretch.'

There was an irony about the other thing. Again and again, to my amazement, I read that Scotland was in advance of England, in all these reforms. But the Scottish Board of Commissioners in Lunacy was separate from England's, and different. The difference was, that the people in charge were not doctors. And they could only advise, not enforce. So that, although Scotland may have had the best lunatic asylums, it also had the worst.

I cannot believe that any was worse than the Lochgrannomhead Burgh Asylum for Pauper Lunatics.

I do not remember life in that place as a continuous rope, or road, but as a series of pictures, like magic-lantern slides thrown on to a whitewashed wall.

I am collected from the workhouse by two men in billycock hats, like those of the police officers who came to arrest Edgar Smith. My memory is frozen at the moment when, gripped between them, I leave the Infirmary Ward. None of the old women I have tried to feed looks up. They have not noticed that anyone has come into the room or is leaving it. They are looking inwards, at nothing. The young girl twitches and dribbles, staring sightlessly at nothing.

If they look at me, they are still looking at nothing, because I am nobody.

The drive. I sit between them. I do not know where we are going, and they do not answer when I ask. I am not worth wasting words on, because I do not exist.

We are approaching the Burgh Asylum, on the edge of a town I recognize as Lochgrannomhead. There is a high, high, black stone wall. There is a great door in the wall, guarded by a man in what looks like the uniform of a prison warder.

We are inside the wall, in a dreary, treeless, featureless park of uncut grass and scrub. We are approaching a range of gaunt grey buildings, three stories high, with little narrow windows, all barred. The main door is closed, and guarded by a man in the uniform of a prison warder.

I am in the office of the Medical Superintendent, with some others being admitted, men and women.

He sits behind a table, a tall, thin, elderly man. His face is kindly, but harassed. There are great piles of papers on his desk. He picks nervously at the papers and at his thin beard.

He deals with each of the new arrivals in a few seconds, after reading documents among his pile of papers. He has difficulty finding the documents. He reads certificates about the wrong person, until an assistant points out his mistake. The assistant's voice is deferential, but his face is impatient and contemptuous.

I am standing in front of the desk, in the clothes the workhouse gave me. He hardly glances up at me. He reads the certificate issued by the very young doctors in Crieff.

'Maniacal delusions. Violent. Violence associated with exhibitionism.' To an attendant he says, 'Ward Seven. Strong dress.'

There is a brief picture as I leave the Medical Superintendent's office. It is of him taking a dark, square bottle out of the drawer of his desk.

All the attendants are dressed as prison warders. I see many inmates, who are doing nothing. They are dressed in a sort of prison uniform, dark grey, and all exactly the same.

My first impression of Ward Seven remains the total impression I had of it. It is as large as a cathedral. The little windows are ten feet above the floor. The beds are eighteen inches apart. There is no other furniture. The walls are of unfaced stone. Once they were whitewashed, but that was a long time ago. There are gas jets high in the walls. The beds are of iron, with straw mattresses. Many have no mattresses, but only loose straw. The straw smells. The ward smells. It seems to be filled with a rancid fog. Attached to the iron frames of many of the beds are straps and chains, placed to go over the ankles, wrists, waists, breasts or necks of the people in the beds.

They are putting me in my 'strong dress', so that I cannot undress myself to indulge my morbid exhibitionism. It is made of some very stiff and heavy material like canvas. The sleeves end not in cuffs but in bags, into which my hands go. I cannot use my hands. There is a heavy leather belt securing my dress round the waist. It is secured not with a buckle but with a padlock.

I have difficulty moving, because of the weight and stiffness of the dress.

I am taken to the day-room. My first impression

of it remains my total impression; there is nothing to add. It is the twin of Ward Seven, except that there are wooden benches instead of iron beds. It is crammed with women, all dressed exactly alike in prison grey. None of them is doing anything, anything at all. Suddenly a fight breaks out between two women. They scream and punch and pull one another's hair. Attendants fall on them, dragging them apart, dragging them away to be chained up, for their own safety, for the safety of others, for the convenience of the attendants.

I am taken to the airing court which is reserved for the more violent women inmates. It is a bare expanse of gravel within high walls. There is nothing in it except the gravel, and a dense pack of women who are doing nothing. Since there is nothing for them to look at, they look inwards. I look at them, but that is worse than looking at nothing.

I am attacked in the airing court. I have never before seen the woman who attacks me. She might be forty or sixty. She is skinny but powerful. I do not know why she attacks me. There is no reason. For no reason, I am the cause of her misery, and the focus of her bitterness. She makes high noises like an animal, like a vixen in the spring. I try to defend myself from her fingernails, but with my hands inside canvas bags it is difficult. Attendants jump on us. She is pulled off me. I am held also, with a force that hurts my arms and breast. I am equally responsible for the fight. It takes two to make a quarrel. I am known to be violent, because I raised a whip against a harmless passer-by. I am to be put in a strait-jacket, until I have worked off my fit of maniac aggression. This will be good for me. It will stop me injuring myself or others. It will save the attendants the bother of supervising me.

I have no clear memory of the strait-jacket, and cannot describe it. I was in the deepest pit of misery and despair, and memory has been merciful. But, in the book I was given, it is described by Sir William Ellis, who was in charge of a great asylum near London, and used the strait-jacket often; he is quoted with violent disapproval by Dr Mortimer Granville, the author of the book:

'The most simple and least objectionable mode of confinement, is that of a pair of wide canvas sleeves, connected by a broad canvas shoulder-strap . . . They ought to come up well on the shoulders and to extend about an inch beyond the ends of the fingers; the part covering the hand should be made of tolerably stiff leather, to prevent the hand grasping anything. They are fastened at the back by two straps, one going from one sleeve a little above the elbow, across the loins to a similar position in the other sleeve; a second lower down, and by three similar straps in the front; the latter being secured by buckles, which, in large establishments where there are many patients to be attended to by one keeper,

157

ought to be locked.'

Mine are locked.

'It is sometimes also requisite to secure the feet. For this purpose we find that a couple of leathern straps, well lined with wool, placed round the ankles and secured to the bed by staples, is all that is necessary.'

In my case, it is requisite to secure the feet. The woollen lining of the straps is not requisite.

Because I have been violent once, I shall be violent again. I am secured at night, by straps about my wrists and ankles.

I do not much notice, because I am drugged. The attendants are empowered to administer the 'House Mixture' to any inmate they think liable to create noise and disturbance at night. It is opium. It is for my own good, and for that of the other inmates of the ward. It is convenient for the attendants, who can sleep or play cards.

A picture I do not have, is that of being seen by any doctor, at any time.

Six

AFTER THREE OR four nights (who counts days or nights in such a place?) I found that I had a violent dislike of being drugged. I spat out my cup of 'House Mixture', when the Attendant's back was turned. I said to myself that I would be my own mistress, in any way I could. Actually this was the only way.

I could not spit out the shackles on my ankles and wrists.

I never after that swallowed any of the pernicious 'Mixture'. I did not sleep so sound, among the moans and snores and twitchings all about me, and in the miserable discomfort of my shackles; but that was something of my own choosing.

I came through the period of apathy, which had been my defence against the intolerable. I became angry and rebellious and watchful. But I hid these things. I imitated the inward-looking passive misery of most of the rest. I play-acted like Edgar Smith when he was 'Doctor Nicol'; like Lady Lochinver when she was being my devoted subject.

I could see that, if this went on too long, the role would become the reality. I would slip back into apathy, and be one with my most pathetic companions. It became quite necessary that I should escape.

Necessary, and impossible.

As soon as I found myself in this mood, I was watchful all the time, looking for ground-floor windows left open, doors not always locked, back-stairs to kitchens, skylights, trapdoors, anything. I was even slimmer than before, because of the diet of the place; I could have crawled through a large keyhole.

But all the keyholes had keys in them, and all the locks were locked. The ward and the day-room had one door each, and the airing court was completely enclosed by its high black walls. Worst, we were watched. Somebody's eyes were on us all, all the time, except when we were locked up.

I tried to make a plan, and came up against blank impossibility. I needed a distraction, to send all the Attendants rushing away; I needed a bunch of keys; I needed a ladder for the outside wall; I needed other clothes than my 'strong dress'; I needed, for those other clothes, an invisible cloak. Lack of any of these destroyed any chance of escape.

There was a matron, second-in-command to the Medical Superintendent, whom we saw as seldom as we saw him. I did not know what either of them did with their time; perhaps she, as well as he, kept a square black bottle in the drawer of a desk.

One day there was a great screaming and commotion, and a pounding of Attendants' feet towards the centre of the storm; and afterwards I heard two Attendants talking, and what had happened was that a violent lunatic had attacked the Matron, and nearly killed her.

So there was at once a new Matron. She seemed to me to share the old notions of madness, and to believe that we were all possessed by devils, or by the Devil. There were more purges, and cold douches, and restraints, and doses of 'House Mixture', by all of which our devils should have been exorcised. She was a big, grim woman. I thought she was not deliberately cruel; but I was not always certain about that. I never knew her name. She had a voice as hard and ringing as that of a Sergeant-Major I had heard drilling a company of soldiers in front of Edinburgh Castle—a voice heard everywhere in the Asylum, rasping down the corridors, and invading the remotest corners of day rooms and wards and airing courts. She had a moderately strong Scottish tone, as though she came from a family of prosperous shopkeepers. I imitated her voice, softly, to myself, as a way of occupying my mind. I almost amused myself. Not to the point of smiling; I did not expect ever again to smile.

It was in the small hours of the morning. Ward Seven sounded like some great cage in the Zoological Gardens, all snorts and whimpers and little, high, heartbreaking cries. The gas-jets were turned low, but there was enough light so that we could still be watched. But, because those of us who were violent were shackled, the Attendant could safely doze in a chair by the door.

Undrugged, I was wide awake, and jumbled, useless thoughts were spinning round in my head. My straw mattress was hard and full of lumps. It rustled when I moved. I could move very little. The blanket they had thrown over me tickled my bare feet and my chin.

The air felt thick as stagnant water, as fetid as a drain. It was very stuffy. For the first time in my whole life I felt ill, weak, wasted. I was frightened of weakness, because if by a miracle a chance of escape did occur, I would not be able to take it.

A bell began to ring, one I had not heard before, a clamorous and urgent bell. Other bells rang, deeper, from all parts of the range of buildings.

It came to me, after a moment of puzzlement, that they must be alarm bells. There was an attempt at a mass escape, or the assassination of the Attendants. Many of the poor women in the Ward screamed and whimpered at the frightening sound of bells in the darkness. Twisting my head, I could just see our Attendant poke her head out of the doorway into the passage.

I heard a man's voice, from a great distance, shout, 'Fire!'

I was shackled to my bed.

There was no sound of fire, or smell of smoke, or glow of flames in the little high windows.

The Attendant ran out into the corridor. The door was slammed. Obviously the key was turned in the lock, but I did not hear it for the clamour of the alarm-bells.

I thought: there is a rule here, that when there is a cry of 'Fire', every Attendant must go at once to help to put it out. I thought: there must be a rule, even here, that if the inmates are in danger, they are to be got safely out of the building; even here, even violent and incurable lunatics would not be left shackled to their beds, to be burned alive. So, I thought, the fire does not immediately threaten us here.

This was the kind of diversion I had been waiting for. And I could take no advantage of it, because of the shackles on my limbs, and because of the key in the lock.

The bells still rang.

After a little, to my surprise, the gas-jets were turned up to their highest, by someone outside in the corridor. The door of the Ward opened. Two male Attendants, in their uniforms like those of prison warders, hurried in. One was a big man, with a full black beard. I had never seen him. Confused, I thought he must spend all his time in some part of the Asylum I did not visit.

Except at times of crisis, or to deal with violence, male Attendants did not enter the female wards. I thought these two had come to release us, and to herd us to safety.

The smaller and slighter of them, whose face I could not see, took the key from the outside of the door, and put it into the lock on the inside. I saw him turn the key. This seemed to me absolutely extraordinary. Fifty female lunatics, about a third shackled to their beds, were now locked into a room with two men, in a building which was at least somewhere near a fire. Awful theories raced into my head.

The smaller Attendant called out, to my utter astonishment, 'Leo!'

'Here,' I cried.

They hurried over to my bed. I saw their faces. I knew them. My heart leapt. They were Simon Donaldson, and the Barone Lodovico di Vigliano.

'Talk later,' said Simon. 'My precious Leo, are you all right?'

'I am now,' I said. 'But how—'

'*Piu tarde,*' said the Barone.

From his pockets the Barone drew a hammer and a cold-chisel, which I knew from the peculiar gleam of the metal in the gas-light. At once he attacked the first of the metal shackles which chained me down. He was a big, powerful man, and accurate with hammer and chisel.

'Quick!' I said, sick with fear that the real Attendants would come back.

'*Prestissimo,*' said the Barone, and even as he spoke the first of the shackles fell away from my left ankle.

I gave way then to a weakness I had so far managed to resist; I burst into tears. I felt Simon's hand on my brow and cheek, and he murmured words of comfort and of love.

The alarm-bells had stopped their agitated pealing. The crash of the hammer on the chisel rang out like an act of murder. Many of the lunatic women were sitting up in their beds, and some were standing, and stumbling about in the garish light of the gas jets. It was a scene from Hogarth or from Hell. The hammer cracked urgently on the chisel, and the chisel bit into the steel that held me. I wanted to speak, but I could not, for my sobs. Still Simon stroked my face, and my shoulder and breast, and whispered loving and lovely words.

And the Barone smote, and the second shackle parted; and those that held my wrists were not so massive.

As the Barone attacked the shackle on my left wrist, I was every second in a worse agony of suspense. If they had stopped ringing the alarm-bells, they had the fire under control. The Attendants would disperse, all running back to their normal duties. Simon and the Barone would be caught, and sent to prison for trying to abduct a dangerous lunatic. And I . . . And I . . . The thought of my own future was worse than ever before, because I was being given hope of freedom.

My left wrist was free. I found that my hand was pressed against Simon's cheek. I thought there were tears on his cheek, but perhaps they were my tears.

The madwomen in the Ward were exciting one another by howling and moving about, and they were agitated and puzzled by the unfamiliar sound of the cold-chisel crashing into my shackles. I remembered, idiotically, that in the old days 'Bedlam' had been the name for a Lunatic Asylum. It fitted Ward Seven that night.

My right wrist was suddenly free. I was unshackled. I sat up on the straw of the bed. I seized and kissed the Barone's hand, which was still holding the blessed hammer. Shameless, I threw my arms about Simon's neck. We kissed one another. I was very certain at last that I loved him. I was still sobbing.

'Now that I have got you back, my very dearest, I will never let you go,' said Simon into my hair.

I embraced him fiercely. I would never let him go, either.

'Come now,' said the Barone. *'Prest' andiam.'*

I saw, through tear-dimmed eyes, that he was smiling through his beard. He wished us well.

166

I stood. I stumbled, weakened by the half-life I had been half-living, and stiff from the shackles. Simon gave a cry of dismay, and supported me with an arm about my waist.

I had never before had a man's arm about my waist. It was comforting.

We hurried as best we could between the crowded beds to the door, the poor lunatics plucking at us, and crying out. The Barone put his ear to the door, to listen for approaching footsteps. We were not out of the wood yet, by a very long way. He shook his head. He could hear nothing, because of the shrieking and gibbering of the poor women.

He unlocked the door, and took the key from it. He opened the door a crack, and peeped out. He turned and beckoned. We slipped into the dim-lit corridor. The Barone locked the door again, from the outside. I saw that this was right. No one would know that anyone had been in, and no one would notice until morning that one violent lunatic was missing. For the same reason, the Barone turned down the gas jets which lit the ward.

We hurried along the corridor. They knew their way, because they were retracing the route they had taken. I felt strength returning with each step, from the fact that I was on my way to liberty; but my legs did not quite agree, and Simon and the Barone were half carrying me between them.

I was no longer sobbing. I was giving thanks to

God for such friends.

We passed the doors of two other wards, locked, unguarded. There was babbling and whimpering from both, as the women had been roused and frightened by the bells. We came to the end of the corridor, where there were iron stairs going both up and down. There should have been a gas-light at the head of the downward stairs, but it did not work, and things were not mended in that place.

We started down the stairs. The Barone's boot-soles rang very loud on the iron steps.

He said, *'Dio!'* and stopped dead.

For a rattle of many feet had started up the stairs. The Attendants were returning. They would be everywhere, in this corridor and the one above. We were trapped.

Suddenly, to my own astonishment, I took charge. I pulled Simon and the Barone up the stairs, and across the corridor to the foot of the other stairs. I hid myself behind the great bulk of the Barone. As the Attendants—I thought eight or ten of them—came to the top of the stairs and into the dark corridor, they would dimly see no more than two men in uniforms like their own.

I called out, very loud and ringing, in the voice of the new Matron, which I had imitated to myself to pass the time, 'Luk sharp, all o'ye—there's fechtin' in Ward Six!'

'Ma Goad,' said an Attendant in a weary voice.

It was probable enough that there would be fighting.

And they all ran away along the corridor, far along to the Ward at the furthest end.

'You've done it,' said Simon, triumph in his whisper, his arm tight round my waist.

'It was lucky the Matron was not with them,' I said shakily, the possibility that she might be there having only just struck me.

'*Andiam,*' said the Barone.

Unchallenged, we went down the stairs and out under the stars. As when I was rescued from Glenalban, I wanted to dance where I stood; but my legs would not have consented to dance.

We crossed the park, myself supported by my beloved friends. Dry grass crackled under my bare feet. If we were seen, we were a patient with two Attendants. No other Attendant would court extra fatigue, on such a night of labour, by interfering with his colleagues.

As we rounded a corner, an acrid smell struck my nostrils: burning: a fire that had been put out with water.

'You started a fire,' I said, this supremely obvious thought having only just struck me.

'In a sort of store-house,' said Simon. 'Piles of straw and blankets and broken furniture. No risk to anybody.'

'Except to ourselves,' grumbled the Barone. 'She go *pouf,* like a *lampa d'olio.*'

'Soon I shall begin to thank you,' I said, with difficulty. 'Soon I shall have words.'

'Later,' said Simon. 'You will need all your strength for the next step.'

And, indeed, I cannot think how they got me up the ladder and down it again on the other side. Simon going ahead and the Barone behind, they somehow got me to the top of the high black wall; there Simon held me, as I would surely have fallen, so weak was I, and trembling so uncontrollably. They had spread a heavy tarpaulin over the top of the wall when they had come in; through it, I could feel the sharp projections of the broken glass built into the coping. I blessed their forethought; without the tarpaulin we should have been cut to ribbons. While Simon held me, the Barone, astride the wall, exerted his great strength, and pulled the ladder up and over the top.

Going down the ladder was worse than going up it, for me and for them.

We went down into complete blackness, which was an unlit alleyway behind a warehouse. The Barone pulled the ladder down, and hid it somewhere. And then, with hardly any words spoken, we were in some kind of gig or trap, which the Barone drove; and Simon supported me still with his arm about me, and my head rested on his shoulder.

'The whole story, when you have rested,' he said. 'I have that to tell you, and other things to tell you. I am going to break my word to your Aunt. I should not do it, but I can no longer help myself.'

'Oh good,' I said dizzily.

'You know, of course, that we must have failed miserably, but for you. But for your courage and initiative, sending those fellows scampering away. It is impossible to believe that a girl who has been living as you have been living, should show such speed of thought, such brilliant intelligence. If anything had been needed to make you irresistible, dearest Leo . . .'

I did not feel irresistible. I felt like a bundle of old laundry. It shows how weakened I was, that a walk of a few hundred yards and the climbing of a ladder should have so collapsed me. Perhaps also it was the violence of the emotion of being free. Perhaps also it was another violent emotion, which I seemed to be feeling in its fullest strength for the very first time. At all events, collapsed I was, and sat helpless as a ragdoll. I would have fallen out of the gig, but for the blessed strength of Simon's arm.

We left the town, and rattled along a country road to a remote house. And then there were lights, and kindness, and a motherly woman; there was a great bowl of bread and milk, and I fell asleep repeatedly while I was eating it; and Simon kissed me goodnight, when the others' backs were turned . . .

'It looked impossible,' said Simon, 'but in the event it was easy. It took time, which I bitterly regret, because it condemned you to spend longer in that hellish place; and it took money, which the Barone seemed not to regret at all.'

171

We were sitting in a new-mown hayfield behind the little farmhouse, where the Barone had rented a couple of rooms. I was wearing my own clothes, fetched from Millstounburn some time before, against the day of my escape. The Barone was away about business—my business. Simon and I were alone together, out of sight of the world as completely as I had been in the lunatic asylum. So his arm could be about my waist, and my hand in his, and my head sometimes resting on his shoulder, and sometimes pressed against his cheek.

No, there could no longer be any doubt in my mind or heart.

'Now,' said Simon, 'we first knew something was strange or wrong from your Aunt Sophia. The fact that you had not written. It was inconceivable that you should not have written, to tell her you had arrived safely, to give her an account of Glenalban, to tell her what your plans might be. She was beginning to be seriously worried, and wrote to tell us so. We knew, of course, that it was Lady Lochinver who had brought you to Glenalban. We tried to make contact with her—for, as you know, she and I had remained in touch. We found out that she had left Glenalban, but we could not find out all at once where she had gone. Well, I knew who some of her friends were, from my days in the Muniment Room. It was a matter of proceeding by a process of elimination. We began, for no particular reason, with her daughter Lady

Stevens. We guessed right first time.

'I had never been there, and was unknown to any servants or local people. So I was able to buy a footman a few drinks, at a modest cost to the Barone, and I learned that a beautiful and very young lady had been brought there by a person called Lord Avington, an Englishman unknown to me, and of whom, in fact, I had never heard. It seemed to us highly unlikely that he had delivered you to Lady Lochinver, being himself part of the conspiracy against you. Why should they involve any outsider in such a ploy? It was obvious that, on the contrary, he had rescued you from some threat at Glenalban—that he was your friend. He would have learned from you that Lady Lochinver was also your friend, as you and I believed. We made a careful note of that name Avington. We thought we might need his help.

'Then what? My drunken footman told me that, after a week in Lady Stevens's house, you were taken off in a carriage to Crieff, and that Lady Lochinver had returned without you. That was all within the footman's observation. It made no sense. Why Crieff? What purpose had you there, and where had you gone from there?

'Getting Lady Stevens's coachman drunk took much longer, and cost much more. But I learned in the end where in Crieff you had gone. It was not so very disloyal of the coachman to tell me, because as far as he knew the errand was entirely innocent. The house of a Doctor Harold Fraser, a General Practitioner of the town. How could this be? You were not visibly ill, as coachman and footman reported it. You took long walks. You ate well. But you went on a visit to a doctor, and did not return. We were two full days speculating on this mystery, and trying and failing to bribe an apothecary and a nurse. And then a dreadful possibility struck us—the one way in which you could be made simply to disappear, and quite legally. You might have been murdered, but not, surely, by a doctor. You might have been abducted, and put on a ship to Brazil. But not by a doctor. No crime was committed by anybody. At worst, if this theory was right, a hint was given to a doctor to act a little unprofessionally.

'Now we were hampered by absence of rank, of official position. The Barone's title did not help us with Scottish petty officialdom. We needed a powerful friend. We remembered Lord Avington. The *Peerage* gave us his address. His household in England gave us, by the penny post, his present whereabouts. We went to find him, and found him. He had not revisited Glenalban, because he had defied Glenalban. He was an ally. He is one. I think I have never seen a man so angry, as he was at Lady Lochinver's treachery. He immediately enlisted himself to help us, and enlisted some formidable local dignitaries to help him, as they would never have helped us. He found out the workhouse you were locked up in—you, dearest and loveliest Leo, in a workhouse! God in Heaven, how could the woman do

174

that to you?—and with more difficulty he found out which asylum you had been put in, and under what name you went there.

'That was the limit of Avington's immediate usefulness, as he admitted and we recognized. You had been certified insane by properly qualified doctors, entirely according to the letter of the law. Only doctors could declare you cured. You were legally committed to the asylum, by a bestial weakness in the law, and it was illegal to get you out of it. A serious crime. I did not in the least object to committing a serious crime for you. The Barone did not regard it as a crime at all. Indeed, as soon as he realized what was involved, he was as excited as a schoolboy. But a man in Avington's position is differently placed—a Deputy Lieutenant of his own county, and so forth. He wished us luck, and pretended not to know what we were proposing.

'Once we had the asylum identified, it was simply the same again. We found the public-house closest to the asylum, on the theory that the Attendants would frequent it. They do. Some of them are shamefully drunken. We thus discovered five important facts, none of which was really in any way a great secret. One, Mary Smith was in Ward Seven. Two, the exact whereabouts of Ward Seven. Three, that Mary Smith was considered violent, and was shackled to her bed at night. Four, the obvious rule that, at a fire alarm, the Attendants are to lock in any patients not threatened by the fire, and are to help to put it out, in case the Municipal Fire Brigade is late or otherwise engaged. And five that, in an isolated part of the grounds of the asylum, a quantity of straw for bedding is stored. The ladder cost a few shillings. The hammer and chisel a little less. The hire of the gig and its horse cost a few pounds—'

'They can trace that to you, perhaps,' I said.

'No. It was hired by a Mr Edgar Smith, of Edinburgh.'

'What?' I said, much startled. 'Why that name?'

'No reason. It was a name that jumped into my head, in connection with you. A pretty safe name, I think, because we suppose it was a pseudonym anyway, and you cannot easily trace a man who does not exist.'

'How did you come by those horrid uniforms?'

'Once again drink. I shall never again approve temperance. Ardent spirits have oiled the wheels of our venture from first to last. We spotted a large Attendant and one of moderate size. We reduced them to insensibility with whisky-and-beer, mixed with an unusual preponderance of whisky. We helped them away from the pot-house, acting their good friends and benefactors. We removed their outer garments. They were not, we thought, in this weather, in danger of catching cold. No doubt they reported that they had been robbed, but they would have suspected passing tinkers rather than ourselves of the robbery. Why should well-spoken gentlemen want the uniforms of Asylum Attendants? They have probably been obliged to replace their uniforms out of their own pockets, but I cannot feel as guilty about that as I should.'

'You make it all sound easy,' I said.

'It was easy.'

'It is not easy to thank you.'

'Oh yes it is,' said Simon, and he kissed me; and I drowned in his gentle, passionate kisses.

I had thoroughly examined myself in a looking-glass, before breakfast, for the first time in I did not know how long. I was dismayed at the pale waif I saw, with lustreless hair and a pinched face, and a kind of dullness, as though there were no life behind the skin of cheek and brow.

I looked at myself again, after a morning in the sunshine—after a morning of hearing all Simon's story, and after a morning of happy courtship, of kisses without number, of hearing and speaking words of love.

One morning. Hardly three hours. A different creature looked back at me from the murky glass. The colour had returned to my cheeks and the brightness to my hair. I saw a face so full of joy and thankfulness and love, that I could truly believe what they said. I could believe I was the most beautiful girl in Scotland.

The Barone came back in the early evening from his business—my business. He exclaimed at the change in my appearance. He said that the sunshine was good for me, and that Simon was good for me.

He had sent a message, highly confidential, by hand, to Aunt Sophia, saying that I was free and safe and well and with my friends.

He had seen the lawyers, telling them that I was back in the world after my disappearance, and that my claim could be proceeded with.

And he had seen a description of me, a hand-bill being circulated everywhere. I was a lunatic with a record of violence. I was very small, and could be overpowered by one or two strong men. I had bright hair and brown eyes, a combination which made me highly distinctive in my own country. There was a reward offered for information leading to my capture. It was, meanwhile, a criminal offence to harbour me, to assist me in any way, or to withhold information about me.

In fact, the Barone's news was a mixture of the best and the worst.

'I am safe here, for a time,' I said.

'But you cannot stay here for ever,' said Simon. 'And you will not be safe here for ever. Our hostess is trustworthy, but she is not a hermit. Her friends come in, for a crack and a dish of tea. It is only a question of time before one of them . . .'

'I can hide, when anyone comes.'

'You cannot spend your life hiding when anyone comes. I have a plan to make you safe.'

'What?'

'I will tell you when it is ready.'

'Your plans so far have been very good. I like your plans.'

'This is my best plan yet.'

He would say no more, but laughed his gentle laugh; and I was sure his plan would be a good one, and I would be safe.

He went out in the morning on a mysterious errand. He would not tell me what he was about, but he looked hugely pleased with himself. His plan was going forward. I would be safe.

We went out into the little patch of flower-garden in front of the farmhouse, after dinner, in the thin darkness of the northern midsummer. There was no moon, but a great scattering of stars. The sweet-scented cottage-garden flowers, wet with the dew, filled the air with fragrance.

Simon said, with a catch in his voice, 'Dearest Leo, do you know the poems of Robert Herrick? He died two hundred years ago, but he says what I want to say to you, now, before we kiss one another good-night. There is a poem called *The Night-Piece*. It is one of the few I know by heart. I shall recite it to you, changing one word.'

I did not think I wanted to hear a poem. But I changed my mind when I heard this poem, in his caressing voice:

'Her eyes the glow-worm lend thee,
The shooting stars attend thee;
    And the elves also,
    Whose little eyes glow,
Like the sparks of fire, befriend thee.

No Will-o'-the-wisp mislight thee;
Nor snake or slow-worm bite thee:
    But, on thy way
    Not making a stay,
Since ghost there's none to affright thee.

Let not the dark thee cumber;
What though the moon does slumber?
    The stars of the night
    Will lend thee their light,
Like tapers clear without number.

Then Leo let me woo thee,
Thus, thus to come unto me:
    And when I shall meet
    Thy silvery feet,
My soul I'll pour into thee.'

He came to an end. He repeated softly, ' "My soul I'll pour into thee." I love you more than I thought possible. I yearn and burn for you. Will you marry me?'

'Yes,' I said into his shoulder. 'Of course I will.'

'That is my plan.'

'You did say it was the best of all your plans.

You are quite right. I like your plan.'

'It makes you safe. Safe from anybody. Safe for ever.'

'I feel safe.'

'As your husband, I shall be legally responsible for you. Nobody can touch you. A hundred doctors can sign their horrible certificates, and we can laugh at them.'

'Oh. Is that the law? Your plan is even better than I realized.'

'There is a Minister a mile away. I went to see him this morning. He is a nice old man, and I told him a very little of our story. Enough so that he understands the need for speed and for secrecy. It is lucky we are in Scotland, and there is no law to prevent the marriage because you are under age.'

'Oh yes. That is why all those English couples run away to Gretna Green, to marry without people's consent . . . Aunt Sophia will be cross with us.'

'Perhaps not so very cross. I am distressed to break my word to her. But, when I gave it, you were not a fugitive from the law. I think that changes things.'

'I think it does,' I said, and raised my face to be kissed in the starlight.

'Tomorrow,' he said, after kissing me.

'What?' I cried; because although I wanted to marry him, I was stunned that it should be so soon.

'I think we dare not wait,' he said. 'The whole

countryside will be looking for you. People like earning rewards. Bright hair and brown eyes are a rare combination. Think, dearest Leo. You will be able to go freely out, to see and be seen. You can go to Millstounburn, and to Glenalban to beard the Grieves in their lair, and to all the lawyers in Edinburgh. Until you marry me, your chin will be forever on your shoulder, and the risk you run continually will be shocking. And if they catch you, and you are not married, no power on earth will keep you out of the Pauper Asylum. But I do not urge this plan only for the sake of your safety. I urge it for the sake of my happiness.

> 'And when I shall meet
> Thy silvery feet,
> My soul I'll pour into thee.'

'All right,' I said huskily. 'Tomorrow.'

We went to the Kirk in the gig the Barone had rented, bizarrely using the name Edgar Smith. The Barone drove; he was to be our only witness. We were not dressed for a wedding; but the Barone made up in his usual magnificence for my shabbiness and Simon's informal tweeds.

A horseman, some distance behind, took the same road as we did. I felt a twitch of uneasiness. As things stood, there was a reward offered for information that would lead to my recapture.

But, in a few minutes, the whole legal position

would be altered. My husband would be responsible for me—for my safety, and for my good behaviour. If he chose to keep me out of the asylum, though I was as mad as a bird, he could do so.

I would be safe. No solitary following horseman could lift a finger to harm me.

We went first to the Manse, to meet the Minister. He had insisted on that. Because I was so young, he had to satisfy himself that I was acting of my own free will, and that I understood what I was about, and truly wanted to marry Simon. He was anxious. He was troubled by the hurry we were in. He had never performed a ceremony of marriage in such a hole-and-corner way; all his other couples had been surrounded by their families and friends, and weeks of preparation had gone before.

The Barone made a contribution to the Kirk's Charitable Fund. I did not know how far this, of itself, laid the Minister's doubts. I thought his reluctance was genuine, a matter of conscience; I thought that my manner and words had more to do with his consent, than the contents of the Barone's purse. Now I am not so sure.

Well, consent he did; and the four of us crossed the strip of grass to the Kirk, which was a little grey unadorned box, some hundreds of yards from the huddle of crofts which made the village.

A horse was tied up near the Kirk. I thought it was the same horse that had been following us.

183

There was no sign of the rider. Simon looked sharply at the horse. The same thought, I was sure, was going through his mind, as had gone through mine. He did not say anything. I was not yet safe, but in a few minutes I would be safe.

The horse's rider was in the Kirk before us. It was Lord Avington.

The expressions of astonishment on Simon's face and the Barone's were so extreme, and so sudden, that they were almost comical. I was sure that the same expression made my face equally comical. The Minister could not understand what had stopped us in our tracks, and caused our eyes to stretch and our mouths to gape.

Lord Avington wore riding boots, and a long cotton coat against the dust of the road. His face had taken the sun; he looked more weather-beaten than before, and even more healthy. He carried his riding whip, and a broad brimmed hat. I could not read his expression. Whatever he was feeling he was hiding.

Until he glanced from Simon's face to mine. And then I saw in his eyes the expression I had seen there before. I had not forgotten that he said he loved me. I had not forgotten the gratitude I owed him. But I had, somehow, in the misery and the turmoil of my life since I had seen him, forgotten the flicker of response which his loving eyes kindled in me.

Well, it was too late. I would be a loving, faithful and dutiful wife. I was about to swear to those things, and I meant to keep my sworn word. I would not, ever again, allow myself a warm response to the love in any other man's eyes.

'What goes forward?' he said, in a voice without expression.

'I am to be safe,' I said. 'I am to be married.'

'I thought it would come to this. He wants what will be yours. He has tried to get it all before, you know. No, Leonora. You will not be married to anybody today, and you will not be married to Simon Donaldson on any day.'

'The Minister is here,' I said. 'The Minister will tell you differently.'

'I will convince you, Reverend Sir,' said Lord Avington to the Minister, 'that you must not perform this ceremony. That, in doing so, you would be inflicting the most dreadful misery on this young girl.'

'He is raving,' said Simon. 'He is jealous. I saw his face when he looked at you, Leo. He wants you. I do not blame him for that. But he shall not have you. I love you, and I have been giving thanks to God that you return my love.'

'Other people have returned what you have called your love,' said Avington, with a new touch of steel in his voice. 'The Minister, and Miss Albany, and the Signore Barone, should hear about these others.'

My mind was racing, and I saw that Simon was right. Lord Avington had told me that he loved me; and I knew—God knows how I knew, in my utter inexperience—that he was telling the truth.

He loved and wanted me, not for the great noble-woman I might become, but for the girl I was.

Well—still my thoughts were racing—did I truly know that last part? His estates might be encumbered with mortgages, for all I knew. He might be on the verge of bankruptcy. He might be desperate for a rich wife, whose fortune he would absolutely control.

Whatever his motive, he wanted me; and he was announcing scandalous rubbish in order to discredit Simon.

It was not that he had come to believe the lies of the Grieves about Simon. It was that he wanted me to believe them. I thought this was a despicable way for him to be playing his game. I said so.

The Minister said, 'We'll no' hae this unseemly disputation in the Hoose of God.'

So we trooped out into the sunshine, and I thought it was the most extraordinary party I ever was a member of.

I thought that, after a little, the Minister and the Barone between them would get rid of Avington, and we could proceed. It could not be too soon for me. But Avington thought otherwise. He was not going to budge, and he was not going to be silent. He spoke reasonably, without heat, but with a note of conviction which the Minister could not have bettered in a sermon.

What he said might have been absolutely true, or absolutely false. It was not obvious which of the two it was.

He said, 'I cannot give you details of the one episode in this young man's history of which I have been made fully aware. To do so would be to breach the most absolute confidence, to break my word to a lady who has done me the honour to confide in me. But you may take my word—you, Reverend Sir,—you, Signore Barone—you, Miss Leonora Albany—my word, as a servant of the Crown and as a man of honour, that the episode brands Simon Donaldson as a cynical, heartless and greedy adventurer.'

'This is slander,' said Simon angrily. He had a right to be angry. He had a duty to be angry. 'I bear you to witness, gentlemen, that Lord Avington is falsely vilifying me in public; I ask you to remember his words, and in due course to repeat them in a court of law.'

'Not so,' said Avington. 'In an action for libel or slander, truth is a perfect defence.'

The Minister looked troubled. I thought he was impressed by Avington's rank and by his apparent sincerity. I thought he was wondering where his duty lay. I thought he was, inwardly, praying for guidance.

I was, too.

The Barone looked wretched. He had been trusting Simon for months, working, spending. He had believed completely in Simon. But it was very difficult to disbelieve Avington.

'It is convenient,' said Simon, struggling to control his anger, 'to make these slanderous allegations, and to be unable to confirm them

187

with even the smallest detail. Your position is adroitly taken, Lord Avington. You pretend that honour prevents you from providing proof of what you say. But I think my friends will demand facts. I think judge and jury will demand facts.'

This was a telling point. The Minister and the Barone were both too intelligent not to appreciate it. If Avington was lying, he was doing so most adroitly; and he was giving himself a beautiful excuse to tell us no facts to justify his charges.

The Minister and the Barone looked as though they were, after all, inclined to disbelieve Avington.

It was the oddest debate anybody ever witnessed. 'This House brands Simon Donaldson as a rogue, and will not countenance his forthcoming marriage to Leonora Albany, spinster.' And we were to vote on this motion, the Minister and the Barone and I; and my whole future rested on the way we voted.

Avington spoke again; and Simon. And they were both, when they spoke, utterly convincing.

Avington said, 'I put it to you, Reverend Sir, that you have known Simon Donaldson for no more than—what?—twenty-four hours. You can know nothing about him except that he is plausible. I grant him the appearance of sincerity. You must grant me that it is, as far as you can know, no more than an appearance. You, Signore Barone, are a man of great generosity and kindness. That has been evident to me in all our dealings. Your instinct is to trust and to believe.

Simon Donaldson was recommended to you in good faith, and in good faith you welcomed the recommendation. But, apart from one brief letter from an elderly and unworldly professor, do you know anything about Donaldson which he has not told you? I understand that you saw no need to confirm anything that he told you about himself, and you did not do so. You could not have done so, or you would not be here. I put it to you—on the hypothesis that he is a liar, you know nothing about him except that he is a good liar. Leonora, you are about to become massively rich, I think. You are not the first rich woman Simon Donaldson has made love to. I know that is true. You do not know it is untrue. I think you are too honest not to recognize the necessity of a doubt. I think you are too sensible, in a matter with such gigantic implications for yourself, for your whole future, to let your head be ruled by your heart.'

There was a long pause. It seemed that Simon, for the first time, had nothing at once ready to say, to rebut these shrewd blows of Avington's. And the rest of us were digesting Avington's words.

'Ye hae planted a wee doot, ma Lord,' said the Minister. 'I'll no' pairform the ceremony the day.'

'I am surprised that a Minister of Religion should break his given word,' said Simon.

But the Minister turned away and left us, and went across the grass to the Manse. He walked like a man who had aged thirty years in thirty minutes.

The Barone looked crumpled. All his usual ebullience was gone. It was as though gas had been let out of a balloon, so that it sagged and wrinkled. Avington had not proved a single thing he had said; but he had sown a doubt. Oh yes, in the Barone's mind he had sown a doubt; and in my mind.

Avington said, 'I am very sorry, Leonora. I am sorry you are hurt. I am sorry that I have been the instrument of hurting you. You need not completely believe me, as long as you do not completely disbelieve me. I think my duty now is to try to prove to you, once and for all, that you must have no dealings with this man.'

'You said you cannot prove it, without breaking your word. Where has your honour gone?'

'Where indeed?' said Simon.

'Come with me to Glenalban.'

'That is madness!' cried Simon. 'Dearest girl, would you run your neck into a noose?'

'Sarebbe la follia,' said the Barone, looking very puzzled at Avington.

Lord Avington ignored them. To me he said, 'We will not go to the castle, of course, but to a secret rendezvous. You will there get proof of what I say. In my company, in my care, you run no risk. I think you know you can trust me. Come. Good God, child, you must *want* to know the truth?'

'I want to know the truth,' I said miserably;

because I was beginning to face the truth.

'You will be fed more lies,' said Simon.

But there was less confidence in his voice. There was the beginning of fear in his voice.

Misery must have shown in my face; doubt; indecision; fear.

Avington said, 'I will tell you this much. And you, Donaldson, will know that your case is ruined. I will take you, Leonora, to meet Lady Flora Grieve.'

'I have met her,' I said. 'I heard her out. I did not believe her then. Why should I believe her now?'

'You did not hear her out, because she did not speak out. She told me what she told you, and it was not enough. She will not want to tell you more, but when she knows the reason I think she will tell you all. Come.'

'I will come,' I said, 'because you are right. I must know the truth.'

Though it would break my heart, yes, I must know the truth.

Simon saw that I was decided to go with Avington. Suddenly he reached into his pocket, and pulled out a small pistol.

I screamed. I had never before seen a pistol held threateningly in a man's hand. I had had no notion that Simon had a pistol.

The Barone, with his heavy stick, knocked the pistol from Simon's hand. It went off as it hit the ground, with a shocking explosion. The bullet sped away somewhere. Avington hit Simon on the jaw, a tremendous blow. I screamed again. Simon crumpled. The Barone caught him as he fell, and laid him on the grass.

'Thank you, Signore,' said Avington.

'I do not know if I thank you,' said the Barone. *'Piccola Contessa,* you will tell me, not what you hear, but whether you believe what you hear. If you believe, I will believe. Ho—this is my pistol. I carry it because my country is full of *ladroni,* bandits. I did not know Simon had it. He took it from my case. He is *ladrone.* Already I begin to believe more and more. I begin to feel myself a very great fool.'

'So do I,' I said.

'Look after *la mia Contessina,* Milor'.'

'Can you doubt it?'

The Barone could not; and nor could I.

Seven

THE BARONE LENT Lord Avington his hired gig, and himself took Avington's hired horse. We left Simon stretched on the grass by the Kirk; and before we were out of sight we saw a woman come out of the Manse to look after him.

Innocent or guilty, he was neither dead nor in danger.

I felt my heart crack, as I went away in the gig with Avington. I felt a volcano of anger inside me; but I did not know at whom it was to be directed. Simon? Avington?

We went into Lochgrannomhead. I shuddered as we approached the dismal town. Avington said I would not be recognized as a dangerous escaped lunatic, in spite of bright hair and brown eyes; it was plain to see, he said, that I was a demure and well-behaved young lady of perfect sanity.

We returned the gig to the livery-stable, and hired instead a travelling carriage. And it was after we had started our twenty-mile journey to Glenalban that Avington told me his story.

'It may have seemed bewildering coincidence that I was in the Kirk this morning,' he said. 'Of course, it was no coincidence at all. After I left you with Lady Lochinver, I quartered myself with other friends, sure that you were safe. I told my household in Berkshire where I was, because I am not in a position to allow myself to drop out of sight. My estates are considerable, my affairs complex, and my duties exacting; I live at the end of the electric telegraph. I am sorry if I sound self-important; the point is that it was perfectly easy for Donaldson and your Italian friend—I think a very good friend, by the by—to locate me.

'They had gone so far in finding you, which was hardly more difficult for them than finding me. Then they stuck. The task they accordingly gave me was beyond them, but perfectly easy for me. A friend of a friend of mine is a Commissioner in Lunacy in Scotland, one of the lay members of the Commission. He could not intervene in any way once you had been certified insane by those ignorant young doctors. But he could put me in the way of finding out what had become of you. It was no secret, you see. There was no official reason why it should be confidential. There was no official reason why I should not be told that you were in such-and-such a place, having been given such-and-such a name.

'I told my friends what I knew, and turned my back on the matter. I had to. On a strict reading, I was already an accessory before the act of a felony. That I warmly approved of the proposed felony was nothing to the point. I could help you most by knowing least.

'Now a new element enters my story, which I speak of with reluctance and embarrassment.

'I saw Duncan Glenalban in London in the spring, and with him his sister Flora. As you know, she is a beautiful and gentle creature, not brilliantly clever—as I believe her brother is—but talented and artistic. I took to calling, quite often, too often. I liked and admired her. I was deeply gratified to realize that my growing admiration was reciprocated. Our acquaintance was only of a few weeks. She had never been south before, and when I had been to Glenalban, she was either invisible in the schoolroom, or, latterly, away with friends. A declaration would have been premature. In any case, I had first to declare myself to her brother; that also would have been premature, a point he would certainly have made. But I contrived an invitation to Glenalban, ostensibly for the salmon fishing. Flora contrived it for me, to be exact; and she knew as well as I did that it was not for the salmon fishing that I was coming.

'Almost as soon as I arrived for my visit to Glenalban, I heard about you. Naturally—you were the first topic on everybody's tongue. So very beautiful. So very young. So very shameless and audacious.

'The next chapter you know. And you know the effect you had on me. You know because I told you. You would have known, I think, even if I had not told you.

'As I said, I went off to Nairn, and quartered myself in a fishing lodge. I flogged the Findhorn with my Silver Doctors and my Durham Rangers, and I was afflicted by conscience. I had led Flora to believe that I was emotionally, ah, committed to her. And I had been. There was no dishonesty or frivolity in my attitude, in any of my actions. I acquit myself of philandering. But my attachment cannot have been very deep. Because, Leonora, it dried up like dew in the sunshine. Your sunshine.'

'That is flattering. But it is sad and bad.'

'It was both those things, and there was nothing whatever I could do about it, except to behave as decently and honourably and kindly as I could. I concluded, consulting with my conscience and my salmon flies, that honesty was the best policy. It isn't always, you know. Kindness sometimes demands—prevarication, white lies. But Flora—she had to be told that—things were not on the footing we had both supposed. I owed it to her to tell her that, and I owed it to her to tell her why. She wrote in reply to my letter, consenting to meet me, and to do so secretly, because I had not obeyed, in her brother's house, the rules relating to the conduct of guests.

'Well, it was a deeply disagreeable scene. I do dislike hurting people, and I hurt her. I know I hurt you today, and I am sorry for that; but I think you are made of sterner stuff than Flora.

'She said, ''But that girl is involved with Simon Donaldson.''

'I said, ''We have all always known that.''

'She said, ''If she is his accomplice, you should be as wary of her as I am of him. If she is his victim, you should rescue her from him. You have been frank with me, Jack,'' she said, ''and, to make you understand, I shall be frank with you.'' She swore me to secrecy, and told me an awful story. It is the one I expect her to tell you. I believed it. You will.

'Well, this put a different and a dismal complexion on everything. I had told Simon Donaldson and the Italian where you were. I knew they were planning to remove you from the place. I knew the Barone was as completely duped as you were—as I had been, by the most plausible villain I have ever met. I feared very much for you. Not for your physical safety. That good Italian could be trusted to guard you—and, in any case, as Simon Donaldson's pawn you had to be alive and well. What I feared was something like today's abortive ceremony.

'So I watched them, while they planned and carried out their abduction of you. They did it very well, I must say—with dash and intelligence and a good deal of courage. Donaldson doesn't lack pluck. At any rate, after you were out, you were always under my hand.'

'Why did you not come to me sooner,' I said, 'with your story which I do not yet know whether to believe?'

'Because I did not know what Donaldson proposed. I could scarcely ask him. I could not ask you. You were never alone, and in any case hardly likely to know. I could not ask the Barone. He went away all day, your first day of liberty, and I could not follow him and keep an eye on you. Which I was determined at all costs to do, after what Flora had told me. My fear was . . . I cannot say this and look you in the eye. My fear was, that Donaldson would force you into marriage, by seducing you last night, which I thought he might have done, because of your gratitude to him.'

'He had no need to force me. He asked me, and I accepted.'

'Because of your gratitude?'

'It did not seem so. I am still not sure that I believe you. I am still not sure that I do not believe him.'

'The man who drew a pistol, to stop me taking you to hear Flora's story?'

'I shall know better what to believe,' I said, 'when I do hear it.'

I did know better what to believe.

The meeting-place was a deserted croft, on a hillside three miles from Glenalban. We

198

approached it by a roundabout way, so that we went nowhere near the castle, and saw none of its people. This remained very necessary.

Lady Flora was already there when we arrived. I did not at once understand how Avington had got a message to her to come, so quickly after the events of the morning. The answer was, that they had made an arrangement, at their previous meeting, that she would come every third day to this place, for news of Simon Donaldson and of me; and this was one of the days.

Lady Flora wore a riding habit. Far away along the hillside I saw a groom with two horses. She was still more beautiful than when I had last seen her, in my prison-cell, because the sun had turned her fair skin to a pink-gold; and because she seemed in her natural element on this wild hill.

When she saw Avington, she reached out a hand towards him, and then pulled it back.

When she saw me, she put a hand to her mouth. I thought she knew immediately why Avington had brought me.

Briefly, Avington told her that I had been rescued from a dreadful lunatic asylum, and then a still more dreadful marriage.

Lady Flora said to me, the words dragged out of her, 'Did you love Simon Donaldson? Do you?'

'This morning I was very certain that I did,' I said. 'Now I am not certain I do not.'

'I was very certain I did, too.'

I suppose I had understood for hours that this was what I should hear. It was the reason Avington could not betray Lady Flora's confidence. It was the reason Simon threatened to shoot Avington, rather than let him take me to hear the story. I had not quite faced the obviousness of it, because I had not wanted to.

'I was only sixteen,' said Lady Flora, looking at me as though pleading for understanding. 'I was still in the schoolroom, being taught French by my governess. I was a child. I had never met anybody, except my family and servants and other children. I . . .'

She stopped. She was blushing. Her eyes were lowered.

'Go on, Flora,' said Avington gently. 'I think you would prefer me to leave you. I think I would prefer to leave. This story makes me too angry. I will not go far.'

Lady Flora nodded.

We sat on tumps of heather by the croft, with a huge blue sky above us, and a brisk wind blowing along the hillside.

In one way, what I heard was not as bad as what I had been led to expect I would hear. In one way it was much worse.

'I suppose the first man in any young girl's life,' she said, 'can easily make a deep impression on her. She has read romantic novels, you know, and dreamed of a knight on a white horse . . . In the ordinary way I would scarcely have met him. I might never have met him. But I went to the

200

library for a book, as he went to the library for a book. I thought it was by accident that we met. He was as shy as I was. Shy and gentle, quite unlike the terrifying gentlemen of my brother's age, that I had only seen at a distance . . . We arranged secret meetings, and went for secret walks. I was flattered, and excited. I was not used to having my face and figure admired. I was not used to being kissed, except by my aunts. It was exciting to feel wicked. He lost his shyness, but not his gentleness. I could not feel afraid of him, of anything he would do. I lost my shyness. I lost my modesty. Not my virtue,' she added quickly, looking at me anxiously, to make sure I did not misunderstand. 'But I am ashamed to remember what—liberties—I allowed him—I allowed myself . . .'

Her face was scarlet.

I said, 'It is brave of you to tell me all this.'

'He said he wanted to marry me. He said he could not face a lifetime without me. I was so proud! And he made me feel—kissing me, and so forth . . . But there was not the slightest chance of my brother consenting, then or ever. I was in despair.'

'So he suggested you elope?'

'He was cleverer than that. He crept into my bedroom, late, knowing that my maid was out for the evening. He embraced me. He recited a poem.'

I had a dreadful premonition.

'It ended with a line about "thy silvery feet". I

thought that was so beautiful that I cried. He said, "I yearn and burn for you". I thought that was even more beautiful than the poem. And so it was I who suggested that we elope.'

'I can understand that,' I said. 'Those words had almost the same effect on me.'

'Those same words?'

'Yearning and burning, and silvery feet. Actually mine are usually pink. Except when I have been going barefoot, when they are black . . . What happened? Why didn't you elope?'

'My maid came back early from her mother's. She saw Simon coming out of my room. She rushed to the housekeeper, who rushed to my aunt, who rushed to my brother. So that was the end of that.' She looked at me again with an air of asking me not to judge her too harshly. 'I was younger than you are now,' she said.

'My great-grandmother was not much older than I am now,' I said. 'And she got into much worse trouble.'

Lady Flora did not understand this reference. She had not been told the full story of my ancestry, not because it was false but because it was true.

She said, 'My brother made enquiries after that, by way of lawyers and so forth. He found that Simon had tried to do the same thing at least twice before. One very young girl who was an heiress. And a rich widow of about forty. That was when he was a student at Aberdeen.'

'Do you suppose the widow had silvery feet?' I asked.

To my joy, Lady Flora began to giggle; and in a moment we were both laughing helplessly. It was not what either of us in the least expected. Perhaps there was a note of hysteria in our laughter. At least, it had the effect of exorcising the spirit of Simon Donaldson from us both. If we could laugh about it, we were not so likely to cry about it.

Still laughing, we embraced.

For myself, I had known quite well in a part of my mind what Flora was going to tell me. Therefore I had known which of them to believe, Simon or Avington. Therefore, when I refused to be convinced, I was lying to the others and to myself. That was, perhaps, because I was unwilling to admit, to them or to myself, how royally, how totally, I had been duped. I had accepted Simon's caresses with joy, and his words of love with pride. I had remembered them first with doubt, and then with embarrassment and anger. Now I could laugh at them, because Flora had started me laughing.

I could have forgiven him a little, for the wonderful 'silvery feet' poem. But he had quoted it as part of his method for securing heiresses. It came out so wonderfully glib, because it was well rehearsed. It became outrageous and comical.

I had a new friend, which was good, because I had lost my greatest friend.

Seeing us laughing and embracing, from a

distance, Avington rejoined us.

'I thought you might have been at blows,' he said. 'I stayed within sight, so that I could catch your sword-points in my cloak.'

'Why should Leo and I be at blows?' said Flora. 'Nothing divides us.'

Well, that was nice, but perfectly untrue. She had forgotten, it seemed, that I was still after claiming her family's castle and estate. Perhaps she thought I had forgotten.

'A question that exercises me,' said Avington, 'is where Leonora goes now. Until—things are a little clearer.'

He meant: until the lawyers have decided who owns Glenalban. It would not have helped the friendliness of our group to have come out and said so.

'I think I cannot ask you to Glenalban, Leo,' said Flora. 'I know you now, and I know that, whatever was planned, it was not by you. Since I was—bewitched—like you—I can understand how it all came about. But my family . . .'

'Will not, as things stand, extend a cordial invitation to Leonora,' said Avington. 'Unfortunately, I do not know this neighbourhood well. If I had been brought up here, I daresay I would know a dozen kindly and discreet farmers' wives who would hide Leonora, and feed her, and wash her clothes.'

'I know some like that,' said Flora. 'One in particular.'

'I hoped you would say so,' said Avington. 'I

did not like to suggest it. I did not like to invite you to defy your family.'

'I am not defying them, exactly,' said Flora, wrinkling her brow. 'I think I am doing my Christian duty. But I am doing it without telling my family. Is that defiance?'

'It is casuistry,' said Avington. 'Don't you think so, Leonora?'

'I do not know quite what casuistry means,' I said. 'But I will accept Flora's offer of a kind farmer's wife who will give me a bed and a bowl of porridge. She need not wash my clothes.'

'She shall certainly wash your clothes,' said Avington. 'You are . . .'

Again he did not come out and say what I was, or might be.

Flora rode ahead with her groom, to make sure that Mrs McPhail would receive a lodger at Achmore, and keep very quiet about that lodger. Avington and I followed in the carriage. The coachman thought our destinations increasingly peculiar.

'What were you laughing about?' Avington asked me suddenly.

'Silvery feet,' I said.

He did not know what I meant. He did not know the poems of Robert Herrick. I would not tell him. He knew that Flora and I had both been bewitched, as Flora said. I did not want to admit that we had been bewitched by the identical words.

I felt like the Chosen People; I was introduced into a land of buttered oat-cakes and honey. Achmore, on low ground near Loch Grannom Side, might have belonged to a different planet from the bleak little croft we had left, though both were on the Glenalban estate. There were fat sheep and cattle, a steading full of ducks and hens, a barn bursting with the new season's hay, and fields of wheat and oats and barley ripening towards the reaper.

I suppose payment was offered. I suppose it was accepted. It was not mentioned when I was by.

No questions were asked. It was enough for the McPhails that I was Lady Flora's friend. They thought she was an angel. There was a long, intricate story about an ill child, and the trouble and expense her Ladyship had been to. I agreed that she was an angel. But I knew how very nearly she had been a fallen angel.

Oddly, this knowledge increased my affection for her. I was thankful to find that I was not the only fool. I was grateful to her for that. I was grateful to her for opening my eyes about Simon; and, for that, there was a little part of me that would never forgive her.

Avington, meanwhile, was to re-establish contact with the Barone di Vigliano, which he could quickly and easily do by way of the Edinburgh lawyers. The point was to see where we stood, and so to decide where we went.

While this happened, I was to wait. I waited for six days.

How greatly did I miss Lord Avington? I simply could not tell even so much. He was kind, amusing, attentive, considerate, gallant, sufficiently handsome. (Simon had been all those things.) He said deeply flattering and exciting things about myself, and his feelings for myself. (Simon had said all those things, and—better rehearsed—had said them better.)

I think I had the wit to realize that I was once again in danger of confusing gratitude with love. But was I not also in danger of suppressing a love which was real, because it was mingled with gratitude? I found that, instead of feeling older as I approached my eighteenth birthday, I was feeling younger. I had thought that, as an adult, I knew my feelings. I now knew that, scarcely adult, I did not.

Flora came to see me on the sixth day. The McPhails treated her like royalty—as her aunt Lady Lochinver had pretended to treat me like royalty.

She showed that she was pleased to see me, and I was very pleased to see her. But she was puzzled, and inclined to be worried. Things were going on she did not understand. There were developments, among the lawyers. She knew this not from Avington, whom she had not seen, but from her brother. But that was all he had written, from Edinburgh, where the business kept him: that there were developments. She wanted to know if I knew more. But I had not seen Avington, either. I assumed that he too was in Edinburgh, if he was needed there, or catching salmon a long way off if he was not. I was hurt that I had heard nothing from him.

For the first time, I thought, Flora was becoming fully aware of what the rest of her family had known all along. I might dispossess them all. I wondered if this would change her loving attitude towards me. I did not see how it could fail to.

I wondered about my own feelings towards Avington; I wondered about Flora's. It was dreadful that such a gentle creature should be hurt twice—by a villain, and then by a man of honour.

My coming into her life was already a calamity.

And yet—and yet—if he fell out of love with her the moment that he met me—utterly amazing as this still seemed—would he not have fallen out of love with her anyway? Perhaps after a few months of marriage? Was that not worse? Had I not, in sum, done her a kind of favour?

I could not lie to myself on these lines for long.

Avington came, in a carriage.

The McPhails knew that he was another friend

of Flora's, and everything in the house was his. Indeed he ate a gigantic tea, in which I heartily joined (my experiences had not reduced my appetite). He was hungry, because he had come straight from Edinburgh, by train to Crianlarich, and then by this hired carriage.

He was aburst with news, but it had to wait until we were alone together. The McPhails were torn between curiosity, hospitality, and the good manners of the Highlands. In the end, we were free to go out into the fat farmland, and he told me his news.

'Things have been going forward apace during the last few weeks,' he said. 'Don't ask me exactly what things. Many of the words involved are Latin, which I have thankfully forgotten. And I know less than nothing about the strange Scottish laws of succession and property. So the fine details of what I heard went largely over my head. However, I think I understand the gist.

'Glenalban's lawyers challenged the very existence of the various deeds and charters which established the Grieves in their stewardship of the castle and estate. There were no such documents to be found in the castle. Of course there were not—Simon Donaldson had stolen them. The Barone's lawyers either had them, or had copies which were attested as genuine. First significant point to the Barone. Glenalban's lawyers then challenged the existence of your great-grandmother's journal, of the marriage certificate, of your grandfather's baptismal record. Or, they

209

said, these things are forgeries. They were shown the originals, at Millstounburn, in the presence of experts. They heard Miss Sophia Grant's account of the discovery of the papers. Second significant point to the Barone.

'Well then, on the face of it the claim looks good. But is there a claimant? Where? She must be produced, or there is no case at all. So everything grinds to a halt. Processes about to be served, if that is the correct phrase, go back into the deed-box. Appointments are cancelled. Actions are struck off the rolls of forthcoming cases. The College of Arms rolls up its parchments.

'Now then, we come to the interesting part.'

'You have not bored me yet,' I said.

'Thank you. You remember that, the very day after you escaped from the asylum, the Barone was away, from early morning until late evening. Except that it was urgent business, you did not know what he was about. I have since heard, from him, that he was most of the day travelling—the route I have come today, but both ways. He had little time between trains in Edinburgh. He dashed across the city—you can imagine that he makes a droll account of that—and spent a few minutes with his lawyers. What he had to say was extremely simple, and of the highest importance. You were found. You were safe. You were you. You see the significance of that?'

'Yes,' I said, 'but before you go on, did he say

what had become of Simon?'

'The Barone doesn't know. Simon has disappeared. I expect it is a thing he has had to do before. I hope he is nursing a sore chin, but I daresay he is quite recovered now.'

'Like Edgar Smith.'

'Did he have a sore chin?'

'No, but he disappeared. That is two people who were quite important in my life, that I shall never see again.'

'Well, you will see the Barone again. He is to be invited to Glenalban. So am I, more or less forgiven. And so, of course, are you.'

'I do not like going to Glenalban. They lock you in wardrobes.'

'Not this time, Leonora. Not this time. You diverted me from my purpose, prattling about Simon Donaldson—'

'Not prattling,' I cried. 'I just asked what had happened to him . . . Very well. I am sorry. Please go on.'

'If you wish further discourse about Donaldson, shall we have it now, and dispose of it once for all?'

'Please go on,' I said, in what I hoped was a dangerous voice.

'Very well. As I was saying, you exist. You can be produced. You can be proved to be Miss Leonora Albany, by, for example, doctors and Ministers in East Lothian. There is a Glenalban claimant, and she has a good claim. It follows that, first, you will probably be Countess of

Albany before the end of the year; and you will probably also be owner of Glenalban. It follows that, second, the present Earl of Glenalban, and his aunts, and their retainers, are now aware of the appalling injustice they did you. They are agog to make amends. I think, if I were you, I should let them. That is why I came here in a carriage, instead of saving time by riding.'

'Why is it why?' I asked inelegantly.

'Because I am taking you away in the carriage, dear goose. I am taking you to Glenalban.'

'This turnabout is a little sudden for me.'

'It is not a complete turnabout. Glenalban will fight you in the courts. The issue is by no means certain. I would fight you myself, in his place.'

'Why could they not have, in the beginning . . . Oh yes. Of course. I was Simon's accomplice. I was branded.'

'Even Flora believed that,' said Avington. 'Even she thought it was right to lock you up. You have forgiven her, I think. Do you suppose you can forgive the others?'

'Not Lady Lochinver,' I said. 'I do not think I can forgive her.'

So, for the second time, I arrived at Glenalban in a travelling carriage, in the evening. The great hills were the same, and the frowning complexities of the castle. As to everything else—dear God, what a difference! No piper this time; no odious play-acting of reverence; no assembled regiments of servants imitating Arabs at their prayers. Just Flora at the foot of the great steps, embracing me, and leading me indoors by the hand.

It was strange to be sitting, in the evening sun, on the terrace which I had seen only from directly above. It was strange to be talking, almost calmly, to the Earl of Glenalban.

I remembered thinking, weeks before, how much Flora resembled her brother. I was struck now by how much Glenalban resembled his sister —tall, slim, with glossy-black hair and wide-apart eyes. There was a further similarity. She had been deeply embarrassed, telling me about Simon Donaldson. Now he was deeply embarrassed. She had avoided my eye. He made himself meet my eye, when he embarked on his apologies.

His apologies were a little stilted. I thought it was because he was unused to apologizing. I could not yet judge whether that was because he did not usually stoop to apology, whatever he had done; or because he did not usually do anything that called for apology. Both, perhaps? He was both arrogant and priggish?

I realized that I knew nothing about him at all, except things that were presumably completely false. Simon Donaldson's account of him, given for one reason. Lady Lochinver's, given for another. Avington had said that he was not really a close friend, but simply an old acquaintance.

Flora simply revered him; her account of him would be perfectly truthful, and perfectly untrustworthy.

Like Avington, I would think as I found. What did I find? A very handsome man, with a severe, humourless face, telling me awkwardly that he was sorry for what he had done.

I could not even tell if he meant it.

He changed the subject, to my relief as well as his.

'I have been to Edinburgh,' he said. 'I think you know why.'

'To try to save your estate from an adventuress,' I said.

He smiled, but very briefly.

It was the very first time I had seen him smile. I had seen him contemptuous and coldly angry; I had seen him deeply embarrassed. The effect of his smile was interesting. But I did not have time to think about it, because he was telling me important things.

He said, 'I returned only a little before you arrived. Consequently, I had not heard until a few minutes ago my sister's account of her meeting with Jack Avington and yourself. I understood about the marriage which Jack rescued you from. We have some experience of that here. But what is this about a lunatic asylum?'

'You did not know?'

'Do you think I would have permitted such a monstrous thing?'

214

'You permitted me to be locked up here.'

'I could not bear to hand a creature like you over to the police for attempted fraud. I hoped you could be persuaded to come to your senses. I hoped especially you would listen to my chaplain and to my sister. Well, you know all that.'

'I would have put it differently,' I said. 'I thought you hoped to terrify me. What did you think Lady Lochinver had done with me?'

'We thought she had succeeded where we had failed. We thought so because she told us so.'

'Did she say she had paid me? Threatened me? Prayed at me? Or simply persuaded me?'

'All four. She said she had convinced you, finally, that your ploy could not succeed, that you were infallibly bound for prison if you persisted with it.'

'You believed her.'

'Why not? It seemed so very probable. She is a convincing lady.'

'She is,' I agreed.

'She convinced us she had convinced you. That you had returned to obscurity, with Donaldson or without him. Remember that we had thought you an impostor. Of course, an honest person might not have been swayed by the arguments my aunt said she used. But an impostor—a tyro impostor, a girl not turned eighteen—oh, we readily believed she had convinced you.'

'She did not even try,' I said.

'But tricked you into workhouse and asylum. Oh my God. I knew we owed you reparation. I swear I did not know how much. I swear that none of us heard a single word about my aunt's manoeuvre. It was unplanned, I am sure. She thought your arrival required action from her, and she conceived what must have seemed a brilliant stroke. It took her a few days to prepare things—that, I suppose, is why you were there for a week. What must have pleased her most was that there was nothing to pay, except a guinea for the doctors. The whole charge of removing you from the face of the earth was transferred from us to the ratepayers of Lochgrannomhead.'

'Well, it was clever.'

'It was devilish. I think she now knows it. That is why she is not here.'

'I did wonder why. I did have an odd feeling, at the thought of meeting her.'

'She had a more than odd feeling about meeting you, I think. I was not here, but I gather the household was much surprised when, almost the moment she heard that Avington was bringing you here, she remembered an engagement somewhere in Fife.'

'I am surprised to have frightened her away.'

'It is more, I think, that you have embarrassed her away. That is a peculiar use of the word, but I think you know what I mean. She could not face you. It will never be easy for her to face you. I think it will be a long time before she does. She was embarrassed to face us, too—myself, my sister, her sister, Avington. At the time, no doubt she thought she was acting in the best interests of us all, as she had throughout. But I think she was appalled at what she had done, the moment she had done it. She would never have told us, and we would never have known. Then, suddenly, she was faced not only with meeting you, but with meeting our knowledge of the atrocity she had committed. I think it will be a long time before she comes back here.'

'She told me she stayed here only to protect your tenants against you.'

'She need not feel obliged to come back here on that account. Can you believe me, Leonora, that none of us here knows anything about that part of it?'

'I will try,' I said. 'But recently I have been asked to believe so many things. I was good at believing things two months ago. Too good. Now I am becoming bad at it.'

'You must believe, Leo,' said Flora. 'My aunt came back, saying that my cousin was better and that you were gone. She said she had paid you some money—fifty pounds. My brother gave her back the fifty pounds. Gracious, he must be cross about that! Not because of fifty pounds, you know, but because of being cheated by his aunt. I don't think she has ever done anything like that before, but being horribly clever once gave her a taste for horrible cleverness, I suppose . . .'

Suddenly, the fifty pounds convinced me. It was not a detail Flora could or would have invented. The Earl must indeed have given Lady Lochinver fifty pounds, and it must have been because she said it was the bribe she had given me.

'I am getting back into bad habits,' I said to the Earl. 'I am beginning to believe people again.'
For the second time, I saw his quick smile.

Once I stood with Aunt Sophia at Prestonpans on the Lothian coast, looking north-eastwards towards Gullane. It was mid-morning, on a day in March of high wind and fitful sunshine. The sea was grey. It looked cold and hostile and dangerous, like the Earl of Glenalban's face when first I saw him. Over Dysart and Kirkcaldy there were black clouds carrying rain out into the North Sea. Suddenly the wind tore the clouds apart, and a broad shaft of sunlight kindled the sea to silver. It was a transformation, a miracle. It was beautiful beyond words. When the clouds closed over the sun again, and the sea darkened, it was not as it had been before. There was something permanent in that momentary change. One could not look at the dark sea with fear or dislike, because one had seen it, for a moment, a sheet of fretted silver.

That was the transformation wrought in the Earl's face by his smile. And, though his face returned again so quickly to its usual severity, I could not look at it as I had looked at it before. I could not be frightened or repelled or angered

—never again, by a face which could be lit by such a smile.

Yes, I was getting into bad habits again. I was becoming dangerously credulous. And I was not only believing in the truth of plausible words. I was letting myself believe in the truth of a smile.

'We were so astonished and delighted, my dear,' said Miss Louisa Frith, 'to learn that you were telling the truth.'

She was still awesomely elegant and fashionable. But she had her nephew's smile.

'Even though . . .' I began.

'Even though you are trying to evict us from Glenalban? But I don't think you will. My nephew has the best lawyers in Edinburgh and London. They will fight fair, but they will fight. What you will find yourself, dear, is not owner of Glenalban, but welcome guest. My own position, more or less. Given all the responsibilities and worries, I think in your place I should actually prefer that. Meanwhile, my sister—my unforgivable and unforgiven sister—made some promises to you about clothes. The very least I can do, by way of making some kind of reparation, is to honour those promises. I shall try to get my sister to pay, but I don't suppose I shall succeed . . . A dressmaker is coming here, from Perth, the day after tomorrow. She is French. You would not think she is provincial. She made this confection. It serves, for the country.'

It did, indeed.

'When you came here, you know,' said Miss Frith, 'our first notion was to hand you at once over to the County Police. It is a very good thing for us we did not. You could afterwards have sued us for I don't know what—false arrest, defamation of character, a whole roster of felonies.'

'I still could sue you,' I said, 'but I think I will not.'

'I will buy you off, with a wardrobe of clothes. As my sister pretended she had bought you off, and cheated my nephew of fifty sovereigns . . . That time you tried to escape, did you hang outside the window by your dress?'

'I nearly died of fright.'

'I don't think you did. But I did, when I concluded that was how you must have managed it. That was why bars were put over the window. I did not want you plunging to your death on the terrace. You hung outside that window, so high about the ground, clinging to your dress? You really did that?'

'I had no rope, Ma'am.'

'You deserve to be Countess of Albany. I don't think you will be, but you would grace the title. You are more of a man than your alleged great-grandfather. You would grace Glenalban, too, but I don't think you'll get that, either.'

She smiled her nephew's smile. We were enemies, and we were friends.

I met the servants who had been my goalers—Mary MacAndrew and Kenneth Doig.

I had seen the Earl's smile for the first time; I had seen Miss Louisa Frith's smile for the first time; and so I had learned something about them. With Mary MacAndrew it was the opposite. That stone-faced, silent creature, who had never shown any expression at all, burst into tears. I found that I was comforting her, which I had not at all expected.

Of course she had only done as she was told by Miss Frith; and she understood the reasons. She thought it was right that I was not at once handed over to the police, right that they should try by all means to persuade me to give up my attempt at fraud; she understood why she was to treat me as she did, and to answer no questions. And she hated every moment. She was thankful when Lord Avington took me away, as it relieved her of a horrid duty.

So she told me, her face wet with tears. I believed her. I was believing tears, as well as smiles.

I had seen Kenneth Doig's smile, come and gone in a wink, like the flame of a dark-lantern, at our first moment of meeting. Now he had no need to switch it off, and did not.

For him, the worst thing about his gaoler-duty was his own enforced silence. He was naturally a voluble man—words fairly tumbled out of him. What he wanted to know, was how I got out of a locked room—or, if I had not got out, how I had contrived to disappear. When I told him, as little

221

boastfully as I could, the torrent of his words was quite shut off. He stared at me with his mouth open, like a fish.

There was one happy but ironic outcome to all this. Mary MacAndrew and Kenneth Doig had known one another only little, before they were thrown together by being my guards. In that time, they were constantly together, and so came to know one another well. And now they were betrothed. It was still a secret, because Mary's father was away, and had not been asked; but they wanted me to know.

'What would you like as a wedding-gift?' I said; and Mary MacAndrew burst into tears again.

I was not put in the King's Room, but an ordinary sunny bed-chamber among other rooms. Mary MacAndrew was to maid me, because she asked to.

And the wheel almost came full circle, because once again I was treated as royalty.

Eight

High summer on high ground was new to me, and beautiful beyond anything I had imagined. I had been confined; I made up for that. I had been undernourished; I made up for that. I had been treated as mad and bad; all the world seemed to be in a conspiracy to make up for that.

People were in the conspiracy, and animals, and Nature herself.

More than anybody else, naturally, I was with the gentle Flora. Though in company she was shy, and seemed somehow soft, she was most active and vigorous when she was walking the hill or riding the glen. She chose me a pony from the stables, a near thoroughbred of the kind they used to call a Galloway, a fast and bold little horse called Peregrine. He was short of exercise when first I rode him, and so was I, so we had a bumpy and perilous time of it. And then he grew used to me, and I to him, and when I went into his loose-box he blew on my cheek, and rested his chin on my shoulder; and I learned that what he liked best was to have his brow scratched with a fingernail. I should not have liked that, but I respected Peregrine's preference in the matter, and every ride began and ended with my scratching him interminably, while Flora and the grooms laughed over the box's half-door.

Flora and I talked about every subject under the sun, while we rode or walked or sat on the terraces; except three. We never talked about Simon Donaldson. We never talked about my impending claim to the castle where we were. We never talked about Lord Avington.

We had no news of Simon Donaldson, and did not expect any. We supposed he was gone forever, out of both our lives.

The legal processes were shortly to be in abeyance, because the courts would be in recess and the lawyers on vacation. Solicitors might still be preparing briefs, but Counsel would not be there to plead them. It was no matter. There was no hurry. With Michaelmas all would march again.

Lord Avington had left Glenalban immediately after he had carried me there. He was welcome, and his breach of the laws of hospitality most heartily forgiven; but he had engaged himself with other friends.

'I am torn,' he said softly to me, as he left. 'I

want to be where you are, but I am not sure it is kind to be where Flora is. I wish I could stop feeling like a beast.'

I thought he was not a beast. I thought I was not one either, but, like him, I wished I could stop feeling like one. I did not know how deep Flora was hurt. I did not ask her. I was glad and sorry that Avington was gone. Flora treated me with loving friendship, though it seemed I had stolen her lover, and I was like to steal her home.

I resolved that, if Glenalban ever did become mine, they would all always be as welcome there as I was, while it was still theirs. This was not a thought to be put into words, to Flora or anybody else.

Miss Louisa Frith was as good as her promise. A French dressmaker arrived, and measured me, and we picked over drawings and designs and samples of material. The dressmaker said, in a mixture of French and English, that mine was the smallest waist she had ever measured. I thought she had made this remark to a great many young ladies, and probably to many ladies not so young. In an astonishingly short time, hampers of gowns began to arrive, as well as silk underclothes and stockings and hats and shoes; and I was able to enter rooms full of strangers without embarrassment.

'Fashion is a fraud, dear,' said Miss Frith. 'We should not value it. But we do. You look better even than I thought possible. You were beautiful before. Now you are scarcely credible.'

I had one truly absurd new dress, with gigantic leg-of-mutton sleeves, and a gigantic crinoline. It made me feel like an overdressed doll, and like a clown. When first the Earl saw it, he gave his rare brief smile, which was like the sudden sunlight on the Firth of Forth.

'It is *meant* to be comical,' I said. 'At least, I think it must be.'

'I was not smiling in derision, Leonora,' he said, 'but in startled admiration.'

His smile had come and gone. It came again, and stayed longer than I had ever seen it stay. I felt myself smiling back. I felt myself blushing. I felt self-conscious in my ridiculous sleeves. I felt hugely pleased with myself, to have aroused startled admiration.

Dear Aunt Sophia answered a letter from Miss Frith, as well as many from myself, saying that she would come to Glenalban in August.

The Barone Lodovico di Vigliano answered a letter from the Earl, saying that he would come to Glenalban in August.

Lord Avington wrote saying that he would come, in time for the first of the grouse shooting.

There was no word from Lady Lochinver. Her daughter wrote to Miss Frith, to say that her mother had gone south into England.

And, week after golden week, the sun blazed on the bare tops of the big hills, and on the shrunken waters of the Alban River; and the wind from the west sobbed in the trees of the lower ground, and combed the dry grass of the hillsides, and set the roses of the formal gardens nodding. The birds fell quiet, but the air of Glenalban was full of laughter and the sound of the hurrying river, and hoofbeats, and the excited barking of dogs.

Riding with Flora, I was astonished at the number of crofts and little farmhouses on the estate. Of course there were great tracts of emptiness, on the high ground where nobody could have lived, but where any kind of farming was possible, farms there were.

There had been no evictions, no threat of evictions. There were some feckless crofters, and some drunken, and some suspected of poaching and of making illicit whisky; but they had wives and children, and those children were safe. The Earl could not be called the best landlord in Scotland, because there were some equally good; but he was as good as the very best. His supposed cruelty was another lie of Simon Donaldson's, told out of spite; another lie of Lady Lochinver's, told out of policy.

Often we stopped at those crofts, Flora and I and our groom—too often, for Peregrine's taste—because the folk came running out of them, calling to us to have home-made barley-water, or tea, or cake. Everywhere Flora was welcomed, because she was loved; and children tumbled round her feet like puppies, and sheepdogs nuzzled up to her like children. I was welcomed, for her sake. I thought that, after a little, I was welcomed for my own sake.

I thought that, all unconsciously, Flora was teaching me how to be mistress of Glenalban.

I thought that I did not want to be mistress of Glenalban. It was in good hands. I had believed lies, which I now knew to be lies. I had believed that it was desirable, necessary, that I should claim my birthright, for the sake of the poor folk on the estate. I now knew this to be needless. I did not want to make so shabby a return for hospitality.

I said to the Earl, 'Sir, I think it is silly for any of us to spend any more money on law-suits. We will tell the Barone to stop. He has spent enough.'

'He has stopped,' said the Earl.

'But the lawyers must still be sending bills?'

'Of course they are. It is a way lawyers have. I never knew such fellows for itemizing every detail of their services. "To writing one letter, one guinea." '

'If they are sending them, the Barone must be paying them.'

'No longer. That responsibility has been transferred. Your case will proceed, Leonora. It is too late to stop now. Why, you would be assassinated by the entire legal profession, as well as the College of Heralds and the House of Lords.'

'But who . . . ? If the Barone is not . . . ?'

228

He would not say who was paying the legal reckonings.

The obvious truth dawned on me, in the middle of the night. The Grieves were indeed making reparation.

I said, 'Sir, this is ridiculous.'

I was wearing again the dress with the enormous sleeves and the crinoline. I had taken a great fancy to it, because it was intensely fashionable, as well as comical.

The Earl assented cordially. 'It is quite ridiculous,' he said, to my surprise. 'Those sleeves are frankly absurd. However, the extremes of fashion suit you, I suppose because you wear them with an air of such confidence.'

'I was *not* talking about my dress,' I said.

'It goes from the ridiculous to the sublime without moving,' he said.

'I am *still* not talking about my dress. Are you paying my lawyers?'

He would not say. He would not discuss it at all. He became almost brusque, in his refusal to speak about it. There was a hint in his manner of the arrogance with which he had first treated me. By this I knew that he was paying the bills, because if he had not been, he would have said so.

He was paying to have himself evicted from his own castle. It was as ridiculous, and as sublime, as the leg-of-mutton sleeves of my dress.

Almost overnight, I was transformed from a girl wearing dowdy provincial clothes, into a young lady dressed in the height of fashion. More people looked at me, more often, and in a new way. Flora began looking at me in a new way; and Miss Louisa Frith; and the Earl of Glenalban. I thought this was because of my new clothes. Then I thought it was something else.

I thought they all knew something I did not know. Well, to be sure, they all knew a vast number of things I did not know. The Earl and his aunt were widely travelled, and widely read. Flora was nearly two years older than myself, and had been to London, and met all kinds of clever and important people, and had started by being far better educated than I was. But there was more to it than that. There was some immediate knowledge they had, relating to immediate circumstances, which they were keeping from me.

Flora said, when I taxed her, that the odd looks I had seen were looks of admiration and astonishment. She said that she and her aunt were amazed that I could carry off such audacious clothes, because I was so very small, and usually only tall women could dress in such a style; but the dressmaker had understood that I could be successfully bizarre; and they both envied me, and that was the look I saw.

Well, it was all possible; but I thought that for the first time Flora was telling me less than the whole truth.

The oddest looks, that I caught least often, came from the Earl. I could not begin to guess what he was thinking. His face was the opposite of mine—except when he smiled his rare smile, and often even then, his features gave nothing away. Perhaps it was natural; perhaps he had schooled himself, in politics and public affairs, to hide his feelings under a mask of impassive severity.

I caught him frowning at me, when he thought I was not looking. I thought it was not a frown of disapproval or of rage, but of calculation. Yet he was paying my lawyers!

I would have been uneasy. I should have been uneasy. But the weather was too glorious, and the high country too beautiful; and, when Peregrine galloped across the mown hayfields, the rush of warm air scoured all uneasiness out of my mind.

Aunt Sophia came, brought in a travelling-carriage sent by Miss Frith. The family left us alone together, for the whole of her first afternoon, with great kindness and tact, so that we could bring one another up to date without any reserve. I had told her in my letters such of my adventures as I thought would not give her palpitations; I still blotted out many of my memories.

She asked me, hesitantly, how much I had been upset, to find out that Simon Donaldson was a cold-hearted rogue. I said that the wound had healed. I thought it had. It was an itch rather than an agony, like a cut that is mending healthily.

'I think the Barone was quite as wounded as you were, dear,' said Aunt Sophia. 'He has been to see me, you know, and he could talk of nothing else! He is vexed at having been duped, because he prides himself on his judgement of people. What a good soul he is! I am glad he is to come here. I shall feel braver, and more at home, when he is with us.'

I also was keenly looking forward to the Barone's coming; I was amused at the thought of his exuberant gallantry, set against the sober reserve of the Earl, and the infinite correctness of Miss Frith. At least he would not be overawed.

Aunt Sophia was, of course. It was obvious to everybody that she was not accustomed to castles; it was also obvious to everybody that she was a lady of breeding, as well as a gentle and lovable creature. Miss Frith took her under her supremely competent wing, and the two of them went off to see local beauty-spots in an open carriage. Aunt Sophia grew pink from the sun, and there were freckles on her temples I had never seen there before.

I asked her what she and Miss Frith found to talk about, on those expeditions in the victoria which sometimes lasted all day.

'You, dear, principally,' said Aunt Sophia. 'Dear Miss Frith is inexhaustibly interested in your childhood, your education, the family, and so forth. I myself supposed that we had exhausted the subject, after our first conversation. But no such thing! Her questions had barely begun!'

Aunt Sophia did not quite say that there were, after all, other topics of conversation quite as interesting as myself; and that she would have preferred Miss Frith to embark on some of them. She could have said so, without wounding me; I would have agreed. I had myself answered a good many questions about myself, from Miss Frith. I did not know why she should want still more details of my uninteresting history.

I caught glances of special oddness when she looked at me, after these examinations of Aunt Sophia. They might have been expressing admiration and astonishment at my new appearance, as Flora said, but I thought not.

'I do not mind Jack Avington coming,' said Flora unexpectedly, when we were riding over a low hill in a bend of the river.

The meadow-pipits flitted before our horses, going *peep-peep-peep* as they settled for a moment on rocks or clumps of heather. Over the hillside beyond the river, a buzzard wheeled, mewing, like a crucifix against the sky. In the river below us I saw a salmon leap. Nature was showing us her handsomest, most generous face: and suddenly Flora was making embarrassing remarks, which I did not want to listen to.

I looked at her anxiously. If she wanted to tell

233

me about the state of her heart, I would listen, because it was my duty as a friend to do so; but I would have preferred another time and place. It was the first time either of us had mentioned Avington in private, though his name had cropped up in general conversation.

'Truly, Leo,' said Flora, 'you are not to worry on my account. Consider your own feelings, and don't be bothering with mine.'

'I don't know my own feelings,' I said.

And she gave me a look quite as odd as any of Miss Louisa Frith's.

Avington, when he came a few days later, showed that he knew his feelings.

He had two private interviews, each lasting a long time, before ever I exchanged a word with him. The first was with Flora. They walked up and down the terrace for an hour. I could see them from my bedroom window, where I sat having my hair cut and dressed by Mary MacAndrew. I could not well see their faces, nor hear a word of what was said. But I thought I knew pretty well what they were talking about. Avington was making sure that in coming back to Glenalban he was acting without dishonour or cruelty; and Flora was telling him what she had told me.

And presently, I supposed, I would be telling him what I had told her: that I did not know my own feelings.

Immediately afterwards, Avington sat for half

an hour with Aunt Sophia. I watched them while my hair dried in the afternoon sunshine. He might simply have been amusing her, and passing the time for them both. I thought not.

I thought Aunt Sophia would approve of his suit, because she must find it impossible not to approve of him. For one thing, it would not matter for my future what happened in the courts of law. For another, his courtship of me would heal as nothing else would any wound I still carried made by Simon Donaldson. For a third, I was fast approaching my eighteenth birthday.

I came face to face with Avington at last, on the terrace where I had been watching him for most of the afternoon. He waved a greeting, and started hurrying towards me. Twenty paces away from me, he stopped dead, with an expression of comic amazement.

'Everybody laughs at this dress,' I said, 'but let me tell you it is the last word of fashion.'

'You simply take my breath away,' he said slowly. 'The jewel is properly set at last. I see that you are Countess of Albany. Nobody could doubt it. They could have, you know, but not now. I wonder Duncan Glenalban bothers to fight the case in the courts. Now, I was going to postpone a proposal to you, until I had adroitly established myself in your good opinion, by catching a salmon, and shooting a lot of grouse, and so forth, manly exploits which would oblige you to view me as a champion, but contemplation of you now simply pulls the words prematurely from my throat. From my heart, I should say. I must try to be elegant as well as passionate. Will you do me the honour to accept my hand in marriage, you unbelievable miracle of grace, beauty and courage?'

'What were you and Flora talking about?' I said.

'You. Myself. Herself. Did you not hear a question I put to you? Is your perfection marred by deafness, or by a perverse refusal to hear?'

He was smiling. He was joking. But he was in earnest. There was no shadow of doubt about that. And he knew that I knew it.

I was elated. He was a truly decent, honourable, kindly and most diverting man. I would be incredibly lucky to meet one I liked better. Sunburned and windblown, radiating health and humour, he seemed to me supremely attractive. He was in every single regard a man I could most happily contemplate sharing my life with. But I was not certain that I wanted to—not quite certain, not quite yet.

'You must give me time,' I said lamely.

'Why? I'll give you all sorts of other things, of course, trumpery affairs like rubies—but why time?'

'First of all, time to hear what you and Flora were saying. Then time to hear what you and Aunt Sophia were saying.'

'How do you know that I have been having these conversations?'

'I watched you.'

'All that age? I am more than flattered. Prolonged contemplation. That suggests that you do not find me repulsive. You may even have detected in me a classical beauty which, as a matter of fact, my mother is the only person to have observed. Also that vigil would have given you time enough. But I daresay your mind was on other things?'

'I was having my hair done.'

'Whoever did it is a master.'

'And so,' I said, 'I was imprisoned in my chair, and I was obliged to watch you walking up and down with Flora, and then sitting beside Aunt Sophia. And I wondered what you were saying, and I still wonder.'

'I like your aunt very much.'

'Well, we can come to that later, and you can tell me exactly what you like about her. First you must tell me about you and Flora.'

'You know, you have changed more than your style of dress. Your character has changed. You are growing rapidly into your new role of tyrant, châteleine, empress. Even a thought too rapidly, if I may inject a note of nervous criticism into a conversation which I intended to be an anthem of praise and supplication on my part, and an almost immediate acquiescence on yours. You are not supposed to give me orders. You are not an Amazon. Or, if you are, I think they would say you were undersized for battle. I am supposed to give you orders, but I doubt whether I shall ever have the courage to do so.'

I burst out laughing. He laughed too. That was what was so very good about him—the laughter that he generated and that we shared. That was one of the most attractive aspects, of the prospect of sharing a life with him.

We bickered amicably, in the golden sunlight of early evening, often making one another laugh. I thought afterwards that it was the most extraordinary conversation I had ever had—even odder than the one in which Avington unmasked Simon Donaldson, outside the little square Kirk. For he was, even as he bantered and bickered, pressing me to reply to a proposal of marriage; and I was pleading for time, and demanding to know how matters stood between himself and Flora, and what Aunt Sophia had said on the subject I was sure they had discussed.

A footman came out on to the terrace, with the gong that was beaten there every evening. It told us it was time to go indoors, to dress for dinner.

'We have by no means completed our discussion,' said Avington.

'We have weeks to finish it in,' I said, 'if you are going to stay here as long as that.'

'My present plan is to stay until I have extracted an acceptance from you, which I shall do by force if necessary. One of those halberds or partisans which Duncan Glenalban so ostentatiously hangs in his hall. A few good jabs with a spear, and I'll soon have you saying "Yes". Of course I shall try first to secure your surrender by means of peaceful persuasion. But I must warn you that my patience wears thin very quickly. I am a most impulsive fellow. Don't be surprised to receive your first stab-wounds about the middle of tomorrow afternoon, if you have not by that time given me a satisfactory reply.'

'There are shields in the hall, too.'

'None that would protect me from the piercing impact of those amazing brown eyes. Inherited, as we know, from your great-grandfather. Really they make all ordinary eyes insipid, colourless, vapid.'

'We must go in and change, or we shall be late for dinner.'

'I rhapsodize, practically in poetry, about your eyes, and all you are thinking about is your dinner.'

'Being proposed to gives one an appetite,' I said.

'Come to think of it, so does proposing. I would have expected to turn away in disgust, from great platters of rich food. But I think I shall fall upon them with every circumstance of gluttony. I beg you will not watch me eating my dinner. I shall revolt you. You will contemplate with abhorrence the prospect of sharing a dinner table, all the rest of your life, with so obscene a spectacle.'

We both laughed, and laughing parted, with nothing decided, least of all what my answer would be.

As I went into the castle from that west terrace, where we had been amusing and enraging one another in the evening sun, I saw the Earl. He turned and strode away, as though to avoid me. He had been watching us. I was sure of it. Watching us as intently as I had watched Avington with Flora, and Avington with Aunt Sophia.

Though he turned away quickly, I had time to glimpse his face. There was no trace in it of the smile I liked so well. It wore a black frown— another of his expressions which I had cause to know.

Had we angered him, by hooting with laughter outside his windows? Had we been boorish and rustic? I thought not—at least, not very. Other people laughed at Glenalban, and dogs barked, and pianofortes were played, most expertly, and with plenty of loud pedal, by Miss Frith and by Flora, and most inexpertly by me. It was a place full of bustling life, and all the mixed noises of activity and sociability. No one had objected to noise before, as far as I knew.

Mary MacAndrew helped me to dress. I was becoming used to being pampered, and it would be stupid to deny that I liked it, because nobody had ever pampered me before. Mary was prattling about her still-secret betrothal to Kenneth Doig, and it was glorious to see the happiness in her narrow face.

As though a coin spun, I saw the other side of Mary's happiness, the exact reverse. I saw misery, in my mind's eye. Not anger, but misery on the Earl's face. It had been a frozen frown. The Spartan boy whose vitals were eaten by a fox would have worn such a frown, and so prevented himself from crying out in anguish.

It came to me that I had been seeing less and less of the Earl; and, when I did see him, it was at meals, or in one of the drawing-rooms, in company with all the others. I was sorry for this, because his conversation was always interesting, and his compliments were welcome because they were rare and because they were meant. It came to me that it was no accident, that we no longer found ourselves talking together, or strolling together.

His misery might be on his sister's behalf, knowing her heart to have been bruised, and seeing Avington enjoying my company. I thought not. I thought it was on his own. The Spartan boy would not have worn such a mask of frozen misery, because that fox was eating someone else's vitals.

And so an astonishing theory jumped into my head. It had simply never occurred to me before; and the Earl had given me no grounds for supposing any such thing.

He was so learned and travelled and experienced. Though he could smile, he was generally serious to the point of severity. He had gigantic responsibilities. Though the same age as Jack Avington, he seemed to belong to a different generation.

If he felt as he looked as though he felt, then my happy comradeship with Jack would, indeed, turn knives in his heart. But why should he, a sophisticated gentleman, a great nobleman, lord of this place, well able to express himself—why should he stand and suffer? He did not know my heart. I did not know it myself. I was not yet Avington's property, and might never be. I might have hated the Earl, for what he had done to me; but he knew very well that I did not. He could have spoken. He could have made a sign. But, instead, he avoided me as though I were a leper.

The supremely obvious explanation came to me, when I lay wakeful in the small hours.

He was drawn to me, but he was repelled by me.

He thought I was beautiful, and he liked my new clothes. But he found me a silly, shallow, ignorant and worthless child. And, indeed, I was. I was inconceivable as his companion, as mistress of Glenalban at his side; I was inconceivable as hostess of political receptions in London, and of great dinners with Prime Ministers and Dukes. Though my face and figure attracted him, my personality and conversation filled him with boredom and disgust.

That must be it, I thought. That explained everything. Nothing else explained anything. I could imagine being torn by such an internal conflict. I could imagine Simon Donaldson arousing physical passion and moral disgust, all at the same moment; I could imagine the misery that one might feel and that one might show. One would find oneself driven to stare upon the cause; but one would have sense enough not to torture oneself, perhaps, by private conversations with the cause.

I felt very wise, making these deductions with flawless logic. I felt very puzzled, and sorry. I felt flattered and angry. I was not, on second thoughts, so very stupid. If I was intolerably young, time would put that right. If I was fairly ignorant, he could put that right. Other clever people had managed to listen to me, without screams of irritated boredom—dear Jack Avington, and dear Aunt Sophia, and Miss Louisa Frith.

But still he was paying my lawyers' bills, with the object of having himself evicted from Glenalban.

It was a great puzzle, and a great muddle; I did not sleep until dawn, and then Mary MacAndrew had much difficulty in waking me.

'I had a long talk to Lord Avington, dear,' said Aunt Sophia after breakfast. 'I have been waiting to talk to you about it, but I had trouble in deciding what to say.'

'Say if you like him,' I said.

'Oh! Yes! That is an important point. I do like him, very much, on brief acquaintance. He has those very pleasant easy manners, and he is full of kindness and consideration! A gentleman, as well as a nobleman, which I think is not invariably the case . . . I understand that he has, ah, conversed with you also. That he has, ah, declared himself to you.'

'Did you give him leave to do so, Aunt Sophia?'

'He said that he could not stop himself from doing so. I was struck by his sincerity, you know. I think he has a true heart! I demurred about the difference in age, but he quite brushed that aside! He said many most generous things about you, which I shall *not* repeat, because those astonishing new dresses of yours are making you disgracefully vain already . . . He agrees that there can be no formal arrangement until your eighteenth birthday—'

'That is only a few weeks off.'

'I demurred also about the *very* short time you have known one another. To be precipitate in these matters may breed the most dreadful unhappiness! But he quite brushed that aside too! Never, he said, had he been more certain about anything! All the while he was in the way of laughing at himself, you know, in that amusing fashion he has, and obliging me to laugh also . . . But, at bottom, I am convinced he is in earnest.'

'Yes, I know.'

'He made the excellent point that while he knew you quite well enough, even after so short a time, for such certainty, he quite saw that you might not feel that you knew him well enough, but that the next few weeks could put that right. To that I had *no* answer.'

'I have no answer, either,' I said, 'to any of it.'

'That is as it should be, dear. Rush into nothing. Think most carefully, and consult your heart and your conscience.'

All this, of course, was quite the proper thing for Aunt Sophia to say. But I was sure she was sure that I would marry Avington; and I was sure that she would pray nightly that I did.

Avington had one matchmaker firmly on his side.

I thought there was constraint between Flora and Avington, although they did not seem to avoid one another as the Earl avoided me. There was no change in Flora's attitude to me. She bore no grudge. I thought she deserved to be loved as she was, by all the folk of the countryside.

Avington was in undisguised pursuit of me, of which nobody at Glenalban could have been unaware. The upshot was reckoned a foregone conclusion, in the Servants' Hall, as Mary MacAndrew reported to me. I suppose that Flora's maid reported it to her, too, in all innocence.

Jack was not always at my side. The castle was filling up with shooting guests and their wives, for the Twelfth of August and the first of the grouse drives. He had to fish with some and ride with others, out of civility to them and to the Earl. He had to engage ladies in conversation after dinner, and turn the pages of their music, and take a hand at cards. These were the absolute duties of a bachelor staying in a great house as a member of a large party; and Jack performed them beautifully. All things considered, it was amazing how often he *was* at my side.

He did not, point-blank, repeat his declaration, his proposal. He made it clear, in a joking way which was perfectly serious, that he *would* repeat it. He paid me many compliments, joking and perfectly serious. But what he was really about was bringing the two of us closer together, so that we knew one another every day more deeply. It was just what Aunt Sophia would have advised.

Though there was nothing arrogant or complacent in Jack's manner to me, it was obvious that he did not entertain the possibility of my refusing him. And indeed, the possibility seemed to be shrinking. Everything was pushing me in the same direction—Avington himself, Aunt Sophia, some of the other guests, who made broad and sentimental hints, even the whole Servants' Hall.

This had a curious effect on me. I did not care to be pushed. Though Jack never *said* anything directly that showed he took my acceptance for granted, he *did* without words show that he took it for granted. And so did everybody else; and I did not care to be taken for granted.

In an odd way, the exceptions to this universal pushing of me towards marriage with Avington were Flora and Miss Frith. When others winked and hinted, or even openly approved, they were silent. They were apt to glance at me, involuntarily; and the odd looks I had seen before came and went in their faces.

The Earl was engrossed in the sporting entertainment of his guests. I hardly saw him at all. Of course he knew about my friendship with Jack Avington. Of course he heard the romantic rumours which kept everybody busy and amused. Of course he had reason to know that they were true. Of course he did not know the outcome. Nobody knew the outcome, though everybody thought they did. I guessed that he was glad to be distracted. I even guessed that Jack was, in a way of drastic surgery, solving his own problem for him.

There were not only rumours about my approaching betrothal to Jack Avington. There were also rumours about my claim to Glenalban Castle. Though nothing had been published or publicly announced, such sensational matters could hardly be kept secret. It amazed some of the visitors that I was kindly entertained in a castle that I was trying to grab from its occupants of three and a half centuries. But other visitors knew better. There was no hope of my claim succeeding. This was, it seemed, the confidential news from Edinburgh. It was colourable; it was not fraudulent; it had been worth bringing; but it was based on flimsy evidence and uncertain law. That was the accepted view in Glenalban, in the first week of the blazing August.

I thought they were probably right, and I thought I was probably glad.

I did not precisely have conversations with anybody about it, because these were kindly and well-bred people who would not have embarrassed me for the world. But I overheard a good many snippets and wisps of other people's conversations.

'It's preposterous, the idea of that chit being owner of all this.'

'Preposterous it may be, dear boy, but damned attractive.'

'The idea, or the little claimant?'

I did not hear the answer: not because I was suddenly ashamed of eavesdropping, but because the two resplendent gentlemen strolled away out of earshot.

It was another foregone conclusion in all their minds, like my marriage to Jack. Still they were all, in varying degrees, agog to know what would happen when the courts sat again and the causes were pleaded. And I understood that there was widespread curiosity, throughout the country, derived from things which were babbled by solicitors' clerks in Edinburgh taverns. This was something that was bound to have happened; but it shows how ignorant I was, that it came as a complete surprise to me.

Jack said, 'What will you do, Leo, if you find yourself owner of Glenalban?'

'I think I would give it back to the Grieves.

But the question is academic. They all say that my cake is dough.'

'I wonder what I hope?' he said. 'Morally I think you ought to win, but I'm not at all sure I want you to.'

That was my position, exactly.

There was a great gala and a great slaughter on the Glorious Twelfth, the opening of the season for shooting grouse. All the gentlemen went off quite early, in knickerbockers and shooting-boots. All the ladies joined them on a hillside, going by wagonette or dog-cart or Highland pony, for a monster picnic. It was still very hot. The men were purple, and had taken off their coats. The beaters and flankers and stops—the army of men and boys who put their lives at risk to make the sport possible—lay panting and scarlet on the heather, but were gradually revived by barrels of beer brought up the hill on donkeys.

I had never seen one of these lavish Highland sporting picnics before, but I had read in the illustrated papers about the Queen's great feasts on the hills above Balmoral. I thought the standard on Albanside must be quite as high as that on Deeside. I was agape, and so was Aunt Sophia. I could not imagine how so many servants, so perfectly point-device, had been transported to this wild place, with white gloves uncrumpled and buttons agleam; nor so much ice, and wine, and linen, and silver, and chairs, and cold salmon; but all the rest took it as a matter of course—or, if they did not, they were better at pretending than I was.

'Are you enjoying yourself, dear?' Miss Frith asked softly.

'Yes, Ma'am, very much. But I am amazed to see that the whole Glenalban dining room is carried all the way up here. Have you a herd of pack-elephants hid somewhere behind the stables?'

She laughed her moderate laugh—not un-amused, but not precisely uproarious. 'Ah,' she said, 'there are a great number of improvisations and short-cuts, you know, which nobody is supposed to notice. The idea is to achieve the maximum of effect with the minimum of hard labour. The servants enjoy it, but not if their backs are broken.'

Miss Frith, like Flora, was unconsciously giving me lessons in how to be mistress of Glenalban.

Two days later there was a greater gala—the arrival of a circus, of a conqueror, of a clown. The event had the air of being attended by military bands and cheering crowds.

The Barone Lodovico di Vigliano came.

He was by now the friend of Jack Avington, Aunt Sophia and myself, and the friendly enemy of the Earl. To all the rest he was completely unknown. He was totally exotic in that place —yet, because he was as always completely himself, he was totally disarming to almost

250

everybody almost at once.

He arrived in his notion of clothes for a Perthshire August—a pale-coloured silk frock-coat, trousers like chequerboard balloons, but pinched in at the ankles, brown button-boots instead of black ones, a scarlet cravat as big as a pillowcase, and a straw hat with a brim a yard broad. Among the sober tweeds and worsteds of the Glenalban party, he looked like a peacock among daws.

He kissed Miss Louisa Frith's hand. I was not sure how she would take an action which, in Perthshire, was as peculiar as it was in East Lothian. But she was pleased. She smiled. I took it that it had happened before, on her travels abroad, but not often. He greeted Aunt Sophia as an old and honoured friend, and kissed her hand. With most of those present, her stock, which had been only moderately high, immediately rose. He bowed deeply to Flora, and less deeply to me. He did not kiss my hand. He called me not *piccola Contessa* or *cara Contessina,* but Signorina Leonora, as though we had never shared adventures and betrayals, and planned my coronation in the Palace of Holyroodhouse. I was surprised, and a little put out. It was the kind of thing which should not matter, but does, when you are not quite eighteen, and long afterwards.

There were some strict gentlemen in the party, and stricter ladies, who were not immediately captivated by this affable eccentric. I think none of them held out beyond the end of the Barone's first evening. He talked much; he listened also. He exclaimed in amazement at the castle, the views from the terraces, the beauty of the ladies present; and at every story he was told. He became effortlessly, and without any apparent intention, the centre round which the party orbited. Everybody wanted to talk to him, men as well as women. I thought his beard was even bigger and glossier than before.

He once or twice smiled at me, that first evening of his conquest of Glenalban, and made little gestures indicating friendliness. But he was constantly surrounded, and we had no chance to talk.

Somebody asked him, as I had done, if his prodigious cane were a swordstick. He said, as he had said to me, that a man needed protection against the *ladroni* of his undisciplined country. He was asked if he had used it; indeed, he said, he had been more than thankful for it; it was not too much to say that it had saved his life. I waited for the story of the melon which he had cut with his sword on the banks of Lake Como. But he told a perfectly different story, about a large Bologna sausage which he wanted to cut into slices. There was a roar of laughter about him, in which Miss Louisa Frith joined, laughing more unreservedly than I had ever seen her do. It was good to see.

I thought that the truth was, that the Barone had used the sword in earnest, to save his own life or somebody else's; but he would never tell a story that glorified himself, but invent one to make himself ridiculous.

I wanted to tell them all the story of the way he rescued me from the Lochgrannomhead Asylum. But the story involved Simon Donaldson, and Lady Lochinver; and so this was not the place to tell it.

He did not join the gentlemen on the grouse-moor in the morning, though he was offered tweeds, and boots, and a pair of guns, and a loader. I did not hear the reason he gave, but it made the solemn Earl laugh as hard as his aunt had laughed.

He joined me instead, where I was sitting with some sewing, among terrifying ladies, on the terrace. He bowed all round; he requested permission from the company to take me for a stroll, since we were old friends who wanted news of one another; he apologized for his intrusion and for taking me away, with a droll humility that made even the grimmest ladies smile.

We went round a corner, so that we were out of sight of the terrace.

'Now,' he said, 'I can kiss your hand, *bellissima e piccolissima reina.*'

And he did so, bowing low.

'I could not speak so, or act so, before all those peoples yeterday,' he said. 'It would not have been *gentile,* I think, to show that I think you are Contessa d'Albini, and *proprietario* of this big house.'

'Oh, I see,' I said. 'Yes, of course, that is right. You do not *have* to kiss my hand, even in private . . .'

'Yes, I do,' he said. 'Now, you do not have to tell me your news, because I have heard it all last night, and again this morning, from one thousand peoples. First, you are even more beautiful than peoples thought, because now you have nice *vestiti.*'

'That is all thanks to Miss Frith.'

'The Signorina Louisa? So? She is kind and generous? That is good. I find her very handsome. But in a different style from you. So—I hear also that you are *spiritosa*—amusing —and not too shy, but also not too bold, so that you please all peoples very much. And I hear that you will marry the Milor' Avington. That is good. I like him. *Mi piace.* You will be rich and a *Miladi* even if we lose the case. And that is good, because I think maybe we lose him.'

'I don't care so very much,' I said, 'but why, when everything seemed so certain?'

'The lawyers have explain, and I have not understand.'

'Why is Lord Glenalban paying our bills?'

'He is *uomo d'onore,* that one. His family owes you much, in *riparazione.* That is first. Another, he thinks I have paid enough, in an affair which is not my affair.'

'Well, that is true.'

'Yes, it is true. It is become quite difficult to get more *soldi* from Italia. They are there, but

254

they are not here. Well now, I have more news. You know your friend, Signor Maitland, with the *negozzio* in Edimburgo. His is now my friend also. That is from Simon Donaldson, of whom we will not talk. Well now, you remember also the *banditto* Edgar Smith, who call himself a different name and come to your house?'

'Yes, of course. But I don't think Edgar Smith is his real name, either.'

'That may be. Such a man has one thousand names. But always he has the *uccello,* the *voglia*—'

He groped for the English word. I looked at him blankly.

'The marks of birth,' he said.

'Birthmark.'

'*Giusto.* So when he is caught he is known. He has been caught. He is in the prison. That is a little bit of good news, to put next beside my large bad news.'

'I think they're both good news,' I said. 'At least, I think I think so.'

Nine

Jack Avington had to go away again.

'I accepted the invitation months ago,' he said,
'before I met you. I have been wondering
whether to make an effort to get out of it, but it
could only be done by telling lies. Remember
Lovelace?

' "I could not love thee, dear, so much,
Lov'd I not honour more." '

'That's a better poem than the last I heard,' I
said. 'No, you must not lie to your old friends.'

'I will be back in good time for your birthday.'

Aunt Sophia was very pleased to hear this.

The party dispersed; people went home or to
other parties. Aunt Sophia said that she and I
were outstaying our welcome. Miss Frith said
that if we stayed for thirty years, we would not

outstay our welcome. Flora said so, too. I thought she truly wanted me to stay. The Earl said the same, in private, to Aunt Sophia, which left her in a flutter of awestruck gratitude. I did not understand why they were determined to make themselves miserable. Left to myself, I would have gone home to Millstounburn, not because I preferred it, but because, in staying, I felt as Jack had said he felt—I felt a beast. But Aunt Sophia was happier than she had ever been, and it was happiness she deserved.

The Earl and the Barone went together to Edinburgh, very friendly and full in one another's confidence. They came back after four days, and the Barone found me on the terrace.

'The news is bad,' he said. 'Still bad. Worse than before. You shall be Contessa if you want, but you shall not have Glenalban.'

A few minutes later the Earl astonished me by proposing a stroll down through the park to the river-bank. He was not a man who strolled. He was always busy. When he walked, he strode briskly, and it was always in order to do something which had to be done.

There was a great constraint in his manner. He seemed to have difficulty with his voice, although, at first, we were simply chatting about the people who had been staying, and about his journey from Edinburgh.

He stopped. He seemed to force himself, as once before, to look me in the face.

He said, 'I think Vigliano has told you. I am fulfilling my legal obligation to you by making you free of this castle and estate, by entertaining you and yours, and by giving you what you require. Your own lawyers have confirmed the opinion of my lawyers as to the effect on your claim of the great period of time during which we have occupied this place, of the impossibility of distinguishing what King James II notionally owned and what we have added since, and of the fact that you demonstrably do not need a castle for political or military exigencies.'

'I think that is as it should be,' I said.

'I believe I can be forgiven for thinking so too. For obvious reasons, and for a much stronger reason which is not obvious. While there remained a possibility of your becoming one of the richest women in Scotland . . . While there was that possibility . . .'

He seemed to dry up. His words stuck. I had never before seen this formidable and splendid nobleman at a loss.

He blurted out, 'Now that I may speak, I can't.'

I stared at him, completely puzzled.

He was scarlet. I had never seen him blush. He made weak, flapping gestures with his hands, like the Chaplain when he was trying to persuade me to repent.

He said, 'You understand, don't you? You surely understand?'

258

'No,' I said, distressed to see anybody so distressed.

'If you were suddenly rich, and I suddenly poor . . . How could I speak to you?'

'Well,' I said stupidly, 'just by opening your mouth, you know.'

He dragged his eyes from the ground, and stared at me.

'How could I declare myself? Declare my heart? Make love to you?'

'Is that what you wanted to do?' I asked, having difficulty now with my own voice.

'It is what I have wanted to do ever since I first saw you.'

'Oh,' I said. 'That was not the impression you gave, when we first met . . . But of course you thought I was a criminal then. How awkward for you, to fall in love with a criminal.'

'No more awkward,' he said, 'than falling in love with a millionairess.'

'I am beginning to understand. That is as absurd as . . . the sleeves of that dress you laughed at.'

'What would the world say,' he burst out, 'if I, newly poor, went trailing after a great heiress? What would my friends say? What would you say? What would I say, myself, to myself? You would never know—never be entirely sure—that I was not another Simon Donaldson. And, worse still, I would never be entirely sure. I love this place . . .'

'So do I.'

'So I thought. How could I dishonour myself, prostitute myself, by marrying for it?'

'It might not strike me like that.'

'The suspicion would never be entirely absent from your mind. Thank God, it no longer arises. You love Glenalban. It is yours, Leonora.'

'Is that what you are offering me, Sir? Glenalban?'

'Glenalban comes with my offer. I am offering you my heart. The lawyers have at last made it possible for me to say so. I have been suffering the agonies of the damned, hiding my feelings so that you would never guess—'

'You did not quite hide your feelings. I knew them. At least, I thought I did. I saw your face—'

'When I had been watching you with Avington? I wondered if you had. I wonder if you can imagine what I went through, watching what I wanted most on earth being publicly and cheerfully taken from me, and powerless to make so much as a gesture—morally forbidden to do anything at all, until the lawyers made up their minds.'

'Oh,' I said. 'I thought I repelled you.'

'What?'

'By being so ignorant and silly and young.'

'Time will put the last right. If the first needs putting right, which I do not think, where lies the problem? The castle is full of books, and the world of places you can see.'

'Well, I did think that myself.'

'And silly? You are the least silly person I have ever known.'

'Even to my choice of sleeves?'

He managed an uneasy smile.

'What gives me agony now,' he said, 'is the thought that I have had to leave it too late. May I ask you . . . I have no right to, but I must . . . may I ask you, how stands your heart with Avington?'

'I don't know,' I said.

'Is that true? Forgive me. The question is unasked. Of course, if you say it, it is true . . . There is then hope for me?'

I thought of the gigantic prizes he was offering me. I thought of his handsomeness, popularity, kindness, sense of duty. I thought of what he had said about himself—about the impossibility of even the appearance of marrying for money.

I looked at him sadly—tall, handsome in a style I had once not liked, usually so immaculate but now, because of the expression on his face, somehow crumpled and woebegone.

'No,' I said.

In spite of what I had been thinking, hearing this word in my own voice startled me so much that I bit my tongue. Was I demented?

'No,' I said again. 'Because of what the world would say, and your friends, and your family, and you, and myself to myself. If I were rich, and you either poor or rich—or if you were as poor as I—then . . . Then I do not know what. I find that the rules you make for yourself apply to me. Everybody knows that I started by trying to take Glenalban. Everybody will know that I failed. Everybody would think, that having failed in one way I took another. Probably they would think that you asked me out of pity, because my disappointment was so bitter. I would never be sure that it was not so, myself. You would never be sure. Everybody knows that Jack Avington has been—courting me. Everybody predicts the result. How will they think, when suddenly I drop him, and grab the chance of a still richer and grander suitor? How would you not suspect that I was mercenary? How would I not suspect it?'

'But this is—as absurd as the sleeves of that wonderful dress!'

'Why is it absurd in me and not in you?'

'I am a man, dearest Leonora!'

'Is a woman no greedier than a man?'

'When a poor man marries a rich woman, there is always a suspicion, usually just, about his motive. When a poor girl marries a rich man, she is suspected of nothing worse than good fortune.'

'If she has just been trying to dispossess that man? The world will know very well what to think.'

'Do you care what the world thinks?'

'I care what I think, and what you think.'

'I utterly absolve you from greed. You yourself suggested to me that you drop your case.'

'Why did you insist on going on with it, Sir?'

'My name is Duncan.'

'To me you must still be "Sir", I think. Why?'

'Because there had to be a resolution, one way or the other. For my sake and for yours. For the sake of tenants and servants, men of business, neighbours. For the sake of the future. We had to know where we stood, now and in perpetuity. If we had let matters drop, then the next generation or the next could have recommenced the whole unsettling and expensive process, with unpredictable results. Nobody's tenure of anything would have been secure. And, supremely, I had to know which one of us two was rich. So that I could lay my heart and my castle at your feet.'

'I could never take your heart, Sir, in case I was confusing it with your castle.'

'I could abdicate here—abdicate all wealth and position. If I got you by doing so, it would be cheap at the price.'

These were the most amazing words that had ever been said to me. I was speechless. But, when I found my tongue, it was to say, 'That is magnificent. But you would never cease blaming me for your loss of everything.'

'I would never cease thanking you for honouring me. Do you think that, if I could make a straight choice between you and Glenalban, stones and mortar would weight heavier than flesh and blood and spirit?'

'*If* you could? Could you not?'

'Of course not. Do you know how many people depend on me? I am bound to offer

263

myself as I am, warts and wealth and all.'

'Do you suffer from warts, Sir?' I asked, startled that such a topic should enter such a conversation. 'You need a gravestone and a hair from a horse's tail and a night of full moon, or so my old nurse told me . . .'

He smiled briefly—the sun on the dark sea. 'It was a remark of Oliver Cromwell's, when his portrait was about to be painted . . . My talk of abdicating my responsibilities is completely empty, the merest oratorical flatulence. What I am asking you to do, Leonora, is not to share the life of the raggle-taggle gipsies, but to share my responsibilities. We work, people like myself. At least, we should. Only so do we justify our inheritances, the monstrous inequity of our good luck at birth . . . Great Heavens, I did not mean to give you a lecture on political economy, or the morality of inherited wealth. But what I do *not* offer you is a life of pampered indolence.'

'That is what I have been living, though, since I came here . . . Sir—'

'Duncan.'

'Sir, I owe it to you to be completely honest, if I can.'

'You can. Only if you tried to be less than honest would you fail. But I dread what follows such an opening.'

'You need not, because it is what I have already said. I am young and ignorant, even if I am not silly, and so I do not know what I truly feel about Jack Avington. But I do know that I

264

could not live with myself, if I had to suspect myself of having married for a castle and a fortune.'

He opened his mouth to say something—even to shout something—but I went on before he had a chance.

'It is no more absurd in me than it would have been, than it was for those weeks, in you,' I said. 'I did think it was absurd in you, until the positions were suddenly reversed. Men have no monopoly of honour or pride. Oh, how pompous that sounded. We are lecturing one another, you on political economy, and I on whatever I am talking about, only I have lost the thread . . .'

'Answer me one last question, Leonora. Could you love me if I were poor?'

'I don't know. I have thought myself in love. I think I am too young for all this. And I do not think a magic wand is waved on one's eighteenth birthday. I think your question does not exist. You are what you are, and part of what you are is being lord of—' I waved at castle, park, river, farms and hills—'all this.'

He heaved a great sigh.

He said, 'You are letting a moral scruple stand in the way of my happiness and, perhaps, your own.'

'You have been doing so for weeks.'

'You *must* admit, in spite of what you said, that there is a difference between men and women.'

'Oh yes. I could not grow a beard like the

Barone's . . . We have only walked a hundred yards. They can all see us, if they are looking this way. What would they be thinking?'

'My sister and my aunt will be hoping for a different outcome to our talk.'

'They know?'

'They have known all along.'

'Oh! That explains some things I found odd. Odd looks. The way they did not seem to take any notice, when everybody was talking as though I was bound to accept Jack's proposal. Miss Frith examining Aunt Sophia about me. Was that on your behalf?'

'Yes, of course, though it was not at my request . . . I do not think, at this moment, I can bear to continue this walk.'

I could not, either. I did not know why I found that I was weeping.

'I can understand you refusing my brother because you did not like him,' said Flora. 'But just because he is so rich . . . ?'

'Ever since all this began,' I said, trying as I spoke to understand myself, 'I have been simply—greedy and ambitious. What was it all for, if not for honour and position and wealth? At your expense—all at your expense. That was how it started, and that is how it has gone on. And now I am sickened at myself that I wanted those things so badly. It seems to me that you were all right about me, when I first came here.'

'No, Leo, no!'

'Your brother told me that he could never have—made love to me—if he was poor and I was rich, because he could never have been sure, in his own heart, whether it was me or his money that he wanted. It is exactly the same for me.'

Afterwards I thought: either I am in love with Jack Avington, or I have lost my reason.

Now it was, beyond question, time I went away from Glenalban.

Miss Louisa Frith said that she would lock me in the wardrobe again, rather than let me go before my birthday, which was two weeks off.

The Earl said that Avington had had weeks upon weeks; and it was only fair that he should have those two weeks, to get me to change my mind.

Aunt Sophia had heard in private from Flora what celebrations had been planned. She was appalled at the thought of our leaving, after what had already been done and spent, for me, secretly behind my back.

So I was overruled, and still I felt a beast.

I was preoccupied with my own concerns—with my feelings and conscience, and in regard to Flora a guilt I could not shake off, and in regard to my moral scruples a suspicion that I had gone crazy—so that I was not at once aware of what everybody else had noticed immediately. It was as obvious, as public, and as popular, as Avington's pursuit of myself.

It was something Mary MacAndrew said, indefatigably carrying the Servants' Hall gossip to my bedroom, that first made me lift my eyes from my toes. I saw what she meant. There was a change in Miss Louisa Frith. Though she kept her awesome elegance, she had lost her severity. She took to relaxing and to laughing. She smiled at the sky and at the trees and at whatever person was by.

Everybody understood the reason except, at first, myself. And then I understood, with a shock of delighted astonishment.

There was a maze of clipped yew-trees below the south terrace, part of a formal Italian garden laid out in the eighteenth century. Once you were well into the maze, you were lost to the world —invisible, almost inaudible because of the denseness of the ancient trees and the mossy paths underfoot. I was once half a morning trying to find my way out.

One day, about noon, I was going with Flora to the herb-garden. We were to pick some aromatic plants, which would be dried, and sewn up in muslin bags, to scent our wardrobes. We passed one of the green, growing arches which led into the maze. From it as we passed emerged Miss Louisa Frith. Her smile was as broad as the archway, and her eyes were dancing. Her hat was a little askew, and her hair a little disordered —amazing and unprecedented sights. She looked a little guilty and self-conscious, and sublimely happy. It was impossible not to smile, at the sight of such happiness.

The Barone Lodovico followed her out of the maze. He was bubbling, chuckling, beaming.

Flora giggled.

I saw that there was a pink flush on one side of Miss Frith's face, on her right cheek. I was puzzled for a moment. People did not blush on one side only; at least, I thought embarrassment sent a blush equally over both cheeks; it always did over mine. And then I glanced at the Barone's beard, and understood what Flora had seen at once, and which made her giggle.

The Barone's noble beard, of which he was so proud, had rubbed against Miss Frith's cheek, and raised that pink flush. He had been kissing her, in the maze. All her new exuberant happiness was explained.

I wondered what the Earl would make of it.

The Earl was delighted. He was so happy to see his aunt happy. He had an immensely high regard for the Barone, like everybody else at Glenalban. He was not only disarmed by the Italian's ebullience and manifest goodwill; he was also—after several long and private conversations—reassured by the antiquity of the Barone's family and title, and the extent of his Piedmontese estates. He had not one castle only, but three, acquired by the judicious marriages of his ancestors. One of the three was high in the Alps; at another he made, he said, most excellent red wine. He had also a town house in Turin, and a villa made out of an ancient tower on the coast near Mentone.

'You have a fourth castle now, Lodovico,' said the Earl. 'You have Glenalban, for as often and for as long as you want it.'

Miss Frith kissed her nephew, a thing I daresay she was in the way of doing, but which I had never seen her do before.

Flora told me that, some time before, her brother had made private enquiries about the Barone. He did so by letter to a British consul in Italy whom he knew. It was not that he mistrusted the Barone, but all that anybody knew about him came from his own words, and was unsupported by any document or by any other person's report. And the Earl had reason to see fortune-hunters behind every bush, after his experience with Simon Donaldson, and with myself.

The report came back from Turin. There was indeed a most authentic Barone Lodovico di Vigliano, a man of scholarly interests, noble beard, extensive estates, and ancient family. He was at present away, believed travelling abroad, as he often did.

There was no bar to the immediate announcement of the betrothal. The celebration would coincide with my imminent eighteenth birthday.

'There is a new fashion here, Leo,' said the Earl, who had taken to abbreviating my name as his sister did. 'You must have observed it. The fashion is for people to fall in love. It is all the rage this summer. My aunt and Lodovico and I and Jack Avington have all done it. You are so desperately fashionable in your dress—I cannot think how you can bear not to join this other fashion too.'

'Sir—'

'Duncan.'

'Duncan,' I said, suddenly finding that this was right. 'I have been wearing fashionable clothes, which make you laugh, because of your aunt's kindness. But I am not the *slave* of fashion.'

What he said was a kind of serious joke, like some of Jack Avington's remarks. It was not entirely ridiculous. The Barone and Miss Frith gave a daily example of happiness which it would have been delightful to follow.

I saw temptation, smiling ever so sweetly. If I could but imagine myself in love with Duncan Glenalban, then I was on a shining highway to a glorious future—a magnificent man, in every regard, my husband—an angel my sister—a palace my home. Since I was marrying for love, I was forging the happiness of my beloved, and money and greatness were irrelevant.

And why should I not be in love with a man whom everyone admired and trusted, and whom I had come to like so very much? Why should I not be in love with a man whose smile was like a shaft of sunlight on the sea? Was not my reluctance to say 'Yes' to the entirely delightful

Avington, to be explained by the fact that all along, unrealized by myself, I was really in love with Duncan?

Oh, it would have been very easy to slide down that treacherous path; and I thought, if I did it, I would be more contemptibly prostituted than the lowest drab in the Gorbals.

That night, at dinner, the Barone was looking comically downcast. He was visibly, if tacitly, begging to be asked the cause of his unhappiness; and it was most obvious that this would be another of his hilarious explanations.

I thought that if Miss Frith continued to laugh so heartily at his ridiculous stories—and I saw no reason why she should not, because they were all ludicrous and always new, drawn from an inexhaustible fund of invention which he pretended was memory—then her married life would be enjoyable indeed.

Usually somebody rose to his bait, and gave him the excuse for his matchless foolery. But that evening we joined in a conspiracy, to tease the poor clown; nobody asked him the question he was waiting for; nobody appeared to notice his histrionic misery.

His betrothed at last took pity on him.

'You are all wondering,' she said, 'why Lodovico is wearing the tragic mask, although you are pretending not to be wondering. I will tell you the reason, because it will take much less time than if he tells it. I have issued an ultimatum. It is me or his beard. He cannot have both. I do not know which way he has decided. It is a close run thing, I think. Either he is moping because he is going to shave off his beard, and so keep me, or lose me, and so keep his beard.'

Flora caught my eye. She touched her right cheek, and giggled. I understood and burst out laughing—Miss Frith did not want a marriage devoid of kisses, but she did not want to lose the skin of her face, by having it rasped away by that great beard.

The Barone groaned, like a victim of the Spanish Inquisition, buried his face in his hands, and caused his shoulders to heave with pretended sobs.

'He has been my companion through all my life,' he said, through his hands, and through his sobs. 'I grow him as soon as I am able, to the despair of *mia povere madre*. And now *questa tiranna*, this lady tyrant . . . *Non posso piu,* no more, I cannot speak for my tears. The day he is cutted off, *caro* Duncan, your river will rise for two metres, because of the tears I will drop out of my eyes—there will be the dangerous floods, many peoples drowned, trees and houses and cattles washed down to the sea—all the faults of *questa crudele,* that lady without heart or pity . . .'

Miss Frith caught my eye and Flora's. She stroked her own cheek, and giggled, which I would not have believed if I had not seen it.

Imagining the Barone Lodovico without his beard was like imagining Duncan Glenalban without his castle, Aunt Sophia without her fluttering and moaning, me without the bright hair and brown eyes of Prince Charles Edward. It was part of him, like button-boots and broken English.

But I saw Miss Frith's point. Her cheek had looked quite sore, the day she came happily and guiltily out of the maze.

The Barone had another few days in Edinburgh, on business of his own. I supposed it was to do with the transfer of money, in view of his approaching marriage.

He came back with news that appalled Aunt Sophia and myself. He had looked in to see Mr David Maitland, our old friend, shopkeeper and antiquary, whom he had got to know in the spring. He had found a police officer on the door, and saw others, through the window, in the shop. Mr Maitland had been killed—murdered, in the middle of the night. His one living-in servant, an elderly man who had been with him for many years, had been struck down with a heavy club, in the near darkness at the foot of the stairs which led from the shop up into the living quarters above. He had barely seen his assailant; he could only describe him as big. Mr Maitland was found lying in the doorway from the stairs into the back of the shop. He had been stabbed. He could have had no chance to resist or escape.

The Police had compared an inventory of the stock, which the servant believed was complete and up to date, with what was actually there. A few small but valuable objects were missing— snuffboxes, miniatures and the like. It was obvious that Mr Maitland had surprised the burglar. But why should the robber have killed him? Why not simply have clubbed him down, like the servant? He was an elderly man, not tall. He represented no threat to a big man armed with a cudgel.

The answer might be, as an Inspector of Police told the Barone, that Mr Maitland knew the intruder. Although it was late, and the shop's shutters up, there was light from the street coming in through the fanlight over the door: enough, perhaps, to recognize a man by.

An oddity was, that the shop door had not been forced, but unlocked with a key. Who could have a key to Mr Maitland's door, other than his servant and himself?

The answer might be, someone who had worked in the shop, and who had taken a key with him when he left. If so, either Mr Maitland had not noticed the disappearance of a key, and so not had the lock changed; or he felt safe in assuming that he would never see that erstwhile employee again.

What employee had there been, who was big, and audacious, and capable of shocking violence?

Edgar Smith, alias Doctor Nicol and who knew what else; a one-time employee who might have stolen a key, or borrowed one and had it copied; who was recognizable even in a bad light by his birdshaped birthmark; who had stolen just such small, valuable objects from that shop before; who was likely to hold a grudge against Mr Maitland for informing against him, and testifying against him at his trial, as the Barone was told he had done.

But was not Edgar Smith in prison? He was not. He had escaped, while being taken from one prison to another.

This was guesswork, but it seemed extremely likely. I remembered the shocking blow with which he had felled the policeman, when he ran away from Millstounburn. It was easy to imagine that man clubbing down an old servant, and stabbing his master to death in revenge, in fear, in greed.

Edgar Smith was at large. No doubt he would commit some other crimes, and violent crimes. Perhaps he would not go to the gallows for the murder of Mr Maitland, but it was easy to imagine that one day he would feel the noose about his neck. It was not easy to imagine that anything would bring him anywhere near Glenalban.

We mourned David Maitland, a man of gentleness, scholarship, and the greatest kindness. We remembered how he had sold things for us, to keep Millstounburn afloat, and taken no commission on the sales.

Now he would never examine the papers in our

attics. Aunt Sophia and I prayed for his soul.

The Barone had other news, for my ears only.

Though he was no longer employing the lawyers who had been preparing my case, he was still in their confidence—or thought he was.

They confirmed to him that my cake was dough, but not quite for the reasons Duncan Glenalban had given me. It was not only because the Grieves had held Glenalban for so long; not only because it was impossible to draw clear lines between what had been James II's and what was their own; not only because I did not need a castle to defend anything. These points weighed, but they were not conclusive. Much more simply, and much more seriously, some vital papers were missing.

'Simon Donaldson and I gave those papers to those people,' said the Barone. 'I am sure of it. Those, with the others. All the papers that we had, we gave them.'

'Do lawyers lose papers?' I asked.

I was not as concerned as the Barone, because I had for some time realized that I did not want Glenalban, and could not have shouldered the weight of such a responsibility; and Duncan Glenalban did, with the utmost competence and humanity.

I thought it strange that I was quite reconciled to not being a millionairess; and my friend, who stood to gain not a penny, was not reconciled at all.

'I think lawyers do not lose papers,' said the Barone unhappily. 'But I think one clerk, maybe with little *soldi* and a large family—I think one poor man can be *corroto*—corrupted.'

'Bribed.'

'Yes. Bribed.'

'But who would . . .?'

'That is why I am unhappy,' he said. 'Who?'

Who stood to gain from my case being lost? Well, who? The answer was supremely obvious, and totally impossible.

But I had thought Simon Donaldson a man of honour.

Suddenly, perversely, I found I was ready to change my whole mind about the whole affair.

I did not like being cheated.

I could not for a second accept that the obvious cheat was the real one. But I *had* been very certain that Simon Donaldson was a man of honour . . .

It was as though my thinking of Simon Donaldson was prophetic. He was seen, some three miles from the castle.

Two stalkers were out, with spyglasses and rifles, looking for a stag which had been wounded. They saw instead a man, by a little ruined croft. I thought, from the description, that it was the one where Jack had taken me, for my secret meeting with Flora. They were a long way away from him. Only with their powerful stalking telescopes could they have recognized him.

Of course they knew him. He had spent many months at Glenalban, and he was given to outdoor exercise and sport. And his height and yellow hair made him distinctive. They were in no doubt.

And of course, after so long, he knew that ruined croft, as a place which nobody went near, as a safe place to hide.

The stalkers made their best speed to the croft. But, from where they were, they had to go far down to cross a burn, and climb again; and by the time they reached the croft there was no sign of their quarry. He had seen them coming down the bare hillside to the burn, and disappeared over the skyline. Only a buzzard could have found him then.

Why was he here? We all asked ourselves, and one another. Not to steal more documents from the muniment room. It was certain he would not dare come near the castle, let alone enter it. Not to repeat his so-very-nearly successful attempts on Flora and myself, with or without the poem about silvery feet.

To meet someone? Who? Had he an ally in our midst? Was he trying to make an ally, with money he had stolen from somebody? Why here, where he was known and hated?

All the folk on the estate were warned to keep an eye out for him; and the few who did not know him were given an exact description. It seemed impossible that, if he stayed anywhere nearby, he could escape the eye of a shepherd or a stalker, or the nose of a sheepdog.

I did not like the feeling of him near. It reminded me of my childish gullibility. Of which I might have been the victim, all over again, with a different liar who had the same motives.

Two days later he was found. He was in the river. He was dead.

His body was found where a fast and deep burn joined the main water, lodged against the pier of a little stone bridge. It seemed that he had been washed down the burn, but no one could guess how far. He had been in the water some time before he was found, but no one could tell how long. They said he had had a knock on the head.

It could have happened in many ways. He could have fallen, knocked his head on a rock, tumbled into the water, and then drowned because he was unconscious. He could have fallen into the water, perhaps trying to cross that dangerous burn, and then knocked himself out on a rock, and so drowned. These accounts of his death were possible, but they did not seem to us likely. He was lithe and active, and he knew how to cross burns.

I thought he had been hit on the head, and pushed into the burn to drown. Probably he had been held under, until he did drown.

Until his body was found, nobody had seen

him, since the stalkers with their spyglasses glimpsed him by the croft. He had lain hid, and come out, probably by night, probably to meet somebody. That person, or another, had struck him down and drowned him. That person might be in Glenalban, of Glenalban, part of the household or the estate; or a person from somewhere quite different; the murderer might have followed Simon, and come to Glenalban only because Simon was there. The brother or father, perhaps, of a girl he had seduced. It was possible.

But the possibilities were infinite. The probability, I thought, remained the same. Simon had come to have a secret meeting with a person in or about Glenalban. And that person, his ally, had turned his coat and killed him. Perhaps because Simon had betrayed him, or was about to do so. From all I knew of Simon, there might be many motives for murdering him.

And everyone on the estate was most strictly asked again, by the Procurator Fiscal and the County Police; and no one admitted having seen him.

I felt strange, that two people I had known should be murdered within a few days of one another. And they had known one another. It was in Mr Maitland's shop that Simon Donaldson had seen Charles Edward's sword, which had sent him to Millstounburn and to me.

It seemed impossible that there should *not* be a

connection between the murders—two victims who had known one another, killed days apart. Had Edgar Smith a grudge against Simon, too? They had met, I thought, in Mr Maitland's shop. There was that link between them; there might be a far greater link. They were both villains. Had they planned some villainy, and had Simon betrayed Edgar Smith, as he tried to betray everyone he met?

This was wild guesswork, and we were all at it all the time.

Once again the Barone shed a new and horrible light on everything.

Once again he drew me aside. His face was deeply troubled. There was no trace of his usual ebullience.

'Leonora *cara,*' he said, 'I am troubled in conscience. I do not know what to do, to speak or keep silence. I cannot talk with any peoples here except only you. I cannot ask my *promessa sposa,* my own Louisa. Nor *sua buona zia,* the good Signorina Grant. And Duncan least of all. Milor' Avington, perhaps, if he was here, but he is not. A man we know was a *ladrone,* a thief and a traitor, is dead. That is good. It was a bad way to die but it is good that he is dead. Probably he was killed for another treachery.'

'That is what I have been thinking.'

'Anybody who knew him would think so. So somebody has treaded on the head of a *serpente.* We are not sad. Almost we praise and

282

thank the man who did it.'

'Almost . . . I think it depends why he did it, whether we praise him.'

'That is exact. Still I say, *il serpente e morto*. It should not destroy the happiness of many peoples.'

'Why should it do that?'

'I will show you why, *carina*. You know that the day after those men saw Simon, I went out with a *telescopo* and a gun and a man.'

'To stalk. Yes. You met Duncan on the hill. I thought it was odd that you should have been stalking in the same place. You might have shot each other.'

'No. We were not hunting the stags.'

'You were hunting the man. I ought to have thought of that.'

'He said he wanted to catch Simon. I knew he had good reason. I wanted to catch him. You know I had good reason. He started early. I did not know which way. I then decided to go also. By chance it was the same way. My man and I, we lay in a place where we were hidden from the stags and from peoples. And with his *telescopo* he stare to one side, and with mine I stare to the other. Up and down, and this way and that way, to search every inch of the ground we could see. I saw *una cerva,* a hind, in a little hollow like our hollow. But it was not a hind. It was a man. It was a hat of tweed on the head of a man of *capelli gialli,* gold hair.'

'Simon.'

'He came out of the hollow and crawled away, like a man stalking. But he was not stalking. He was crawling to be not seen. But with my big *telescopo* I saw him well. I said to the man that was with me, "*Eccolo!* There he is." But my man was not with me. He had gone to another place. I did not hear him move, because of the loud wind on that hill. And then another man, he come from that same hole in the ground. He looks slowly all round. He does not see me, because I am hidden in my hole, and my *telescopo* only is push through some grasses. He walks towards me. Soon he will see me. I stand up. He looks very hard at me. I shrug my shoulders. I say I have not seen any peoples, any Simon. He says he has not. I do not tell my man that is with me, or the *polizia,* or Louisa. If I tell them, horrible troubles come. Why should I make horrible troubles, to destroy my marriage that is not yet, to destroy my friend, when a very wicked man is dead?'

'Who was talking to Simon, in that hollow?'

'Duncan Glenalban.'

Ten

I PUT A hand to my head. It was not that I had not been expecting that answer, but that I had.

The Barone and I discussed the implications, from every side, hour after hour: what had happened, and what he should do. I had never before seen him so serious for so long.

It was, at last, clear to us. Much guesswork was included, but we thought our guesses were good.

Simon Donaldson knew that firm of Edinburgh lawyers very well—the ones who had been preparing to evict Duncan Glenalban and install me in his place. He had been to see them first, about my affairs, long before the Barone had even come to Scotland. If there was a dishonest clerk in their offices, then Simon's trained nose would have sniffed him out. Possibly he discovered some misdeed of the clerk, and so had him in his power if he needed him.

Things progressed, and my case looked strong. It was strong. Duncan Glenalban took over the responsibility of paying the lawyers, with the very convincing explanation that matters had to be brought to a permanent conclusion, for everybody's sake—an explanation which had totally convinced me and, I suppose, everybody else. He had probably not found the dishonest clerk out—the clerk had found him. The clerk had abstracted the vital papers. Duncan either had them now, or had destroyed them.

Simon Donaldson extracted from the clerk, who was in his power, the facts about the theft of the papers, about the bribe the clerk had been given. We wondered what had given Simon the idea that such a thing had happened; we concluded that Simon had put the clerk up to the whole thing—the removal of the papers, and their sale to Duncan. For this put not only the clerk in Simon's power, but Duncan also.

Simon, we thought, wrote to Duncan by the penny post. It was a letter which was not seen by Duncan's secretary or by anybody else. It was blackmail. Duncan was holding his millions, by dint of the stolen papers. He could spare a few thousand for Simon.

Duncan replied, probably to an accommodation address in Edinburgh—a tobacconist or bookseller or solicitor. Duncan said that he agreed to pay, to buy Simon's silence. He told

Simon to come to Glenalban. He appointed a meeting place. It was unfortunate that Simon was seen by the stalkers, but not fatal. Duncan knew every inch of his lands, and could arrange to meet Simon quite safely. What he could not do, or said he could not do, was to produce overnight the amount of money in cash that Simon was demanding. That seemed to us a likely reason for their having a second meeting.

They must have thought they had a narrow escape—the Barone, they thought, had very nearly seen Simon. But the Barone was a good actor. He convinced Duncan that he had seen nobody. By this time they had arranged their next meeting, for the following night. Duncan said he would bring the money. Instead he brought a club. They met, and Duncan killed the blackmailer, by hitting him on the head and drowning him.

Where was Duncan believed to be, when Simon was killed? Why, asleep in his bed. He could get out of his own castle in the middle of the night, unobserved. Avington and I had done it.

Why had Duncan sought to make love to me? It was a subtle version of his aunt's strategy, of Lady Lochinver's passionate Jacobite vapourings. She had put me off my guard, and caused me to trust her completely. He had done exactly the same thing. He could not have shut me up again, in wardrobe or asylum—the Barone and Jack Avington knew too much about all that. So he sought to trap me in a different prison, one that

287

was inside my own head.

Would he in truth have married me, if I had accepted him? Yes, perhaps he would. For two reasons, each on its own perhaps enough. I thought he *did* think me beautiful; physically he *was* attracted to me. I thought that there he had spoken the truth. He was in consequence prepared for me to share his life at Glenalban, as his property; he was not prepared for me to own it. That was one reason. The other, we thought, was that as his wife I *was* his property. I could never again make legal claims against him. I was a spent force. He was permanently safe.

We debated, the Barone and I, which of these two reasons would be the stronger to the Earl. We took unexpected sides, perhaps. The Barone thought my beauty would have been the stronger reason; I thought my legal helplessness would have been stronger by far.

I wondered drably how far Miss Louisa Frith—how far even Flora—had been privy to the Earl's stratagem.

And we could not make out what the Barone ought to do. Anything he did would almost certainly be purposeless—cause misery, bring about no justice. The Earl would flatly, and apparently incredulously, deny having met Simon Donaldson. Surely he would be believed, against a comical foreigner. It would go ill for any policeman who thought otherwise. The Barone might not be suspected of malice, but of faulty eyesight, or of seeing what he wanted to see, because he was obsessed by the desire to see it.

I wondered if Miss Frith's surrender to the Barone were not another example of the same stratagem. Even Flora's regard for Avington. Were they all Simon Donaldsons, treacherous manipulators of other people's feelings?

He had said that, if he had been poor and I rich, he could not have spoken to me. He had said that, if he could have forgotten his responsibilities, he would have thrown away Glenalban to have me.

I was sickened not only because he had said these things, but because I had believed them.

And then a thought struck me, which had been amazingly slow in coming. He had connived at my being put in the Lunatic Asylum. He, involved with Hospital Managements and Lord Lieutenancies and such, would have been far better qualified than Lady Lochinver to arrange it all. What had happened, I thought, was that I had run to her; she had sent immediate word to him; he had found the doctors; and all else followed.

Lady Lochinver was not far away in England because she was too embarrassed to face me. She was away on his orders, in case she gave his part in it away to me.

I could not leave, without giving the reason. With

my birthday imminent, with all the preparations so far advanced, I could not get up and go from Glenalban, taking Aunt Sophia with me, without the reason. I could not give the reason, because the Barone and I had excellent guesses, but no evidence.

He said that he would get the evidence. I did not know where he would find it, with Simon dead and the dishonourable clerk keeping as quiet as a mouse. I thought that, if he found it, his heart would be broken; because he would find that the whole family were of the same kidney.

Meanwhile I was committed to my birthday party, the horrible charade of rejoicing. I dreaded it. The worst was to see Aunt Sophia innocently looking forward to it, excited as a child; and Flora and Miss Frith and the Earl pretending to look forward to it.

The Barone had asked the Earl, some time before, if there were any empty croft or little farmhouse he could use as a retreat. I had not heard about this. There was no reason that I should, although it was no secret. It was not to be a place for assignations with his beloved, because everything between them was public and above-board; it was a place for assignations with his Muse. He was writing an epic poem about the *Risorgimento*. He had been coy about this, except to Miss Frith, for fear of mockery. There was no mockery, when his reason came out. It seemed likely that he would write a marvellous epic, since he was so learned, and felt so strongly and generously. I was not certain I would read quite all of it, as my recent experience of poetry had not been happy.

It would have been possible to find the poet a room in a tower somewhere, quite isolated, in a place as big as Glenalban. But such a thing would not have served in the same way. He would have been conscious of crowds of people near, even if he could not see or hear them. He would have wanted to join them. He would have joined them. He needed to be somewhere where he could not join anybody, where there was no temptation to drop his pen and rush out to make people laugh.

There was no empty but habitable house on the estate when first he asked, but now there was one. It had been rebuilt after a fire, and was now ready. It was to be occupied by a new tenant, but not until the spring. Food and drink could be sent by Miss Frith; probably, I thought, taken by her. He would not be there all the time, but he was desperate to be there some of the time, or his epic would never be written.

He said that, however much glorious poetry was pouring out of him in his solitude, he would be back for the celebration of my birthday. He said this because other people were by. He knew very well how I felt about that celebration.

The Earl of Glenalban proposed to me again; and I refused him.

I found I had forgotten that though his mouth was broad, his lips were thin; that though his eyes were fine and wide-set, they were a cold cruel grey.

I found that his smile was a fraud. It was not sunlight on sea, but gaslight on a stage illusion, such as I had seen with Aunt Sophia at Christmas entertainments in Edinburgh.

'I beg you to reconsider, Leo,' said Flora. 'I beg you to accept Duncan, for your own sake as well as for his.'

Once again, I thought she knew something I did not know.

'You will tell me if this is final, Leonora,' said the Earl. He no longer shortened my name. I did not know why.

'It is final,' I said. I no longer called him 'Duncan'. I knew very well why.

Flora, understanding that my answer was final, was in pitiful distress.

What did she know, that I did not know?

They told me Jack Avington was come back to Glenalban, to my relief and joy and confusion. He seemed to me one rock in a heaving world. The Barone was my only other rock. All the rest were traps, or painted canvas.

As once before, I saw him talking to Flora before he talked to me.

But he saw me very soon. He looked to me better than ever—a miracle of health and humour and sanity.

I asked him about his grouse-shooting and his deer-stalking and his friends in Argyll. He waved away my questions, because he had more important things to talk about.

He said, 'I hear that Duncan Glenalban has done a turnabout, a somersault, a spin.'

'I think he has done more than that,' I said.

'The moment my back is turned, he declares himself your suitor. Flora tells me he would have done it long ago, but for not knowing who was rich and who was poor. I thought she must have got it the wrong way round. I thought a fellow would woo a rich girl if he found he was poor, but Flora says not. I suppose he has cut me out.'

'Why do you suppose such a thing?'

'Because he can offer you ten times my modest competence.'

'No. You can offer me what he cannot.'

'Better trout fishing than his. I can't think what else.'

'Well,' I said, embarrassed, 'I mean honesty, and sincerity, and so forth. I like those things.'

'Yes. So do I. So does Glenalban.'

'You know him to be honest?'

'I believe him to be so. Why not?'

'You said you did not know him very well. Not well at all, you said, although you were at school together.'

'Come to think of it, that is quite true. After

spending so much of the summer here, I came to think he and I were intimates. I like and respect what I see, but I daresay I don't see very deep. Often it's better not to, I find. You'd lose half your friends if you knew their depths. Better not dig too deep. Awful things crawl out.'

'You have to dig deep, when you are thinking about marrying somebody.'

'Have you dug any distance into me, Leo?'

'Yes. To the bottom. Nothing has crawled out.'

'Will you marry me, my dearest girl?'

I opened my mouth to say 'Yes'. The words that came out were, 'I don't know.'

He sighed. 'Absence has not made the heart grow fonder. The barrel-organ plays the same tune. Well, you are not yet eighteen. And at least I am back, to counter the sinister efforts of Duncan Glenalban.'

'I am glad you are back.'

'That is absolutely the first unreservedly amiable thing you have ever said to me.'

I laughed; but it was a short unhappy laugh.

I wanted to confide in him. I could not do so, without asking the Barone; and the Barone was away in his retreat, composing Alexandrines.

'I wish my conscience allowed me to seize you and kiss you,' said Jack. 'I am staggered at the moral strength which stops me doing so. You're so beautiful I want to scream. I am mad with love for you. I must go and swim in the river, to cool my blood. Speaking of which—I have been out of reach of newspapers—is it true, this rumour I hear, of Simon Donaldson being found in the river?'

'Yes. We think he was killed.'

'The police, Flora says, are quite sure he was killed. I should think he had a thousand potential murderers, including you and Flora and myself. But what in the world brought him here?'

'We think we know,' I said. 'I will tell you, but only if the Barone gives me leave.'

'The epic poet. I suppose he is writing in Italian? I hope so, because I shall not be obliged to read it, because I shall not be able to read it. He has become your uncle, Leo. It's a very good thing. He is more use to you than your aunt, much as I like Miss Grant. What have I become? Your cousin? If you say that I shall go and swim in the river.'

I laughed; but it was another short, unhappy effort.

Jack was a haven, the still centre of the storm, asylum most unlike that in Lochgrannomhead. I felt safe when I was with him and when I thought of him. I felt comforted and confident.

And so I had opened my mouth to say 'Yes', and the words that had come out were 'I don't know'.

I had a new hat in which I much admired myself. It was a kind of overgrown Highland bonnet, in a bold check of brown which matched my eyes and red which was supposed to intensify their brightness. From it stuck, directly upwards, a bunch of tail feathers of a cock pheasant, a foot and a half long, so that, when I wore the hat, I felt like not one but several members of the Company of Archers in Edinburgh Castle.

Jack Avington said my hat was by a Tam-o'-Shanter out of an opium-eater's dream. The Earl of Glenalban smiled at it, in the days when he smiled in my direction.

When I was happy, putting on that hat made me burst out laughing. When I was sad it cheered me up. That day was eminently a day to be cheered up by an extravagant bonnet, so I wore it for an afternoon walk.

It was a solitary walk. Flora had letters to write; Jack had salmon flies to tie; Miss Frith had a conference with the housekeeper in the linen room; Aunt Sophia had a croft to visit, with an illustrated Bible for the children (she had brought the missionary zeal of East Lothian to the heathen of West Perthshire); the Barone Lodovico his epic to write, in his remote retreat.

It was no longer possible for the Earl and me to walk together. He had in any case gone off alone with a gun to shoot pigeons, wearing his rust-coloured shooting coat, and with a Labrador retriever at his heels.

The sun was bright, but there was a cold east wind—the first cold wind of the autumn. It was a day for brisk walking. Hard exercise was what I needed; I hoped it would take my mind off my doubts and dismals.

But it did not. Try as I might to concentrate on the little scurrying clouds, the thrashing branches, the flocking peewits and the piping titmice, I could not rid my mind of the things that weighed it down.

As I walked down through the trees of the park towards the river, I thought about the enormous merits of Jack Avington, and my inability to say 'Yes' to him, as though some bit of my mind snapped on the word like a mousetrap. He was lovable, but I had to suppose that I did not quite love him, and never had, and I did not understand why. I questioned myself, and got no answer. I thought there was no answer. I did not quite love him, and that was how it was. It was such a pity.

My thoughts turned from my own unimportant affairs to larger matters, to conspiracy and murder. I brooded about the theory which the Barone and I had constructed, which answered everything as nothing else could. I examined it again, trying to be perfectly logical, which did not come easy to me.

There were some guesses in our theory, like the dishonest clerk in the lawyers' office. But these guesses were not essential to the theory. Duncan Glenalban, or some creature of his, could have stolen the vital papers in some other way; and Simon Donaldson could have found out about it in some other way. The central facts which we knew to be facts stood firm in the middle of everything. The papers were missing. The Earl had met Simon in secret, and denied doing so. Simon was dead. It was nearly certain that there was a connection between all these, and that the connection was the reason for Simon's death. Any other explanation was terribly farfetched.

Would the Earl of Glenalban commit murder? Almost anybody would, who had as much at stake as he had. Almost anybody would, to silence a blackmailer. He was a tall, powerful man, a sportsman. He could murder. He was about to be blackmailed, by a deeply treacherous man. He had to murder. He did murder. I did not see how this conclusion could be avoided.

I came down into the belt of trees by the river, out of sight of the castle. The birds and I had the world to ourselves. The ground rose steeply to the east, and suddenly I was out of the wind, and the sun was hot. I realized that my racing thoughts had caused my legs to race. I had not noticed how hot and exhausted I was getting, because I was preoccupied, and because of the keen wind. I sat down, collapsing at the foot of an ancient oak tree, like a half-empty flour sack. My glorious and ridiculous hat felt like a feather pillow on my head, suddenly intolerable. My brow tickled with the woolly stuff. I tugged off my hat, and felt the sun on my temples. I put my hat on a small, dense bush of holly which had seeded itself amongst the roots of the oak— deposited it on top of the bush, which gave it an air of raffish vanity. The bush became a green and prickly young lady—like myself, in both regards—making shameless advances to the oak tree.

I closed my eyes, seeing and feeling the sunlight through the lids. I was glad to have the oak tree for my back, and glad that it was so old that many of its branches had fallen off, and let the sunlight through.

I heard the shrill shriek of a blackbird, as something startled it in the undergrowth of the wood. I wondered idly what had alarmed it. It was supremely unimportant; it was not a fox, at this time of day. Not a hawk, when the blackbird was in the shelter of trees. Not a wild-cat, on this low ground. Perhaps a farmyard cat that had gone wild, or a stray dog. Perhaps a person. But I had seen and heard nobody. I wondered why anybody would be in that piece of woodland in the middle of the afternoon. Somebody going to the river, somebody the Earl had asked to fish? But it was not on the way from anywhere, the castle or the main road or the village. Someone shooting? But the grouse lived in heather on the bare hillside, not in trees; and the partridge shooting was still a week away, and the pheasant shooting two months.

A gamekeeper? But this little bit of woodland was not preserved. The nearest pheasant coverts were a mile away.

All that could bring anybody here was the chance of a wood-pigeon. Destructive vermin in the cornfields, and delicious eating in a pie or on a piece of toast . . .

The Earl was out after pigeons. This wood was a place he might try. He would enter it as stealthily as possible, hide himself, and keep perfectly still; for wood-pigeons are shy and clever birds, who seem perfectly aware of the difference between a walking stick and a shotgun. Perhaps he had just come into the wood, and startled the blackbird. That would annoy him, because it would alert the pigeons in the tree-tops.

I did not want to share the wood with the Earl of Glenalban. If I got up and left it, I would scare the pigeons, and spoil his sport. Did I care if I spoiled his sport? I did not care to be mean-minded, petty, vindictive; he might be all that I thought him, but I could not be childishly spiteful to a man who had asked me to marry him, the very day before. It was best if I sat quite still. It was best if he shot or did not shoot, but in either event went away out of the wood without seeing me.

There was a shot, much nearer than I had expected—the great boom of a sporting shotgun. And another, immediately. Both barrels of his gun. Shot tore through the leaves beside me. I heard the patter of pellets on twigs and leaves. I shrank back, startled. I had been nearly in the line of fire, though safe behind my oak tree. He had seen a rabbit. A rabbit, five feet above the ground?

I saw that my hat had exploded. It was

shredded, by two charges of shot. Its tattered remnants had been knocked by the second barrel off the holly bush.

Whoever fired thought the hat was on someone's head. My head. No one else had such a hat. Whoever fired thought he had blown my head open, when he saw the hat disappear.

Would he reload at once? Would he come and inspect his handiwork? I could not run and hide, without making a noise he could not fail to hear. There were dead twigs and dead leaves everywhere. If he heard them rustle, he would know I was not dead. The undergrowth was not thick. He had a trained dog with him.

I was very frightened. I made a plan. If I heard his footsteps crunch over the wood's floor towards me, I would jump to my feet and run. I would run in a zig-zag through the trees, like a snipe over a bog. I would be very difficult to hit, and soon I would be out of range of a shotgun. He could run after me. No doubt he could run faster than I, because his legs were longer. But if I ran directly towards the castle, he could not follow me far, shooting as he went.

I heard a crunch, of feet on twigs and leaves. I tensed myself, to jump to my feet and run, if they seemed to be coming towards me. They were going away. He was content. He was sure he had done his business.

I suppose his idea was to dispose of the body later, or get someone to do it for him. Or let me be discovered, and supposed the victim of an armed poacher whom I had surprised setting a deer-trap in the wood. It was likely enough. Every year, somewhere in Scotland, a keeper was killed by a poacher.

I peeped round the trunk of the oak, through the leaves of a clump of hazel.

I saw, disappearing through the wood, exactly what I expected to see. A rust-coloured shooting coat.

I crept out of the wood. I ran all the way back to the castle, my chin on my shoulder. I saw no sign of the rust-coloured coat. Of course, he would make sure it was seen a very long way away, as soon as possible.

I ran across the courtyard and into the great hall. I was hatless, my hair wild, my face crimson. My breath came in deep, shuddering gasps. I passed an astonished footman. I passed Flora, coming out of a morning room. She gave me a shriek, and put out a hand to me. I brushed passed, wordless. I ran to the smoking room, where Jack had been tying his salmon-flies. I burst in. He was there. I thanked God. He gave me a look of utter astonishment, and jumped to his feet. I collapsed into a leather chair. I struggled to get breath enough to speak.

He said, 'Whatever has happened, Leo, you are safe here with me.'

As soon as I could I said, 'Yes. I feel safe. Duncan Glenalban has just tried to kill me. He thinks he succeeded.'

Jack sat down suddenly, as though he had been

hit on the head as hard as Simon Donaldson was. I thought he believed me immediately, not because what I said was probable, but because I said it.

I told him exactly what had happened.

He said slowly, 'It was an accident. It must have been. Obviously he was not shooting at a pigeon. They never go near the ground in a wood. Or a rabbit or any other ground-game. A squirrel. Possibly a rat or a weasel, but I should guess a squirrel.'

'How could he have thought my hat was a squirrel?'

'It was half obscured by leaves—in the shade of the trees . . .'

'It was perched right on the top of a holly, in full sunlight. Do squirrels have pheasant-feathers sticking out of their backs?'

'It was *that* hat? In full view, in full sun? But he could not have supposed anybody was wearing it.'

'Yes. Because of where I had put it, it would have looked from where he was exactly as though someone was wearing it.'

'In any case, who but a raving madman would wantonly destroy a hat with both barrels of a shotgun . . . I find it difficult to get to grips with this, Leo. Duncan Glenalban is in love with you.'

'He is more in love with Glenalban. He said to me once that he was not, but today shows otherwise, I think. Oh. I have just realized something, and I wish I had not.'

'Tell me.'

'I think I had better tell you everything. What I have just realized is about Flora.'

'You *cannot* suppose Flora knew about such a shocking thing?'

'She came to me yesterday. It was after I had refused Glenalban. After I had said it was final. She said I must reconsider. I must marry him. It was for my own good. She was trying to warn me. She was telling me that if my refusal was really final, then I was signing my death warrant. I am sure she didn't want me killed. But she couldn't come out and say that is what would happen, if my refusal was final.'

'If she didn't want you killed, that is exactly what she should have done.'

'No, Jack. Think. She wanted me alive because she likes me. She wanted me to marry her brother, so I would stay alive. But she would hardly say, "Marry him or he will murder you". I mean, it is not endearing, in a prospective husband.'

'I see your point . . .'

'And she gave me another of those odd looks.'

'I can see how she might do that. Assuming that you're right about what happened, was it a *crime passionnel?* Was it that if he was not to have you, no one was?'

'No. It was this.' I waved round the big, dark, comfortable room.

'But he has this safe. Your case is lost.'

'I wonder. We have the fact that my case is

lost only from Duncan Glenalban himself, and from lawyers he is paying.'

'If your case is *not* lost, and you will *not* marry him, he does have a motive. My God, he does have a motive. Little as I can bear to think it of a friend. Anyway, he will hardly try again in front of me.'

'I am quite safe now. I am as safe as I feel.'

'But, Leo, I cannot be at your side all day and night.'

'Not all night, no . . .'

'I think I should take you to the Barone, now at once.'

'I think that is a really good idea.'

'We'll creep out, as we did once before. Nobody will know where we're going. When I come back, nobody will know where I've been. You won't want to hide in the croft for ever, but it will serve for a day or two, perhaps. And we can make a plan. The important, immediate thing is to get you to safety. If Glenalban tried once he will try again. I still can't quite believe any of this—'

'You would if you saw my hat.'

The Barone was extremely surprised to see us. But he seemed glad, although we were interrupting his epic poem.

His quarters, the little rebuilt farmhouse, were cosy rather than spacious, but perfectly comfortable. The food which Miss Frith brought or sent him was most already cooked—I saw half a cold roast turkey on the scrubbed kitchen table—and he was perfectly capable of frying a rasher for his breakfast, and of making coffee. He said he made much better coffee than the servants at Glenalban, because he made it much stronger. A woman came in for an hour each morning, to clean the house. He would not have her more than an hour, he said, because she broke his concentration with her mopping and scrubbing.

The epic was progressing, but slowly. A table in the parlour was covered with sheets of foolscap paper, themselves covered with very bold black writing, full of alterations and crossings-out.

'The civilities having been performed,' said Jack, 'let us get down to business. First your story for the Barone, Leo; and then, I hope, the other things you wanted to tell me.'

The Barone was, of course, as stunned as Jack had been. But, instead of sitting down as though hit, he bounced up, charged out of doors, and plunged about the steading like an angry bull. He roared like a bull, too.

At last he calmed down enough to say to me, 'This proves we were right, *cara.*'

'Right about what?' said Jack.

'All the rest,' I said. 'Simon Donaldson, and the stolen papers, and so forth.'

'You've left me behind,' said Jack. 'Do you know why Donaldson came here, and why he was killed?'

'*Credo di si,*' said the Barone.

And so we told him what I was morally sure had happened. And in the telling I became more sure, because I had been thinking about it so much, and the pieces fitted together better.

It took a long time, partly because the Barone from time to time plunged out of the house again, to relieve his feelings by charging and bellowing; partly because Jack interrupted with a lot of questions. They were good questions, and we had good answers to them.

When at last we finished, Jack sat in silence for a long time.

He said, 'It is all horribly convincing, even to Glenalban arranging for your committal to the asylum, Leo. But there is one weak link. One unanswered question. One serious flaw in your theory.'

'No, there isn't,' I said.

'Listen. Documents have disappeared which, if produced, would provide Leo with a strong case in the courts. Their disappearance destroys her case. I accept the probability that Glenalban caused them to disappear. I suppose he either has them or has destroyed them. That being so, *what need to kill Leo?*'

'Well,' I said, 'as I said before, it must be that my case is really much stronger than they say. Or would be, if the lawyers weren't being paid by the Earl. And, if that's so, I might one day get different lawyers and start all over again. I might do that tomorrow. It *must* be so. If not, I'd still have my hat.'

'Then the missing papers are *not* crucial to your case.'

'Perhaps important rather than crucial,' I said. 'If they're not there, Glenalban has a good case, one that's worth fighting. If they are there, he has no case at all. Something like that.'

'If they're not there, Glenalban has a good case,' Jack quoted back to me. 'And they're not there. Why kill you?'

'I should think it's like getting at a horse before a race,' I said slowly. 'I have never been to the races, but I heard all about a dreadful episode at Musselburgh, from our gardener at Millstounburn. The man who owned the favourite had the second favourite poisoned. Just to make extra certain, you know.'

'Improving the odds,' said Jack. 'A prudent course, if disgusting. And Duncan Glenalban is an outstandingly prudent man. Yes, I suppose it comes out like that. I'm not completely satisfied by your logic there. It still seems to me a weak point in your theory. There must *be* vital documents in the business, as well as those which are no more than important. Why not steal them?'

'Because the truly vital ones have all been copied,' I said, 'and the copies countersigned by bishops, or something.'

'Steal the copies too.'

'But they're spread all over the place, in the College of Arms and the University and so forth.'

'You have an answer for everything, Leo, but a trace of puzzlement lingers in my mind.'

'Not in mine. I was shot at by a man in a rust-coloured coat.'

'I can see how that increases conviction. Nothing like the rattle of musketry, to rid the mind of doubts. What do we do now, Barone?'

'You go back to the *castello,* and you very secretly bring back to this place the Signorina Grant.'

'Aunt Sophia?' I said. 'She won't like it here as much as Glenalban. And I don't see why anyone should want to murder her. Or is there a Grant claimant for Glenalban?'

'You must have a chaperone, Leo,' said Jack. 'It was stupid of me not to have thought of that.'

'I am not so *very* old,' said the Barone. *'La mia carissima* Louisa will not be happy if I am alone, all one night of summer, with the most beautiful girl in Scotland. And you, *cara,* would have no *reputazione.* You would be as dead as though Glenalban had shotted you.'

Of course it was true. He was not old, and I was almost eighteen. Being shot at, and so forth, had driven the social rules out of my mind. But Aunt Sophia would make everything respectable. Besides, she was devoted to the Barone. Under all the circumstances, she would be reconciled to the farmhouse for a day or two.

'How will you get her secretly out of the castle?' I asked Jack.

'I shan't try to. We will go publicly. I will be

taking her to a croft which she would never find on her own, where the children are in instant need of an illustrated Bible.'

'What will you say when you come back alone?'

'That she is returning later, in another carriage, with a doctor or some such. I shall not have met the doctor, nor heard his name. I shall merely have heard that he is to visit the croft, to examine a child suspected of measles, and that Glenalban lies on his way home. The arrangement will have made itself.'

'Come to think of it,' I said, 'how will you explain leaving with me and coming back without me? Several people saw us go.'

'I took you, at your request, to the main road between Lochgrannomhead and Crianlarich. You were to be met by a friend with a vehicle, who was to take you to one of those places, or perhaps somewhere else. I do not know the identity of the friend, or how you communicated with him, or where he is taking you, because you refused to tell me any of these things. I did not wait for your friend's carriage, but left you by the side of the road. You insisted on this improper arrangement, because, I thought, you did not want me to see who your friend was. I think it is all convincing. I think it will add a nice touch of mystery and confusion, to divert everybody from the truth.'

'That is quite good,' said the Barone, in a tone of grudging approval.

'Won't Glenalban be amazed,' I said, 'when they tell him I was running about the castle after he'd killed me.'

'Perhaps he'll think it was a ghost,' said Jack. 'Like Banquo's, you know, after Macbeth had him killed. Perhaps Glenalban will expect you to shake your gory locks at him at his dinner table, but nobody else will see you, and they'll think he's gone mad . . .'

The Barone, on whom this reference was apparently lost, was becoming impatient. Jack drove away, in the dog-cart he had borrowed. I waved until my arm ached.

It was still early evening. The disc of the sun was only now being nibbled by the hill-tops. It was extraordinary that so much had happened in so short a time. Jack had driven like the wind from the castle to the farmhouse; I hoped he would come more sedately with Aunt Sophia, because she was a nervous passenger.

The Barone said that he had made a plan. It would involve our going immediately to Edinburgh. It would mean my missing my eighteenth birthday celebrations. I did not mind at all. We would have a much better party, in Edinburgh, or at Millstounburn—just me, Aunt Sophia, the Barone, and Jack Avington.

The Barone would have to go back to Glenalban, before setting off for Edinburgh. This was reasonable. The clothes he had at the farm were those of an epic poet and Italian patriot. They were sufficiently bizarre there; in Prince's Street they would have caused a crowd to gather, and the Barone to be arrested for a breach of the peace.

He said that Aunt Sophia and I would be quite safe for a few hours on the following day. He showed me the massive lock on the farmhouse's single outside door, and the padlocks on the heavy shutters. Coming from the peaceful Lowlands, I might have thought these defences absurd on a little farmhouse. But I knew now that things were different in the wild Highlands. There were roving bands of tinkers, brutal, greedy, almost inhuman; some said that they were mongrel gipsies, some that they were the savage descendants of the small, desperate clans proscribed after my great-grandfather's hopeless rebellion of 'forty-five. They preyed on isolated farms, stealing everything, sometimes killing, then melting away into the hills. Especially they were dangerous at this time of year, when the harvest was in, the meat hung, and the brine-barrels full of fish. And Highland farmers had to travel a long way with beasts or produce to market, leaving their wives and children unguarded for days and nights. Those great padlocks and bars of iron were very necessary. It was comforting to see them. Aunt Sophia and I could withstand a siege, if Glenalban chose to besiege us.

As to the Barone's plan, he would not tell me. It would not be complete until we had reached Edinburgh. Obviously it involved lawyers. It involved Jack Avington, on whom we knew we could rely. I thanked God for two such friends.

It was dusk when Jack came back with Aunt Sophia. She shrieked when she saw me, because Flora had told her of seeing me run like a madwoman through the castle, scarlet and hatless and with a shocked expression on my face. Jack had told her a little, as they came along in the dog-cart; but, as he told me aside, he thought she should be sitting safely in a chair when she listened to the whole, not perched on the seat of a dog-cart.

He had already told his story to Duncan Glenalban, about leaving me beside the road. He said Glenalban had been utterly dumbfounded. Well he might be, that I was alive and well.

Jack had to get back at once, to make his story about Aunt Sophia credible. He pressed my hand as he left. I was never nearer loving him.

The Barone said that, before he went back to Glenalban, he must shave off his beard. It would be a lengthy and agonizing process, as well as heart-breaking. But we knew of his betrothed's ultimatum, and the baring of his face could no longer be delayed. He put a great kettle of water on the kitchen range to heat. He said he would need that and more, and that he would have to sharpen his razors fifty times.

Before he withdrew, to make this terrible sacrifice on the altar of love, he locked the door, and closed and barred and padlocked all the shutters. He said we would have no visitors in the night, but it was foolish not to take such simple precautions. He had no weapon, because he had left his swordstick in the castle.

As soon as his water was hot, he went out into the kitchen to shave. I told Aunt Sophia as much of the story as I thought she could stand. She did not at all want to go to Edinburgh. She was appalled that I would miss my party. But I could not give her the full reasons, without shocking her more than I could bear to.

She still wanted me to marry Jack Avington. We were on safer ground, when I tried to explain to her my feelings for Jack. She was distressed on his behalf and on mine. But she owned, in the end, that one could not commit oneself for a lifetime without perfect certainty.

Every so often, our conversation was punctuated by a howl of agony from the kitchen. He called out that he was not slashing himself but merely removing layers of skin.

I noticed that he had taken the keys out of the front door and out of all the padlocks on the shutters. I wondered idly why he should have done so.

He came at last, beardless, back into the parlour. His face was not unpleasing. It was perfectly familiar to Aunt Sophia and myself. We had seen it in the spring, at Millstounburn. It had a birthmark, resembling a bird, beside the left ear.

Eleven

EDGAR SMITH SAID cheerfully, as though I had asked a question, 'Yes. Those padlocks keep people in as well as keeping them out.'

His voice was as I remembered—pleasant, educated, with no trace of any foreign accent.

He said, 'There were just four people who could have exposed me. Mr David Maitland. Poor foolish Simon Donaldson. And your good selves. I would not have had to kill anybody, if my dear Louisa had not insisted on the nudity of my face. But, once I discovered the extent of her private fortune, I was quite resolved to marry her. Besides, I have contrived to convince myself that she pleases me. She will not visit my castles in Italy, because I have none. Fortunately, I no longer need castles in Italy, or even in Spain; I have the unfettered use of a castle in Scotland. It

315

is the culmination of a career in which effort and talent have been only intermittently crowned with the success they deserve. Of my many marriages, only one produced the dividends I expected. Do I bore you? I think not. You know, there is that in the artist—and I am indubitably an artist—which requires recognition and applause. But the nature of my art forbids my allowing anyone to see the fulness of it. Simon Donaldson knew most about me, but he was in the same line of business— indeed, we were once rivals, which was how we became acquainted—and he was never more than grudging in his appreciation of my skill. I cannot expect you to applaud me, but I cannot resist this unrepeatable chance to extract your recognition of my achievements. I can speak to you freely because, as you will already have realized, you will not repeat what I say. Except perhaps in Heaven, which I do not expect to visit.'

I cannot analyse my feelings. I had no feelings. I was numb. I knew that Aunt Sophia and I were dead. We had to be dead, because we knew that bird-shaped birthmark.

Suddenly I said, surprising myself, 'Have you killed the policemen who came to arrest you at Millstounburn?'

'No, Leonora, if you will allow me to continue to call you so. One saw me only in the distance, and running away. The other I hit while he was rushing at me. I was deliberately contorting my face. There is no possibility of his identifying me, on oath, in a courtroom. It is not so with the four of you. I quite regret the implications of that. I was sorry to kill poor Simon, and sorrier to kill David Maitland. I shall be sorrier still to kill the amiable Miss Grant, and as for you, dear Leonora, I shall be disconsolate. Not inconsolable. Louisa and her bank-books will console me. But I shall be sad. Oh yes. For a poet to destroy a thing of rare beauty—I shall be sad.'

During this chilling rubbish, I was trying to think. The keys of the door and padlocks were in his pocket. They could be got only if he was unconscious. If Aunt Sophia created a diversion (as he and Simon Donaldson had, at the lunatic asylum) I could perhaps jump for some weapon, and hit him on the head . . . Could I, hardly more than five feet tall, and weighing no more than a squirrel, knock unconscious a big, powerful and healthy man?

I could try. Our last state would not be worse than our first, because our first was as bad as it could be.

There was a poker by the fireplace.

Edgar Smith's eye darted very quick from me to Aunt Sophia and back again. He was alert, wound tight as a fiddle-string. Nothing would pass him by. He saw my eye on the poker.

He excused himself, with a show of elaborate courtesy, and put the poker next door in the kitchen. I half rose to my feet, and sat down again. There was nothing in the parlour that made a weapon of any kind.

He had said he was unarmed, as a reason for

all those padlocks. I did not now believe him. I was right. From the kitchen he came back into the parlour with both hands full. In one hand was his swordstick, in the other a double-barrelled shotgun.

'Was it you who tried to shoot me?' I said.

'Your beautiful hat. I was so sorry about the hat. I do not think I quite hid my surprise, when you knocked on my door this afternoon.'

It was true. He had not hidden his surprise, but he had hidden the reason.

He put down swordstick and gun where he could reach them and I could not. He stretched behind, to a cupboard, and pulled out a rust-coloured coat.

'It is amusing to reflect,' he said, 'that I acquired this coat on Duncan Glenalban's recommendation. He told me that, for rough shooting in August and September, the colour was ideal. It matched turning leaves and dying bracken. I followed his advice with some reluctance. A coat of this hue did not suit my performance as an eccentric Italian aristocrat. It was altogether sensible, practical, conventional, and I was being none of those things. But, pressed by dear Duncan, I allowed the little tailor in Lochgrannomhead to make me a coat of this stuff. Which enabled me to impersonate him to anybody who saw me, from a distance, by the river. Including yourself. A pretty irony, I think.'

'Quite pretty,' I said.

There were two things uppermost in my mind.

I clung to them, in case my courage suddenly went from me, and I blubbered and knelt and pleaded. I did not wish to do that, in front of Edgar Smith, in front of Aunt Sophia.

She seemed calm. She knew exactly what was happening, and why. She had the courage of her steady faith. If I had courage, I thought, it was not quite of that sort. She stretched out a hand towards me, and I took it. Edgar Smith's hand flickered towards his shotgun; but he dropped it.

The two things in my mind were that I would *not* break down in cowardice or despair. And that we must keep the man talking—boasting—revealing himself—as he said he longed to do, and as he would never have such a chance to do again. While he talked, we were alive. When he stopped, we were dead, because if he did not want us as an audience, he did not want us at all.

He would talk vaingloriously, because he was proud of himself. He might relax his alertness, in clouds of self-esteem. From that, something might come. It was a very small chance, but it was our only chance.

Aunt Sophia's fingers, squeezing mine, said that we must be wide awake and brave. Mine, squeezing hers, said that there might be something else to hit him with, besides the poker.

I said, as firmly and as graciously as I could, 'Will you tell us the story of your life, Mr Smith?'

'With pleasure,' he said heartily. 'No one has ever heard it. You are privileged. I would say uniquely privileged, but as there are two of you, I think that would be a kind of solecism. I should start by correcting you. My name is not Smith.'

'We did not suppose it was.'

'What is it, you ask? I have none. So begins my story. My mother was English, governess to the children of a banker in Turin. Her employer, by her own later account, was a man of solid affluence, but without charm or culture. It was scandalous that a creature of her breeding and education should have been the vassal of such people. Unfortunately she had had to leave England somewhat hurriedly, and seek employment very far away. She told me scraps of that story, during my strange childhood, but never the whole story. She had been employed in a similar capacity, but in infinitely better circumstances, in London. The family of a judge. She was caught stealing. She ran away before she could be arrested. The same thing happened subsequently, in Italy. She was not so quick. She was arrested, and went to prison. I was quite sad, because it was embarrassing for me to have a mother in prison. That is one half of my inheritance—a superior and educated voice, a wide and general culture, an admiration for poetry and art, and a disposition to steal.'

'Do you steal papers in important law suits?' I asked, to make sure that he went on, and on, and on. Also, I was interested in the answer.

'Yes, of course. I could not have my Louisa deprived of her fortune—myself deprived of my

320

fortune. But that comes much later in my story. I am telling you of my parentage, so that you will understand how triumphantly I have overcome the disadvantages of my birth. My father was a groom employed also by the banker. I never met him. The union was not blessed by the Church, since my father was already married. I believe he was a fellow of great adroitness, great charm, and his chief diversion was causing young females to fall in love with him. Others prefer manly sports, cards, the theatre, wine. My father liked women. He was very successful by my mother's somewhat embittered account. Behold the other half of my inheritance. The two together dictated my choice of career which, as you know, has now reached its triumphant culmination.'

'Not quite yet,' I said.

'Aha! Will you try to stab me with my sword-stick, as I stabbed David Maitland? Club me with this knob it has, as I clubbed his servant, and Simon Donaldson? Or shoot me with this fowling-piece borrowed from the gunroom at Glenalban, as I shot your delectable hat? I know you have courage and resource and quickness of mind, Leonora. Without those qualities in you, we would never have got out of the lunatic asylum. But abandon any such ideas, child. I am much stronger than both of you together. And I move much quicker than you would think, to look at me. I have had to move quick, many times . . . My mother was dismissed by the banker, of course, as soon as her condition became evident. She was naturally deserted and disowned by the groom my father, who thought the destruction of one life was sufficient penance for the sin they had committed. My mother was in some distress, until my birth and for some months after it. Then she fed herself and me by earning silver in the only way open to her. There were times when she found a protector, and we lived in moderate comfort. There were times when she had to put me in the care of some old woman, and take to the streets of Turin. In some ways, perhaps, an undesirable upbringing for a child. In others, richly educational. As a one-time governess, my mother *was* a woman of culture, and her voice was educated. Culture and speech she most assiduously taught me, when the exigencies of her profession allowed. Though my life was in the back streets of Turin, I could pass as an English gentleman. In those back streets I learned Italian also. I spoke both languages with equal fluency. It has been most useful to me. I would recommend any young fellow embarking on my profession to master at least two languages. It gives one so many choices of personality.

'So I grew up, developing my talents in all directions. I would have liked to have been slim, to have displayed the elegance of figure of a Simon Donaldson. I was not made in that mould, so I made the best of what I was, and became instead a lovable clown. It does quite well, I think? I am the licenced buffoon of Glenalban? I adopted—perhaps by inheritance, perhaps by her example—my mother's taste for stealing. It is something I have always enjoyed. Ordinary, humdrum mortals can have no idea of the sheer exhilaration of a successful theft. I adopted, at the same time, my mother's enthusiasm for the arts, which was quite genuine in her and is quite genuine in me. It is, perhaps, my greatest enthusiasm, after money. As soon as I was old enough—and it would seem astonishingly young by Northern standards—I mounted my father's hobby-horse. But I saw that he had misunderstood his own life—underestimated his own talents, perhaps. He was always an amateur. I became a professional.

'I travelled widely. This was agreeable, and also necessary, because I was repeatedly married. With one exception, my marriages were a grave disappointment. The fortunes I had expected to control had either been grossly exaggerated to me, or they were under the noses of trustees and lawyers.

'I grew a beard. It had the effect of hiding the little blemish which you will have observed, beside my left ear. It had the effect of making me resemble the great Garibaldi, who was and remains my hero.'

'I thought I recognized you, when I saw you with your beard,' I said, because a silence had fallen, and silence was dangerous.

'You did recognize me, even though I had a

beard. I told Simon Donaldson what to say. He was to say that you had, of course, seen engravings of Garibaldi in the illustrated papers, and that the likeness you saw was to them. I expect he laughed a little at my vanity. You would have liked me more, rather than less, for my harmless desire to resemble my hero. And you forgot Edgar Smith.

'Well, I found I had too many wives in Italy, and too many names. I went to France. I spoke a little French, as many of the people of Piedmont do, but only a little. France was a struggle. I found myself in Rouen, a dreary grey city but a place of much wealth. My beard was at its biggest and my manner at its merriest. I adopted a splendid name, and presently identified and pursued the spinster sister of a great merchant. I did not know or care what he bought and sold; only that there was a great deal of it, and the sister had remarkable jewels. I became aware that, between the secret meetings she was having with me, she was having secret meetings with somebody else. A man in my profession develops what is, perhaps, a sixth sense in these things. I waylaid him with my swordstick in an alley. He said that he had been aware of me, too, and suggested that we be not rivals but allies. He said there was enough in that treasure-house to be divided. He was tall, with yellow hair. He cultivated a shy and gentle manner. In all respects he and I complemented one another. Any lady who recoiled from one of us might embrace the other. At that time he called himself Sir Gordon Crocker. Under this alias, he was as careful to avoid persons from Britain, as I was to avoid any Italians. I lent him a little money. We went into partnership. We failed with the merchant's sister, owing to the malignant intervention of her brother; but by this time, and to a qualified extent, we trusted one another.

'He told me an astonishing story.'

'About Glenalban,' I said.

'He was very angry. He had been within a whisker of securing a fortune beyond his dreams, or even mine, and the purest bad luck—the premature return of a servant—had cheated him of it. He nursed a bitter grievance. However, while there he had made a number of quite authentic historical discoveries, of which you know. He was sure some use could be made of them.

'I devised the use that could be made of them. Poor Simon was a clever lad, in some ways far more highly educated than myself, but he did not have my breadth of vision. Or, of course, my experience.'

Aunt Sophia sniffed. Our hands were still clutched together. I was not sure if the sniff was simply a sniff, or a comment on what Edgar Smith (or whatever he was called) was saying.

He smiled blandly in her direction, as though taking the sniff to be a comment on his words, and welcoming it.

He went on, 'The documents Simon had taken

from Glenalban proved, as you know, that the castle was the property of any legitimate heir or heiress of King James II. Very good. We had to produce one. We wanted a man, or a woman, who looked like the portrait of any of the Stuart princes—as close a resemblance as possible. James I, Charles I, Charles II, James II, the Old Pretender, the Young Pretender. Any of these faces would do. Our candidate could be of any age, and come from any country. The other thing we needed, of course, was documentary evidence that our candidate *was* a legitimate descendant of James II. It was fortunate that we had Simon's expert knowledge.'

'His knowledge of old documents?' I said.

'A knowledge of old documents which enabled him to simulate them.'

'Forge them.'

'It is not always necessary to call a spade a spade, Leonora. It is not always desirable or prudent.'

There was a hint of harshness in his voice. I felt the pressure of Aunt Sophia's fingers on mine. This was the man who had killed David Maitland and Simon Donaldson, and who had fired two barrels of shot into my hat.

'What form our simulated documents would take,' continued Edgar Smith, once again bland and cheerful, 'would naturally depend on our candidate. If an elderly Frenchman with an uncanny resemblance to James I, for example, we would construct one set of evidence of his

326

legitimacy. If a middle-aged lady in Rome with a startling similarity to the Merry Monarch, another. Our search for a candidate might take years—we recognized that. But we need not be idle in the meantime. We could scrape incomes in other ways. We were bound to be obliged to do so, and we agreed that we could do so better in partnership. It was desirable that we should trust one another, up to a point. It was impossible that we should trust one another completely. Nobody but a madman would trust either of us completely.

'We agreed to go about the world, as we had been doing, but with the difference that we would be looking, always looking, for faces like the faces we had studied. It made a new interest for us both—almost a kind of game. In Paris I thought we had arrived. I saw a lady of about thirty, who looked, I thought, much like Charles II—those bold eyes, those black curls . . . She was a Levantine, wife of an importer of almonds and dates. We were days trying to make her understand what we wanted of her, and when at last she understood she began to scream and scream . . . It was one of the times when I have had to move rapidly. Her husband had a very fierce moustache, like an Albanian bandit . . .'

He chuckled richly, remembering. Another silence fell. To fill it, I said, 'But you went to a professor. At Aberdeen, I think. The professor recommended Simon.'

He laughed. 'That was our account of how Simon and I became acquainted, yes. You heard that account from him and from me. That I wrote to a professor with whom I had been corresponding for years, on matters connected with my own historical researches. That he replied, recommending Simon as a colleague or assistant. That Simon came to Italy to meet me. I had not been corresponding with any professor. I did not know any professor. I was not engaged in any historical research. Nobody recommended Simon. Nobody would have recommended him, after what had occurred at Glenalban. But you heard the same story from two people, so you completely believed it. Indeed you had no reason to doubt it. If Simon and I were plausible, then so was the story of how we met. What was necessary was that we should tell exactly the same story. We took care to do that.'

'You were very clever,' I said, putting a sickening note of admiration into my voice.

'I don't think you mean that,' he said, 'but, if you do, you're right. We were very clever. I was very clever, and I made use of particular advantages which Simon had. Education, for one. A tall, slim figure. Attractive yellow hair. An air of shyness, so that he seemed disarming and trustworthy. Great advantages.'

I felt angry, because I had been the dupe of all these things.

'However,' Edgar Smith went on, 'in October of last year, exactly ten months ago, neither his advantages nor mine were profiting us. Our fortunes were at their lowest ebb. We were in Brittany, where people keep their purses buttoned. We had gone there in pursuit of two sisters, one widowed and one unmarried . . . That story I shall not tell you, as it ends in failure and humiliation. Well, having got to Brittany, we could not afford to leave it. We found ourselves in a little town called Lamballe, near the coast, not far from St Malo. We had rooms in the Tour d'Argent. After a week they presented us with the reckoning. We could not pay. It was highly embarrassing.

'We had heard of another Italian, who had taken a villa outside the town. I kept well out of his way, for good and obvious reasons. It was easy to find out everything about him that anybody knew, in that small place. He was a grandee, a baron. He was rich, he was Piedmontese, like myself. He was a big man, with a big beard. He was some kind of scholar—a thing I had never been, nor pretended to be—and he was in Brittany to study the stone circles of the Druids. Apparently there are many such things in Brittany. I would not give sixpence for a sight of all of them, but this Barone Lodovico di Vigliano was reported to be fond of them.

'I observed him from a safe distance, going out of his nice rented house, by himself, in a pony-trap. He went to measure and examine these idiotic bits of stone, which everybody made such a fuss about. In appearance he was not really at all like me. But we were about of an age, about of a size and shape, and we both had full black beards. There all similarity ended. I was disappointed, because a very good idea had entered my head . . .

'By this time the landlord of the Tour d'Argent had impounded our belongings. Things were desperate for us. I had a pistol.

'Simon was engaged in seducing a chambermaid at our hotel, so that we could with her help rescue our possessions. That was a necessary task. I undertook the other necessary task. I entered the rented house, when I knew its occupier was out in his trap. I knew from days of observation that there were three servants only. I threatened them with my pistol, and locked them in the coal-cellar. I searched the house, and found a useful number of gold coins, as well as other portable and saleable objects. Most unfortunately, the Barone returned and surprised me. He rushed at me, with a chair held over his head in order to smash me to the ground. He was far too brave. I was compelled to shoot him. I ran away, with my new possessions. I was quite stupid. I should have shot the servants too. They could describe me. Eventually they would get out of the coal-cellar, and then they would describe me. So I altered my appearance. It was extremely simple. I shaved off my beard. The change, you know, is total. It is quite remarkable. It is more difficult to recognize a man you have known with a beard, when you see him clean shaven, than the other way about. I was safe from arrest for a little, but for hours rather than for days. So Simon and I went to St. Malo, and took a boat to England. It was all a new world to me. I was prepared to love it, for my poor mother's sake.

'Simon was homesick for Scotland, so we took the train from Portsmouth to London, and from London to Edinburgh. The gold coins made everything easy and pleasant, but they would not last for ever.

'From Edinburgh, I wrote to a friend in Turin, asking for all he could find out about the Barone Lodovico di Vigliano. He was most helpful. I was in a position to describe accurately the Barone's possessions and interests. I was in a position to be the Barone, when a suitable moment arrived. For the time being, in Scotland, I was a Scotsman, or an Englishman, speaking in the educated voice my educated mother had taught me, which you are listening to now. At any moment I could become Italian, or a mixture of the two.

'We looked in the windows of jewellers' and goldsmiths' shops, but stealing from them would have been extremely dangerous. To have been employed by one of them—that would have been helpful. But none would employ either of us. We met an attitude of suspicion which bruised our feelings. We looked in the window of Mr Maitland's shop of antiquities. It was as full of valuable things as any jeweller's. I secured a position with Mr Maitland, telling him an excellent story, and pleading misfortunes which were not entirely fictitious. I used the name Edgar Smith.'

'Why?' I said.

'Why not? What have you against such a solid, unpretentious, respectable name? Well, after I was established as an employee of the shop, Simon came in the character of a customer. Together, as was natural in our two roles, we examined much of the contents of the shop. Simon was by now an expert in all matters connected with Prince Charles Edward, in order to prosecute our grand design the moment we had found a candidate. He spotted the sword which you had sent. He knew what it was. I, working in the shop, knew where it had come from. It was I, in fact, who had opened the parcel in which you sent it.

'I also knew, from Mr Maitland, about the chests of papers in your attic. I did not know what they were—nor did he—but I knew of their existence, because he had told me how he looked forward to examining them. I should explain that my manner to Mr Maitland was not like anything you have seen. I was an eager and docile pupil, diligent, respectful, hard-working, grateful for his trust in me. I was ignorant about antiquities, but not about poetry and painting. On these subjects, I impressed Mr Maitland with my knowledge and enthusiasm, which were perfectly genuine. For all these reasons, Mr Maitland told me more than he would have told an ordinary assistant in his shop. He told me about those papers; and he instructed me in the value of various antique articles. I was interested in those which I could put in my pockets, and sell without risk.

'Now you see the advantage of the collaboration between Simon and myself. The sword would have meant nothing to me. Simon could never have discovered where it came from. But put our knowledge together . . .

'For a time it seemed to me an intervention of Providence, an extraordinary coincidence, that Simon and I, of all people, should find such a relic, considering the plan we had. But really it is not. We had been looking for anything that would help us, for a year and a half. We were alert, all the time, for any useful face and for any useful object. It would, I think, have been odd if we had not found something, in the end. It is even odd that it took us as much as a year and a half to find something. I do not include the Levantine lady in Paris . . .

'Why did you come first, and alone?' I said.

'Ah. I had not intended to come so soon, and I had not intended to come alone. I had not intended to be dismissed from Mr Maitland's employ, but to leave it at a moment that suited me. But he caught me taking some coins out of the cashbox, when I was certain I was alone in the shop. He dismissed me. I left, with my pockets full. If I was to come to Millstounburn, it must be at once, that same day. I came, I saw, I almost conquered.

'Of course, what I found was our candidate—a young lady with an unmistakable look of the Young Pretender. Called Albany, a name Simon had told me the Prince used. Who had sent that sword to Mr Maitland to be sold . . . I am sure I looked wildly excited. I was. There was no need to conceal the fact, if I was Dr Colin Nicol, the antiquary.

'But I had to go and hide, after that unseemly brawl with the policeman, and Mr Maitland's knowledge of the contents of my pockets. If I had been caught, I would have been sent to prison. That would have been highly inconvenient, as well as uncomfortable. Also, it would have given Simon a clear field, without either my guiding hand or my participation in the profits. I had to remain in touch with Simon, but out of sight of anybody else.'

'So Simon came to Millstounburn instead.'

'He had been away, on projects of his own. I believe there was a widow in Stirling . . . By the time he returned, I was out of sight, waiting for my beard to grow. Nobody in Britain had seen my beard. I was not sure how long it would take for my beard to transform me back into what I had been. That is why Simon told you that he did not know—that I did not know—how soon I could leave Italy. By this time, of course, we had reinvented me, as his patron and colleague and fellow-scholar. He told you all about me, I believe. When you met me, I was much as you expected. Of course I adopted the name and style of the man I had killed. This was partly because, if enquiries were made to Italy about the cheerful Barone, the answers would be satisfactory. Partly because I was in possession of some small pieces of precious metal—a flask, a watch, that kind of thing—with monograms and crests which fitted my new identity. This impersonation would not have done in Italy, or even in France. But it did admirably in Scotland. There was a very faint chance that some Briton, travelling in Italy, had met my original. I decided to ignore the chance. It was a small risk. I was more likely to be exposed as a fraud if I adopted a completely fictional identity.

'So Edgar Smith, in hiding, died a slow death during the winter, and Lodovico di ViglIano was reborn. As soon as my beard concealed my face, and more especially my birthmark, you had the pleasure of receiving me at Millstounburn. And listening to a style of speech which I had devised, perfectly comprehensible to you, yet continents away from the voice of Edgar Smith.

'By this time, we knew that we did not need to forge any papers. Simon had examined those journals, with you, while my beard was growing. He had established that the journals were authentic—that you were authentic. We felt like men grubbing in the earth for pennies, and being handed sacks of gold on golden trays.

'We began the legal business. It made serious

inroads on my stocks of gold, but it was a necessary investment. And the rewards would be incalculable. We had always adopted a flexible approach, prepared to adjust our strategy to circumstances. The relevant circumstance here was that Simon's skill caused you to become attached to him. And I suppose you know the law—if all had worked out as we planned, Simon would not have been consort of the mistress of Glenalban, but himself master of Glenalban. It is an excellent law, I find—the instant and automatic transfer of wealth from bride to bridegroom, at the moment of their marriage. I am about to benefit from it myself, to a scarcely credible extent. I hope they never change that law . . .

'Most calamitously, Simon had meanwhile allowed himself to be outwitted. Over a long period, and totally. Yes, by Lady Lochinver. I feel a reluctant admiration for that pestilent woman. She knew—they all knew—that Simon was vindictive, as well as—we need not blink the word—avaricious. She rightly feared future trouble, an attempt at revenge. As an insurance against it, she pretended she stood his friend, prepared to betray her own nephew on Simon's behalf. He confided in her, confident of her support. It was a dreadful mistake, but it was not altogether foolish of him. Her support would have been an enormous help. It appeared that it was being just that, until the moment you were locked in that cupboard . . .

'I have said that Simon and I trusted one another, but only to a qualified extent. With your knowledge of him, you will appreciate my need for prudence. It was entirely possible that, when the prize was in his grasp, he would suddenly decline to share it. For that reason I abstracted certain documents from those which we handed to the lawyers. The lawyers assumed that those documents, which they had seen but not copied, were amongst those which we gave them. They proceeded on that assumption. The documents were to be produced at the proper time—at a time when I had made quite certain of my own legitimate share of Simon's wedding portion.'

'Legitimate?' I said.

Aunt Sophia's fingers tightened on mine. His temper was not quite predictable.

'Well, I had worked for it all as hard as he had. I was the mastermind throughout. I accept that "legitimate" was an ill-chosen word, though I question your wisdom in pointing that out. Let us say "equitable". At any rate, as I told you with perfect honesty, without those papers your claim to be Countess of Albany remained unanswerable, but your claim to Glenalban became thin to the point of disappearance. With the papers, that too approaches the unanswerable. In effect, having those papers enabled me to control Simon.'

'Where are they now?'

'Here.'

'Safe?'

'Safe in that box on the table. But to be burned in the morning. I no longer wish claims to be made on an estate part of which belongs to my betrothed. Besides, tomorrow there will be no legitimate descendant of King James II. The deeds will have become irrelevant, except as historical documents which hold no interest for me. We are jumping about. Let us return to the chronological. The date of the abstraction of the papers was about that on which Lady Lochinver lured you to the castle, and my beloved Louisa locked you in the cupboard. We knew nothing about that at the time, until Avington told us. What an agreeable fellow he is! So very trusting. And you know how necessary he was to your abduction from the asylum. The account we gave you of that was exactly true. I prefer truth, when possible. One cannot be caught out by it.

'And then it seemed, to Simon and myself, that your incarceration and liberation would work powerfully in our favour. You were hunted; as his wife you were safe. And you were so grateful! He had been so gallant! Our visit to the Kirk followed immediately and inevitably. What we did not know was that Avington had followed us; and we did not know that Lady Flora had told him her story.

'The effect of Avington's intervention, there at the Kirk, changed everything. It put Simon entirely out of the running. But not myself. Rather the contrary. Like you, I had been Simon's dupe. I knew nothing of the episode with

Lady Flora, nothing of his other conquests. I was as shocked as you were. You were even sorry for me. I could continue to fight our battles, Simon's and mine. I could go as a welcome guest to Glenalban, vouched for by you and by Avington, and, as to the rest, relying on my performance, which I had now polished, of a rich, eccentric and affable buffoon.

'Simon had wit enough to see, even while Avington was destroying him in front of you, that I must not be destroyed. I could salvage almost everything, as inmate of the castle and friend of its owner. But he did not want things to proceed on those lines, if he could possibly prevent it. He did not want to lose you.'

'Is that true?'

'He did not want to lose the future owner of Glenalban.'

'That does not answer my question.'

'With Simon? Yes, I think it does. He thought there was a chance he could retrieve himself, recover your good opinion. But not if Avington took you to Lady Flora. Hence my pistol, which I really didn't know he had. I can understand why he did it, but it was a mistake. I had to hit him with my stick. That proved me your ally. In fact we all gained something from his folly, although all Simon gained was a bruise . . .

'When I had duly been made welcome at Glenalban, I told you Edgar Smith was in prison. I did not say which prison, or under what name he had gone. That was so that no busybody could make any useful enquiries in the matter. My purpose was to reinforce, more surely than ever, the division between Edgar Smith and myself, our absolute separateness. There had always been a chance of your recognizing me. Small, but there. I might have a mannerism of which I was unaware, of rubbing my nose in a certain way when I was listening, or a way of crossing my legs in an armchair. I have observed such things in others. One does not observe them in oneself. Such a thing would possibly light a spark of memory in your mind, and then you would stare and stare at me . . . I mention this to show you how careful I have been, what trouble I have taken, how richly I deserve to succeed.

'Soon after I came to Glenalban, another factor entered the situation which profoundly affected my plans. I discovered that Miss Louisa Frith could be rendered fond of me. I amused her, intrigued her. She had never met anybody like me, in Scotland or on her travels. I should think not, indeed! I made private enquiries, and discovered the extent of her personal fortune. Well, you know, in the profession from which I have now retired, there are times for siege and times for assault. This was a woman to be swept off her feet. It was a time for boyishness. I was *very* boyish.

'I now, Leonora, lost all interest in your affairs. You could marry Avington, or Duncan Glenalban, or who you liked. If you found your crock of gold, I was rather pleased than sorry, so long as my own was not threatened.

'And then it was threatened.

'My Louisa surprised and delighted me by her enthusiasm for kissing. There has not been much of it in her life, I suppose, and she was making up for lost time. The Scottish are energetic people, and their vigour on the field and the deer-forest is carried into their caresses. I was expected to respond with equal vigour, and did so, knowing that each hearty embrace made more certain my comfortable old age. But my beard scratched her cheek. It had happened before, but not to such a painful extent. Northern women have more sensitive skins than Latins, and my Louisa's is like a rose-petal. I could not refuse her request. Especially as it was not a request but, as she herself defined it, an ultimatum.

'Action had at once to be taken. Most of it, fortunately, was simplicity itself. It was entirely possible that I should be taken, at some moment in my married life, into Mr Maitland's shop, or meet him under some other circumstances. After all, I expect to frequent artistic circles in Edinburgh. There was a substantial risk that he would see me. If he did, he would undoubtedly know and expose me. Naturally I had had a copy made of the key of his shop door, and naturally I had taken it with me when I left him. I thought it might one day come in useful, and it did. I still had my beard, of course. He did not know me. How could he? He thought I was an intruder, as, indeed, I was. I did not give him time to raise the alarm. I was not troubled by his servant, who hardly saw me. Once again I took a few articles —things I could conceal about my person—to make it appear that robbery was the whole motive of the crime.

'I was a little worried that you might reflect on the coincidence that I was in Edinburgh, on a very brief visit, on the very night Mr Maitland was killed. I reinvoked the ghost of Edgar Smith, caused him to have escaped from prison, caused him to have a grudge against Mr Maitland, for the latter's non-existent evidence at a non-existent trial. All this provided, or confirmed, by a fictional conversation with a non-existent Inspector of Police. You believed me completely, did you not?

'I turned to the problem of Simon. He would not immediately expose me, but he would black-mail me by threatening to do so. You will agree that that was an intolerable prospect. So I sent for him. We remained in constant touch. He could write to me freely at Glenalban. It is not a house where people read the private letters of others. At least, I do, but I am exceptional in that as in so much else. I liked him writing to me here. Each letter addressed to the Barone di Vigliano reaffirmed my new identity.

'I told him I could smuggle him into the castle, and he could help himself to miniatures and silver. It was a chance he had been pining for, ever since his expulsion. Revenge as well as

342

profit. But he was right not to risk attempting it without a friend in the garrison.

'The silly fellow let himself be seen. It did not greatly matter. Indeed, it probably enhanced the credibility of the story I told you, that I had seen him in secret conference with Duncan Glenalban. I made a rendezvous with Simon. I emerged quietly from the castle, which I had not attempted before; but I knew it could be done, because you had done it. I met him. He was enthusiastic about stealing the miniatures. He was also enthusiastic about sharing my new fortune with me. I held him under, with my stick. Thus I did not even get my boots wet, which might have been hard to explain.

'Then I came to you with my story, and with my distress. I did that well, too, I think? My motive there is probably obvious to you.'

'No,' I said. This answer would still keep him talking. Besides, it was true.

'If I could persuade you to suspect Duncan Glenalban of named and nameless crimes, then you would be on your guard never against me, but always against him. Together we formed that theory, that Duncan had stolen the documents, that Simon had found out and threatened to blackmail him. You know, that theory was so good, I was almost believing it myself.

'Meanwhile this farmhouse had been rebuilt and furnished, and Duncan lent it to me.'

'Why did you want it?' I asked.

'Why,' he looked at me in surprise, 'to write my poem.'

'You really are writing a poem?'

'It has been in my mind for years. I have never had leisure or peace of mind enough to tackle it. I assure you, I have never been so happy as in my solitude here, producing what I believe to be a work of beauty. I would like to paint also, but that talent is denied me. Also I could come and go as I pleased, observed only by the birds of the air, carrying a gun and a spy-glass if I wished. This afternoon I did so wish.'

'How could you know I was going for a walk?'

'On a fine afternoon, have you ever not done so, since you have been here?'

'How could you know I would be alone?'

'I did not. But I know the routine of Glenalban. Naturally, by now. I know that on Wednesday Lady Flora devotes the afternoon to letters, and my Louisa devotes it to some housekeeping task. I knew you would not walk with Duncan Glenalban. There remained only Avington.'

'Suppose I had walked with Jack?'

'Then you had longer to live.'

Aunt Louisa's fingers now clutched mine so tight they hurt. She was hearing things we had not told her.

'How did you know,' I asked, 'what road I would take?'

'I did not need to know, in advance. That is the merit of a spy-glass, together with the

344

knowledge that from Glenalban most walks start from the terrace.'

'You must have entered the wood as I did, or after I did. How did you cross it so quietly?'

'Ah. You do not know a tithe of the advantages of an upbringing like mine. To write an epic poem, yes, I am capable of that, because I was brought up to it. To enter the bedroom of a sleeping man, even of a man not quite asleep—to cross it—to leave the room with his watch and money, yes, I am capable of that too, because I was brought up to it.'

'You wore that reddish coat so that I would think you were Glenalban, if I saw you?'

'Not at all. I did not intend you or anyone to see me. I did not think, after I had fired, that you had seen me. I did not think you would see anything, ever again. That is why I was so surprised when you came here. I wore that coat when I went out with a gun, because it is the coat I wear when I go out with a gun. That you should think it was Glenalban who shot at you merely provides an amusing irony. It is not at all credible that Glenalban should try to kill you.'

'Yes, it is, I mean it was.'

'No, child. Avington put his finger precisely on the weak point of the theory which accused poor Duncan. If he had stolen documents that destroyed your case, he had no need to murder you. He might have done one or other, to keep Glenalban, but it was absurd to suppose that he would do both. I had not suspected Avington of so much intelligence. His objection was unanswerable. You did your best to answer it, which was most amusing for me to listen to, but your logic was not good. His was better. It should have led you to conclude either that somebody else had stolen the documents, or that somebody else had pulled those triggers, or that somebody else had done both those things. I was in some fright that Avington would follow his own argument to its logical conclusion. But you beguiled him out of his logic, child. Whether permanently or not I don't know. It will not matter. There will never be a charge of attempted murder brought, because there will not be a witness. Just hearsay from Avington and from me. And, of course, Duncan can probably prove he was five miles away, full in view of a dozen people.

'Well, well. When Avington brought you here, I was surprised not only that you were alive. Also that I was being given a second bite of the cherry, as my poor mother used to say. And he fell in immediately with my idea that he should bring Miss Grant here also. It shows how completely he trusts me, doesn't it? My one fear now is that my dearest Louisa dislikes my birthmark. Perhaps I shall be allowed moderate whiskers—enough to cover it, not enough to lacerate her cheek. I shall suggest that. There will be many things to discuss between us.'

'I don't think,' I said, 'those discussions will take place.'

He looked at me, his eyebrows raised over the

big, bland, not unpleasing face which I remembered so well from so long ago at Millstounburn.

He wondered what I meant. I wondered what I meant. I meant nothing at all. I simply wanted to keep the conversation alive.

While it was alive, we were alive.

I had an inspiration. I said, 'We are not the only people who can recognize you.'

'Yes.'

'Customers, in Mr Maitland's shop. Are you going to kill them all? How will you find them? One day one of them will see you.'

'I was not employed in the public part of the shop. I was at the stage of being a sort of apprentice, learning the trade. My duties lay in the storeroom and workroom behind. The only customer with whom I dealt was Simon Donaldson.'

'There is Mr Maitland's servant.'

'He was on holiday, throughout the few days I was there. That should have been obvious to you. He is alive.'

'Oh . . .'

The little parlour of the farmhouse was bright and comfortable. It had three ways out. One was the open door into the kitchen, in which an invisible lamp was shining. One was the incongruously massive front door, the key of which was in Edgar Smith's pocket. The third was the archway at the foot of the narrow, winding stairs. There was no hall or passage—simply the arch and immediately the dark staircase. The

347

bottom two steps were visible from the parlour. Then the staircase twisted to the right, beyond the back wall of the parlour. Upstairs, I supposed, there were two bedchambers—one for the farmer and his wife, when they took occupation in the spring, and one for their children. In one, Edgar Smith had made himself comfortable, with fine linen and blankets from Glenalban. There was no possibility of us reaching those upstairs rooms. There would have been nowhere to go, if we had reached them.

In the parlour, the oil-lamp on the table spread a golden light on the pages of the epic poem; and on the cheerful moonlike face with the bird-shaped birthmark; and on the narrow features of Aunt Sophia, who sat straight-backed and dignified in her wooden chair, as she always did, and as she had unsuccessfully taught me always to do . . . My mind unaccountably sped backwards down through the years to my childhood, my happiness, her love and care for me. Her reward was a dingy and secret end at the hands of a monster. And she was here entirely because of me—because of my ancestry, because of my ambition and greed. It was not to be borne. It was not to be allowed.

'You will not discuss your whiskers with Miss Frith or anyone else,' I said, 'because you will go to the gallows. We shall send you there.'

'From the grave?'

'From the witness box.'

'Brave words, Leonora. And, like most brave

words, the purest nonsense. Well well, I have indulged my hunger to tell somebody my story. The hour of my dinner is approaching. Talking so much has given me an appetite, to match the thirst which it has also given me. I shall eat and drink more comfortable in the knowledge that there now stands no impediment to my future luxurious felicity. How elegant my language has become, suiting its subject. My poor mother would be proud of her last pupil.'

He picked up the shotgun. It was pointing between Aunt Louisa and me. I wondered which he would shoot first. I hoped it would be me.

'There will be bloodstains,' I said, my words coming out a little high and strained, try as I might to be brave. 'They will catch you by the bloodstains.'

'How you are struggling to postpone the inevitable. I scarcely blame you. Miss Grant is more stoical. She has hardly contributed to our little symposium. The chairs need repainting, as you see. The paint is quite chipped. I have a pot of paint and a brush, sent up here at my request by my dearest Louisa. Had that not been the case, you would be sitting elsewhere. I shall paint the chairs. I shall enjoy doing so. It is a rewarding task, because so pleasant an effect is achieved with so little labour.'

'The floor.'

'Your chairs are standing, as you can see, on a little piece of shameful rug. It is all holes and frayed ends, bare patches and stains. I have been intending for days to burn it.'

'Lord Avington knows we are here.'

'Avington will be told that you have gone, on my advice and at my charges, to Edinburgh. I suppose he will continue to believe that Glenalban tried to kill you. It will be interesting to see what comes of that.'

'You will find our bodies hard to dispose of.'

'With the whole of the Scottish Highlands for their reception? With all night to spend? With a pony and cart? Do you know how deep some of the peat-hags are? No, and nor does anybody else, because when a sheep stumbles into one it is never seen again. The mud closes over its head, and it sinks, and sinks, and sinks, and within minutes the mud has oozed itself smooth again, and you would have no idea that anything had fallen into it. Duncan Glenalban was kind enough to warn me most particularly against the peat-hags. That is how I know what they are called.'

He pulled back the two hammers at the breech of the shotgun, cocking it. The gun was one of the new breech-loaders, invented in France only a dozen years earlier, and arrived in Britain hardly five years before. The new gun could be reloaded in seconds. It was a good gun for a murderer.

The two clicks of the hammers sounded as loud as shots, in the quiet little room.

Twelve

'THAT WILL BE enough, Mr Smith,' said the Earl of Glenalban.

He came down the last two steps of the little dark staircase. He was wearing a rust-coloured shooting coat, and carrying a shotgun.

Edgar Smith spoke the truth when he said that he could move very quick. He spun round in his chair, and at the same moment fired. The boom of the gun was shattering in that small space. But Glenalban moved equally quick. He must have been expecting Edgar Smith's spin. He dropped to the floor. Not knowing what I was doing, not having the smallest notion of a plan, I jumped out of my chair and threw myself at Edgar Smith—not at his person but at his gun. It was just as he fired again. I spoiled his aim, but not enough. Glenalban gave a cry. He was hit. I

351

could not tell how badly. He was not dead. Edgar Smith threw me off, so that I crashed into a corner of the room. All the breath was knocked out of my body. To my absolute amazement, and still in the same blink of an eye, Aunt Sophia had also jumped up, faster than I had any idea that she could move, and seized the swordstick.

Edgar Smith broke his gun at the breech, and pulled two fresh cartridges out of his pocket. In a matter of seconds he would be ready to fire again, at the injured and helpless Glenalban. I was fighting for breath, winded, powerless to move. Aunt Sophia pulled the sword out of the swordstick.

Even as Edgar Smith reloaded and cocked his gun, Aunt Sophia stabbed him in the thigh, as hard as she could, with the sword. He gave a great shout, and dropped his gun. I managed to crawl forward towards it, but before I reached it Glenalban, crawling also, had reached it and thrust it away out of Edgar Smith's reach. On his knees, he pointed his own gun at Edgar Smith's stomach.

Edgar Smith was clutching his wounded thigh, looking at it incredulously. Blood was oozing between his fingers.

Speaking through clenched teeth from the pain of his own wound, Duncan Glenalban said, 'Between you, you saved my life. Thank you.'

I tried to speak. I could not. I was still winded.

Aunt Sophia said, 'You saved ours, Sir. Thank you.'

'Are you all right, Leo?' said Duncan, not taking his eyes off Edgar Smith.

'No,' I managed to say. 'But soon yes.'

And soon I was almost as good as new, though stiff and bruised from crashing across the room.

'Are you strong enough to hold this gun?'

'Only just,' I said, taking it from him without shifting its aim from Edgar Smith's chest.

Duncan was still on his knees. He could not stand. He reached out for the chair that Aunt Sophia had been sitting in. He dragged it across the floor, and put it in front of me, so that I could rest the barrels of the gun on its back. And still the aim of those barrels was Edgar Smith's bottom waistcoat button.

Duncan said to Aunt Sophia, 'Please see if you can find a clothesline, or any bit of rope in the kitchen.'

'You are wounded,' she said. 'Is it your leg? We must look at that first.'

'Not first but second,' said Duncan. 'We must truss our fowl first.'

Obediently Aunt Sophia trotted out into the kitchen. She found at once what every farmhouse kitchen had, a coil of hempen line for the washing to be pegged to. Duncan made two tight turns round Edgar Smith's chest and upper arms, and tied him to the back of his chair.

Edgar Smith was still clutching the wound Aunt Sophia had given him, and watching the blood ooze, with a kind of stupid blank expression, as though he had been cheated, and

353

could not make out how it had been done.

'I think you had better keep hold of the gun, Leo,' said Duncan. 'But, if you have reason to shoot, make it his legs. He must be alive for the gallows. Besides, you are too brave and too adorable to be killing people with guns.'

'Adorable?' I stammered, as stupid as Edgar Smith.

'Yes. Will you marry me?'

'Yes,' I said.

'First things first,' said Aunt Sophia severely, coming back from the kitchen again. 'I have put some water on the heat. We must cut away the leg of your trousers, Sir.'

'But they are new trousers.'

'You can get other trousers, but not another leg.'

They were both quite calm. I did not understand how they managed it. My heart was still thudding from the wild terror and excitement of those few seconds of violent action; and from the Earl's proposal; and from my unexpected 'Yes'.

I was as astonished by my own sudden certainty as by anything else that had happened.

Aunt Sophia cut away Duncan's right trouser-leg, just above the knee, with a knife she had found in the kitchen. I did not watch them afterwards. I could not, without taking my eyes off Edgar Smith. I was thankful, though I despised my squeamishness. I heard grunts of pain from Duncan, which he tried to suppress. Each one tore at my heart.

'We must get all the shot out at once,' said Aunt Sophia, in the tones of a strict teacher of infants. 'Each of these pellets could fester, and then you would lose your leg.'

They were a long time about it. Aunt Sophia would not let Duncan tell us his story until she had finished. She said it would distract her from digging out the pellets. There were not so very many pellets. A full charge, at point-blank range, would have blown his leg off, if it had not blown his head off.

Suddenly Duncan said, after stifling a yelp of pain, 'I don't want you to say "Yes" just because of the events of this evening, Leo.'

'I seem to have changed my mind about a lot of things,' I said, trying to concentrate on the job I had been given.

Aunt Sophia found a clean linen sheet in a press, and tore it into strips. She bandaged Duncan's leg. He was easier. His face was drawn with pain, and he could put no weight on his leg.

He said, 'I suppose we had better minister to the wound you so gallantly made, Ma'am.'

'I suppose so,' said Aunt Sophia without enthusiasm.

'The rules of war, you know. Humane treatment of prisoners.'

'Pooh,' said Aunt Sophia. 'But he should be able to walk to the gallows.'

There was not much she could do with a deep and narrow stab-wound. She staunched the bleeding by bandaging a pad very tight over the place. Duncan held the shotgun. But it seemed to me needless. Edgar Smith was a man in a stupor; he was like one of the silent, motionless lunatics I had lived among.

Eventually he was done. The furniture was put back on its legs. Aunt Sophia and I heaved Duncan into a chair, from which he could watch Edgar Smith. A little blood was mopped up, and the swordstick wiped. Duncan pushed a rag through the barrels of Edgar Smith's gun, which was his own gun; he said that, if it were left fouled overnight, the metal would be corroded.

'One of us could get back to Glenalban,' said Duncan, 'to set their minds at rest, and to bring a conveyance to get us home. But . . .'

'Out of the question, Sir,' said Aunt Sophia, who had adopted an air of authority I remembered her attempting ten years before. 'You are in no state to move an inch, except in a comfortable carriage. Nora has had both mental and physical shocks. I would never find my way! We must resign ourselves to staying here until morning. That creature said that a woman comes in to clean the house, daily, in the morning. She shall take a message to the castle.'

Duncan smiled.

The sun came out over the iron-grey waves of the sea. It was no fraud. I reached out suddenly, shamelessly, and took his hand. He squeezed my fingers as Aunt Sophia had squeezed them, when we were in the Valley of the Shadow of Death.

'All that horseplay,' said Aunt Sophia, 'has

given me an unaccountable appetite.'

Duncan laughed. I had a great desire to kiss him. I could not make out what had happened inside me.

Dubiously I said, 'Shall I cook something?'

'No, dear,' said Aunt Sophia. 'You had better leave it to me.'

Aunt Sophia continued to forbid Duncan to tell his story, until we had eaten. She said it would be bad for our digestions, after so much excitement, and lead to inflammation of Duncan's injuries. He and I obeyed meekly. We stared at one another, as though in discovery, and held hands like children.

We had some cold bird, and potatoes which Aunt Sophia fried, and excellent cheese. We had one glass each of Duncan's own best Burgundy, which Miss Frith had sent up to the farmhouse.

'Any more would be dangerous for us all, for different reasons,' said Aunt Sophia. She firmly put the cork back into the bottle, and the bottle away in the kitchen.

And at last I was permitted to hear, and Duncan to tell, what had happened to bring him to the bottom of the farmhouse stairs.

'I came back from shooting,' he said, 'to find odd things going on. Flora told me that Leo had come rushing along the passages like a tempest, in a state of distraction, and many degrees below the usual level of her formidable chic. Almost immediately afterwards she disappeared with Jack Avington in a dog-cart. It did not seem like either an elopement or an abduction. I could not see why it should be in the nature of an escape. What had Leo to escape from? She had the love and protection of too many people, rather than too few. Nobody knew where they had gone. We assumed they would return. Meanwhile nothing could be done about it.

'Jack did return, after a long time, alone. He had a story ready. Two stories. One about Leo, one about you, Miss Grant. I would not be here if Jack were a better liar. His stories were simply no good. He had taken you to the main road, Leo, to meet an anonymous friend, who was to take you to who knew where? What friend? Communicated with by what means? Taking you away for what purpose? And Miss Grant had to go without a second's delay to a croft, of uncertain locality, inhabited by a family of unrevealed name, with an illustrated Bible for which the children could not wait until morning, thence to be brought back by an unnamed doctor, on whose way home Glenalban lay . . . This was all so ridiculous that I almost believed it, except for the uneasiness in Jack's eye. So truthful a man shouldn't attempt such tactics.

'I couldn't begin to imagine what any of this meant. But I decided to follow your dog-cart, Miss Grant, and some instinct made me bring my gun. It soon became obvious where you were headed—the road to this place goes nowhere else. I was able to follow you at a safe distance, because I knew where you were going, and to double round and get here ahead of you, because I was on horseback.

'I was completely baffled, as you may imagine. There was no reason why you should not visit Lodovico in his retreat. But why in the evening, and why make a secret of it? I scented some very peculiar conspiracy. I couldn't begin to tell you, from sheer embarrassment, some of the wild theories that went through my head.

'Because I knew where you were going, Miss Grant, I was able to get here before you. I let my horse go, ran a little, and walked a little, and crawled a little, and was under the walls of his house when you arrived. I could do no more until the commotion of your arrival, or I would have been heard. I climbed in an upstairs window, while Lodovico was banging about, locking the shutters and so forth, covering any sound I made—'

'Climbed in?' I said. 'How?'

'Have you ever heard of a farm without a ladder in the steading? How do you suppose they make stacks of their hay and ricks of their straw? Also this house has just been rebuilt, after it was gutted by fire. I supervised the rebuilding. I know it inside out. I knew which upstairs window I could break without being heard from the parlour. I crept down the stairs under cover of Lodovico's voice, when he was boasting of his exploits. In that vein, he would drown a platoon of soldiers crossing a barrack-square paved with broken glass.'

'You sat there listening,' said Aunt Sophia, 'all the time he was talking?'

'In one sense I owe you an apology, Ma'am,' he said. 'I could at any moment have ended your discomfort and peril.'

'That would have been *quite* wrong,' said Aunt Sophia. 'You would have cut short his confession.'

'That is what I concluded. The more the better from him, I thought. Even to his plans for, er, eliminating the two of you, and disposing of your mortal remains.'

'Then you were so brave,' I said, very close to tears at remembering the lovely shock of his sudden appearance.

'I had this gun. It is easier to be brave when you hold a gun. You had no gun, Leo, when you jumped like a fury on an armed man. You had no gun, Miss Grant, when you ran and took his sword.'

'You were braver than I was,' I said.

'No. You were braver than I, both of you.'

'This is a sterile argument,' said Aunt Sophia, as dry as when she told me she would not treat me as a Queen.

'We can continue it in private, darling girl,' said Duncan, smiling at me; so that my fingers wriggled in his, like eels in love with their trap. 'Can you now overlook my fortune and my castle?'

'Yes,' I said, with difficulty. 'I will be brave about them, too.'

'What was the theory this fellow was talking about? That you and he worked out together? About my stealing documents from the lawyers, and having secret meetings with Simon Donaldson? And then trying to shoot you?'

'I cannot possible tell you, ever,' I said. And immediately told him.

He whistled, when I had finished.

Aunt Sophia looked gravely disapproving.

'And you had Jack Avington believing it, too,' said Duncan. 'I thought his manner to me was odd, this evening. You had him whisking you away from the awful dangers of Glenalban to the safety of this fellow's protection . . . I can see why you turned a little chilly towards me, dearest goose. One minute cheating you of your birthright, the next murdering Donaldson . . .'

'It is unkind of you to make fun of me,' I said, with an attempt at dignity. 'It was a very good theory.'

'Oh yes, my love,' he said quickly, *very* good . . . I can tell you what I am dreading. Telling my Aunt Louisa what we have heard tonight.'

'I think you may leave that to me,' said Aunt Sophia.

'Would you do that?' he said, startled.

'As a woman, I can better understand her feelings. I can better soften the blow, the many cruel blows.'

'It would be an uncommon kindness.'

'A common one, Sir, I think.'

He bowed his head, rebuked by a goodness even I had not fully understood.

'I have just realized something,' I said. 'Duncan, what do you really think of Jack?'

'A very good fellow indeed,' he said instantly, 'Kind, decent, generous, courageous.'

'Yes, that is what I think. And he saved me from dreadful things, and he thought he was saving me from even more dreadful things, and I liked him very much, and he made me laugh, and I never quite fell in love with him. I could *not* understand why. I do now.'

Duncan looked at me, eyebrows raised, almost but not quite understanding.

'You were partial to Lord Glenalban from the beginning, dear,' said Aunt Sophia. 'I knew. I was quite sorry, because I am very attached to Lord Avington.'

'You *knew,* Aunt Sophia?' I said. 'How did you know?'

'By the fact that you refused Lord Avington, without being able to give a reason,' said Aunt Sophia. 'A man you knew to have every admirable and amiable quality. With whom you were on terms of intimate friendship. Why should you refuse him, if you were not in love with somebody else?'

'That's what Flora thought,' said Duncan.

He moved his injured leg, unthinking. He let out a gasp of pain.

'Please be still,' I cried, clutching his hand as though one of us was drowning.

'I will, when I remember . . . Flora was sure you would come to me in the end, dearest Leo. I tried to share her optimism. There was almost no moment when I honestly did share it. She will be happy. You did say "Yes", didn't you? It wasn't a trick of the sound?'

'Flora,' I said, remembering. 'She almost warned me not to refuse you. She said, for my sake. I thought . . . Dear God, I thought she meant you would kill me if I refused, because you might lose Glenalban. And she was quite against my being killed, I thought . . .'

Duncan laughed. Aunt Sophia looked shocked.

'She is so much in the way of admiring a much older brother,' said Duncan deprecatingly, 'that she convinced herself that your happiness depended on me as much as mine on you.'

'It does,' I said. 'Another thing has come clear to me. I would never have believed that I would actually attack, bare-handed, a man as big as that, with a loaded gun in his hands . . . But his gun was pointed at you. I think, if it had been pointed at anyone else in the world—even you, Aunt Sophia, even Flora, even dear Jack—I would never have had that—fit of madness. But I wanted you alive. I wanted you. Oh dear, I am as selfish and greedy as ever I was . . .'

'I can't get up and kiss you, curse it,' said Duncan.

I threw myself to my knees by his chair. He kissed me. My arms were tight round his neck.

First our lips and then our cheeks were pressed together.

Into his cheek I said, 'I see what your Aunt Louisa meant. Please don't grow a beard.'

I felt his smile on my own lips, when he kissed me again.

When I emerged at last from the heaven of that awkward embrace—and I only did so because my beloved was beginning to hiccup from the pain of his wound—I saw that Aunt Sophia was sedulously looking away, stiff as a ramrod, like a seated statue entitled 'Tact'.

Edgar Smith was looking inwards, I thought, at the future he had lost and at the future he had gained.

We sat up for all that remained of the night. None of us slept. I could not have slept, for happiness and excitement. Duncan could not have slept, for the pain of his leg. Aunt Sophia would not allow herself to sleep, because convention demanded that Duncan and I, together in the small hours of the morning, be respectably chaperoned. Edgar Smith did not sleep, I thought, because of the monsters in his head.

Mrs McGill, a bustling little body, arrived on foot at nine o'clock. She shrieked when she saw how large a party was sitting having breakfast in the parlour. She shrieked at the bandage on Duncan's leg, and that on Edgar Smith's.

She hurried away to tell her man to run to Glenalban for two carriages. She was to tell them to get the County Police, and the Procurator Fiscal from Lochgrannomhead.

Edgar Smith ate no breakfast, though we offered him what we had. He did not seem to hear our voices, or see our faces.

The carriages arrived. The coachman and four footmen were saucer-eyed with curiosity. In the dog-cart came Jack Avington with Flora. Flora gave a little scream when she saw the bandage. Then she saw that Duncan held my hand. She looked from his face to mine. She laughed with sudden happiness. It was moving to see that gentle creature so joyful at another's joy.

Jack followed her eye, and saw what she had seen. He grinned ruefully, and shook Duncan by the hand that was not holding mine. I burst into tears, grieving at another's grief.

Two footmen lifted Duncan into the first carriage. He tried to stifle a grunt of pain, too proud to show weakness in front of his sister and friend and servants.

He called to me, as though suddenly remembering, 'Smith said something about a box. The missing papers. You should have them, Leo.'

I had entirely forgotten about the box, the papers, my claim, and all. There had been more important things on my mind. There still were. But Duncan insisted that we salvage the papers, and send them to the lawyers. I thought I had better begin as I meant to go on—I had better obey, as well as love and honour, as presently I would swear to do before an altar.

The papers went on my lap, as I sat beside Duncan in the carriage. I did not look at them. I did not care about them.

Of my days in the Lochgrannomhead Asylum for Pauper Lunatics, I recorded that I did not remember a continuous passage of the days, but a series of distorted lantern slides. So it is of the days that followed the autobiography of Edgar Smith, the battle of the farmhouse parlour, and my unexpected betrothal to Duncan.

I see myself contemplating the strength and symmetry of Duncan's face, and wondering how I could ever have supposed it any but the most perfect in the world.

I see dear Flora's selfless joy, as she welcomed me as a sister.

I see the fallow deer flicking through the shadows of the great elm trees of the park.

I see Miss Louisa Frith, emerging after two days spent in the solitude of her room, faultlessly elegant as ever, her head held high. I marvel at courage greater by far than any I showed, when in a moment of madness I threw myself at that gun.

I see Jack Avington leaving, his smile a little twisted, but firm on his face; and Flora's smile sitting no easier, as she watches his carriage away.

I see my own unhelpful tears, as I learn that not every story can have a happy ending; and that, for there to be a silver lining, there must be a cloud.

I see Duncan's first attempt to walk, with a stick; and his smile, when he found he could.

That smile—that smile. My mind held an album of pictures of that smile.

The last day of August was my birthday. I wished that Jack had stayed, but I understood why he did not. That was the only shadow on a day and night of gold. Blurred gold, for me; I was drunk for twenty hours, not with wine but with happiness.

I remember the beginning. Mary MacAndrew gave me a birthday gift, when she called me in the morning. It was a little needle-case, delicately embroidered with tiny flowers and birds. I wept and embraced her. I was weeping and embracing people, thereafter, for twenty hours. Never can a small and undeserving female person have been shown such love and goodwill.

There was formal announcement of our betrothal. I remember no word of the kindly speech made by the Earl of Draco, when he proposed the toast to us; I remember only the smiles and cheers, and my sensation of being carried through warm starlight on a chariot drawn by swans.

'Leonora,' said Duncan.

367

I had gone out to join him on the terrace, after breakfast. It was two days after my birthday—thirty-five hours of official betrothal. He had been up very early, about farming business. I had not. I had gobbled my breakfast, most unladylike, because time was wasted that was not spent with him.

With Simon and Jack I had wondered how one could recognize authentic love in one's own heart. The question no longer arose. It answered itself. I would have done murder for Duncan, committed treason, flattened cities.

Why did he call me 'Leonora'? Why had he no smile for me?

He stood, holding his stick, which he still needed. All the marks of pain had been gone from his face. All of them had come back.

'The lawyers,' he said.

'The lawyers,' I repeated stupidly, the words meaning nothing to me. 'Is your leg hurting? Have you done too much this morning? I keep begging you, darling, not to tire yourself.'

'The lawyers have met together, yours and mine,' said Duncan. 'With the papers we sent. The ones Smith took. The result is a foregone conclusion. I am advised not to go to court.'

I looked at him blankly. The most horrible suspicion jumped into my mind. He was a man of scrupulous honour. Too scrupulous. He carried it to absurd lengths. Before, he had not made love to me, although he loved me, *in case* I was rich and he poor. Now he *knew* I was rich and he poor.

'It doesn't make the slightest difference,' I said. I tried to speak lightly, reasonably, although I was scared to death. 'It is as Edgar Smith said, that night in the farmhouse. The moment we're married it's yours. All the documents and deeds and arguments are aca-academic.'

'You refused me,' he said drably, 'in case the world confused love with greed, in case you yourself did.'

'When I refused you, I did not know I was in love with you. You do know you are in love with me. It is very astonishing that you should be, but you say you are, and I believe you, if only because I want to . . .'

'Do I, now, know I am in love with you? That was the point you made about yourself. You said that men have no monopoly of honour.'

'Since we are repeating old conversations,' I said, 'you said to me, after you were shot, that I must forgive you for being so very rich, and overcome my scruples, or something like that, because we loved one another. If you could say that, why can't I?'

'We must repeat yet another conversation,' he said. 'When a penniless girl marries a rich man, the world gives its blessing. When a penniless man marries a rich woman, the world sneers behind its hand. How could I know, in my heart why I married you?'

'Because you asked me when I was penniless.'

'No. I had heard Edgar Smith. The missing documents were on the table in the parlour.'

'Oh. That is true, but . . . Are you accusing yourself of asking me to marry you, with your poor leg full of shot, because you knew I might win Glenalban?'

'How can I not accuse myself? At any rate suspect myself? I did know you might win Glenalban. And in that knowledge I asked you.'

'And in that knowledge I accepted you. I admit I wasn't thinking of it at the time . . .'

'I did not think I was thinking of it,' he said. 'I thought I thought of you. Now I cannot know what I was thinking then, or what I am thinking now.'

'Try thinking of me again.'

'You and Glenalban are fused now, inseparable. You must grasp the central point. Suppose the case were fought and I won it. In marrying me, you would not become owner of anything, except what I specifically gave you. Put it the other way about. In marrying you, I would become owner of everything, and you would be left with only what I specifically gave you.'

'I shall be happy with what you give me,' I said. 'If I may wear dresses with sleeves that make you laugh . . .'

'It would be your own that I would be giving you! What fairness is there in that? It would be obscene, dishonourable, humiliating!'

'Am I to understand, Sir,' I said, drawing myself up to my full height, and trying, with terror in my heart, to be as dignified as an archbishop, 'that you are withdrawing your proposal of marriage? Is that honourable?'

'You know it is.'

He turned and limped away, his face as full of pain as in the moments after he was shot.

My mind was numb with misery. I ought to have foreseen all this, and I had not. He ought to have foreseen it, and he had not. Both of us had known, if we thought about it, that with the missing documents restored, my case was good, and perhaps unanswerable. Both of us had put the whole matter out of our minds—I because I did not care, he because of his wound and because of his love. Now a letter from the lawyers had jolted him out of his happy oblivion, reawakened that prickly conscience, so that it filled him with poisoned pins.

The trouble was that, in his own terms, he was right. To withdraw his proposal was honourable. In defiance of all logic, and of all the things I had said, there *was* a difference—a poor girl could decently marry a rich man, but not the other way about. A hundred years hence it might not be so; but in that year it was profoundly so.

I tried to make a plan, though my mind was not in a state for making plans.

Could I make all my property over to him, by irrevocable deed of gift? Secretly, so that he did not know I was doing it until after I had done it? I thought not. I was old enough to be married, but I was three years short of my legal majority.

I did not think a minor was allowed to give away the moon.

Could I convince him that I loved him so much that his tender conscience was breaking my heart, that I would die of misery without him? I thought not. My heart would break. But I would not die. He knew that. And if by any such means I lured him into marriage, he would still never be sure of his own motives.

Could I convince him that he loved me so much, that Glenalban was no more than icing on the cake? Devise a situation where he must rescue me from a treacherous river or a savage bull? And thus reveal his heart to himself?

He had already done that.

And he was still lame. He could walk only slowly, with a stick. Heroics would be impossible, for many weeks yet.

I stared sightlessly at the sunlit park, sloping down to the Alban Water. It was mine, and it was death to me.

Luncheon took place normally, which somehow amazed me. After such a morning, life could *not* continue in its accustomed grooves; but it did.

I had no appetite. This was so rare that Aunt Sophia looked at me anxiously.

Duncan had not yet said anything to anybody. Nor had I.

I did not want to go down to dinner. But I thought I should imitate Miss Louisa Frith. I decided to dress with special care, and to hold my head high.

By a familiar magic, no less mysterious because it happened so often, the Servants' hall knew the story by evening. Mary MacAndrew looked stricken. I truly believed that my happiness had become as important to her as her own. Hers was assured; mine had been assured, and it was in ruins.

Next day at luncheon Duncan quietly announced that he was going to Edinburgh. There was to be a meeting between himself and both sets of lawyers. What was to be arranged was the transfer of property deeds from his name to mine. They would be put in the hands of Trustees.

Everybody nodded. Nobody could believe that it was actually happening. Nobody could think of anything to say.

Breaking a silence that had become painful, Miss Frith said to me, 'Congratulations, dear.'

'But I don't want it!' I said.

'I know. But we all know that it is your right.'

'I don't want my right,' I said. 'I want . . .'

I did not finish my sentence. I did not need to. They all knew what I wanted.

Duncan excused himself, rose, and went to the door. He turned, and said, 'I shall not be coming back. They can pack my personal things and send them on. I shall see you all again. Or perhaps not all.'

Flora suddenly said, 'Shall I come with you?'

'No!' I almost shouted. 'Because one person

goes mad, the rest need not. This is your home.'

Duncan went through the door with no further word. The footman closed it behind him. It did not signify that we were playing this scene in front of half a dozen servants. Anything they did not know about it, they soon would. It was their right to know; it was their home too. And none of it could be any sort of secret.

'It is a very moral form of madness, dear,' said Miss Frith presently.

'I know,' I said. 'It is duty and conscience and pride and so forth. I wish none of those words had ever been thought of.'

'From duty he has maintained the Glenalban that you see.'

'Yes. And from duty I shall have to try to do the same, if I must, but I had much rather he went on doing it, and then I could help, if he told me what to do, but now he never will . . .'

And then I did exactly what I had vowed I would not do. I collapsed my forehead on to my arms on the table, and burst into violent sobs.

'If I were you, Nora,' said Aunt Sophia, speaking loud so that I could hear over my sobs, 'I would find that dreadful man's swordstick, and stab Lord Glenalban in the leg—his good leg, I think it ought to be—and go on doing so until he gives up this nonsense.'

I raised my head, to stare at her in amazement. My face must have looked horrible.

'I do not like seeing you unhappy,' said Aunt Sophia, by way of explanation of her advice. 'I do feel that you and Lord Glenalban are ideally matched. I feel a duty in the matter quite as strong as his, to promote your future happiness. It has been my responsibility, ever since your dear mother left us. I feel a sense of responsibility for this betrothal, also, since I had the honour to be present at its inception.'

She was making excuses. She knew her suggestion was monstrous and unthinkable.

'I would use a pin, rather than the swordstick,' said Miss Frith. 'A good long hatpin.'

'You had better do it at once,' said Flora. 'He's leaving directly.'

I goggled at these amazing ladies.

'We don't care who owns what,' said Flora. 'We want you to marry Duncan.'

'The pin of this brooch,' said Miss Frith, removing a jewel from her bosom. 'Two inches long, and something to get a good grip by. Hurry, child, you'll miss him.'

So I rubbed away my tears with my knuckles, most unlike the mistress of Glenalban, and ran down into the courtyard. A travelling-carriage was waiting. Duncan had not yet come out. He was expected any moment. I jumped into the carriage. I thought I saw a look of understanding on the stolid face of the footman who held the door. I even thought I saw the suspicion of a wink.

I drew the curtains over the windows of the carriage, to darken it. I made myself as small as I could, in the corner. He might not get into the carriage, if he saw from the ground that I was in it. Once he was in, and the door shut behind him, I could follow Aunt Sophia's plan.

I could not believe I had heard what I had just heard. I knew Flora was fond of me; I thought Miss Frith also. It jolted my heart to realize how much they loved me.

And, in Aunt Sophia, duty, morality, conscience were the stars she steered by. She should have approved of Duncan's rigid adherence to his code of honour. When she pretended to speak from a sense of duty, she was fibbing, and she knew it. She suggested the swordstick!

Duncan was helped in. He murmured surprise at the unexpected darkness of the carriage. He leaned out of the open window, to call a last instruction to his valet, who was to follow in another carriage with the boxes; he was still leaning out when the carriage started. Then he relaxed back into the seat. Thinking himself alone, he allowed himself to groan at the pain of being hoisted in. Then he saw me.

'Leo,' he said, 'this is only more pain for both of us—'

'No,' I said, 'only for you. I am to stab you with this pin until you promise to marry me. Again and again and again. It was supposed to be in your good leg, but it will have to be in your bad leg. It will hurt horribly. Wouldn't it be best if you promised straight away, so I don't have to stab you, which I am not looking forward to, although I can see it is a good plan . . .'

'You're demented,' he said. 'You've stumbled over the edge into lunacy. The real thing, this time. I shall have to take you back to the asylum in Lochgrannomhead. You were to stab me again and again and again, until I promised . . .'

I heard that his voice had changed. I saw that his face changed. He was smiling. I burst into more tears, and dropped my pointed weapon.

He took me in his arms, and I wept over his waistcoat.

'I'm defeated,' he said. 'I cannot withstand the threat of torture. I do promise to marry you. But it is simply to save you from the sin of stabbing me in the leg.'

And he called to the coachman to turn round; and we rattled home to Glenalban.